Cranford E

Wherever the siblings of Cranford Estate go, scandal is sure to follow!

As the future marquess, William must marry appropriately, yet he's tempted by his close friend's sister, Anna... A most inconvenient attraction indeed!

Tilly flees London with her reputation in tatters! And promptly meets Lucas, the Earl of Clifton, and his adorable baby nephew. But with scandal hot on her heels, will she make a suitable wife?

Eligible bachelor Charles is stunned when strikingly unconventional Lucy goes out of her way to avoid him. They have a connection, but Lucy is hiding a heartbreaking secret...

Read William's story in
Lord Lancaster Courts a Scandal

Tilly's story in
Too Scandalous for the Earl

And Charles's story in
Scandalously Bound to the Gentleman

All available now!

Author Note

Scandalously Bound to the Gentleman is the third book in the Cranford Estate Siblings trilogy.

I have thoroughly enjoyed writing this story, which is about Charles, a diplomatic envoy working for the British government, and Lucy Quinn, an independent woman with a troubled past. The beginning of the story is set against the colorful backdrop of India, where Charles's and Lucy's attraction to each other brings them together. It is in the palace of the Rajah of Guntal where they share a magical night of love. Having experienced an unhappy affair in the past, Charles is in no rush to step up to the altar. Lucy has also suffered a trauma in her life and is as reluctant as Charles to wed. It is agreed there will be no commitment and afterward they part, Charles for England, Lucy to remain in India.

Unfortunate circumstances and a child born as a result of their night together force Lucy to leave India for London. Here she meets Charles once more, and after much soul-searching, they eventually resolve their conflicts.

Scandalously Bound to the Gentleman is a story of hope and a passionate search for love and happiness with many pitfalls along the way.

Scandalously Bound
to the Gentleman

———

HELEN DICKSON

HARLEQUIN® HISTORICAL™

Recycling programs for this product may not exist in your area.

ISBN-13: 978-1-335-59609-3

Scandalously Bound to the Gentleman

Copyright © 2024 by Helen Dickson

For questions and comments about the quality of this book, please contact us at CustomerService@Harlequin.com.

TM and ® are trademarks of Harlequin Enterprises ULC.

Harlequin Enterprises ULC
22 Adelaide St. West, 41st Floor
Toronto, Ontario M5H 4E3, Canada
www.Harlequin.com

Printed in U.S.A.

Helen Dickson was born and still lives in South Yorkshire, UK, with her retired farm-manager husband. Having moved out of the busy farmhouse where she raised their two sons, she now has more time to indulge in her favorite pastimes. She enjoys being outdoors, traveling, reading and music. An incurable romantic, she writes for pleasure. It was a love of history that drove her to writing historical fiction.

Books by Helen Dickson

Harlequin Historical

Caught in Scandal's Storm
Lucy Lane and the Lieutenant
Lord Lansbury's Christmas Wedding
Royalist on the Run
The Foundling Bride
Carrying the Gentleman's Secret
A Vow for an Heiress
The Governess's Scandalous Marriage
Reunited at the King's Court
Wedded for His Secret Child
Resisting Her Enemy Lord
A Viscount to Save Her Reputation
Enthralled by Her Enemy's Kiss
To Catch a Runaway Bride
Conveniently Wed to a Spy
The Earl's Wager for a Lady

Cranford Estate Siblings

Lord Lancaster Courts a Scandal
Too Scandalous for the Earl

Visit the Author Profile page
at Harlequin.com for more titles.

Chapter One

1817—India

Enclosed by hills carrying the bounteous colour of an Indian summer through the glare of the sun, Charles didn't see the danger coming. He rode over rocky ground, his animal guided by his sure hand, its hooves negotiating the loose scree. Suddenly his groom shouted something that sounded like danger, but even though Charles's mind leapt to alertness, it was too late. His horse, spooked by a large snake that slithered from the rocks and across its path, reared, its front legs frantically pawing the air and throwing Charles from the saddle. The next thing he knew he was hitting the ground and rolling down the hillside into a gully below. Pain shot through his thigh, followed by a blow to his head as it made contact with a large boulder, halting his fall. Darkness engulfed him.

How long he had lain there he had no idea as he slipped in and out of consciousness. With a grinding pain inside his head, half opening his eyes, through a haze he saw a bullock cart drawn by two skinny-looking oxen making its way towards him. A woman sat inside the cart, guiding it between boulders strewn on the ground. A plague of flies had descended on him, but there was nothing he could do about it. The cart stopped beside him. The woman spoke to his groom in what he recognised as Urdu. She remained in the cart while someone lifted him inside. The bullock cart began to move off.

It rumbled over the uneven ground in sweltering heat. Each jolt was agony to him. The journey seemed endless. He opened his eyes, his faltering gaze settling on the woman. She was wearing traditional garments— the long skirt with a blouse and a billowing scarf that covered her head and floated in the breeze, the delicate fabric the colour of scarlet threaded with gold.

His gaze became fixed on a long strand of hair that had escaped its confines. There was something not quite right about it, he thought. It was light blonde in colouring, most strange, he thought, for an Indian lady. As he continued to slip in and out of consciousness, in his lucid moments the long strand of light blonde hair—lifting defiantly in the breeze like a ship's sprightly pennant— continued to hold his attention.

He couldn't remember being lifted out of the cart. Some hours later he was aware of a wet cloth being applied to his brow, cooling, welcome. Soft words were murmured, the sound comforting along with the tinkling of bangles.

'Mr Anderson?'

A woman's voice.

'Tilly?' his voice rasped.

Disconnected memories flooded his mind. He was delirious, dreaming of his sister again surrounded by pastures green in the country of his birth. A searing heat tore through his right thigh, combining with the pain inside his head. Where in God's name was he? What had happened to him? He remembered being thrown from his horse and nothing else.

Voices drifted towards him in the darkness. He attempted to move, to raise his head, but his eyelids were weighted and the pain inside his head and leg was unbearable. His bloodshot eyes blinked in puzzlement. He couldn't understand why the face bending over his was shrouded in a swirling haze.

'He has a concussion,' the voice said, a soft voice, a caring voice.

'Perhaps it's as well he's out of it until his wound has been treated. Have him brought to the treatment room. I'll give him something to dull the pain and see what can be done to save his leg.'

'He's in a bad way. Will he make it?' the female voice asked with concern.

'He's strong and healthy. It always helps.'

The agony of being lifted on to a stretcher was too much. A merciful darkness descended once more.

The fever gradually left Charles. There was a babble of voices all around him. His eyes flickered open. As the haze lessened, he brought his gaze into focus. He didn't recognise where he was. Noting the other beds where injured British and Indian men lay, he realised he was in an infirmary, a small, whitewashed affair. Two women and a man bustled about, tending to the other patients. He tried to raise his head, but the room began to spin. He squeezed his eyes tight. The sudden movement made his head feel as though it would explode.

He tried to remember what had happened. When he had set out from Madras, the landscape had stretched out before him, clouds of dust stirred up by his horse's hooves settling on his coat and that of his groom. Mile after mile, hour after hour, they had climbed hills and forded rushing streams. He loved riding over the Indian plains, mysterious, still unknown to him after four years in India, despite his curiosity and desire to know more. They had been riding for four days when his horse threw him.

After a while he carefully blinked his eyes open, relieved to find his sight no longer quite so blurred. A woman approached his bed with a bowl in her hands. She murmured a few words of conventional greeting, placing the bowl on a low table, but when she looked at him a sudden feeling of unease caused him to start, his scalp prickling. It was the woman who had brought him here in the bullock cart, he was sure of it, but she was no longer dressed in Indian clothes. She was studying him with a cool interest, her expression immobile and guarded. His eyes met the steady gaze and for one discomforting moment it seemed that she was staring into the very heart of him, getting the measure of him, of his faults and failings. He had never seen eyes that contained more energy and depth.

'You're awake at last,' she said.

His mouth was as dry as a desert. With patience, she held a cup to his lips. The cool water was a welcome relief to his parched throat. On a sigh he placed his head back on the pillow. 'Thank you. How long have I been out of it?'

'We brought you in two days ago. You are in a small hospital in Nandra in the state of Puna, close to the border with Guntal. Do you remember what happened?'

'My horse threw me. How bad is it?'

'Not good.' She stood aside as a man came to the bed and began removing the dressing from his leg.

'I'm Dr Patrick Jessop—at your service,' he said without raising his head as his piercing eyes scrutinised the wound. 'The muscles in your thigh were badly injured when you fell—thankfully no broken bones, which would have complicated matters. I've managed to suture the wound back together, but it will be a while before you can bear your weight on it. It's a nasty wound and it's possible it will leave you with a limp, but we'll have to see.'

'At least my leg is still attached to the rest of me— thank the Lord—not forgetting yourself, Dr Jessop,' Charles uttered, staring at the middle-aged doctor, for the lilt of the voice was unmistakably Irish. He met twinkling grey eyes in a face tanned dark. He looked at the woman.

She didn't crack a smile or even blink. When she looked at him her stare was forthright. 'You should. You also suffered a head wound and developed a fever.'

'Which I am relieved to see has left you,' Dr Jessop said, prodding the flesh around the wound, causing Charles to grimace with the pain this caused.

Slowly the pain subsided a little and Dr Jessop stood back and looked down at him. 'You're Irish,' Charles remarked, wondering why he should state the obvious.

'Sure I am—from County Wicklow, but it's a long time since I saw the Old Country. I'm a surgeon by profession. I've worked for the East India Company for more years than I care to count, but my work extends beyond the Company. Many residents of Nandra and the villages beyond seek my services when they are in need.'

'I imagine a trained surgeon is a treasure in such a remote place as this.'

'I go where I'm needed. There's no lack of work to be done—soldiers to patch up after some skirmish or other.'

'We're glad to have you at the hospital for a while, Dr Jessop—to make use of your skills,' the young woman said, gathering up the soiled dressings.

'I sure have my work cut out. We can mend broken bones and wounds incurred in fighting, but nothing can keep out the disease, the fevers and the gangrene that creep silently and infect people without notice until it's too late and kills so silently.

'I'm due to leave any time soon—to get back to the regiment in Madras. I can't say I won't be glad to leave the state of Puna. The territory is too unsettled to be easy. I will leave you now. It's been a long day and I'm ready for my supper. I will leave you in Miss Quinn's capable hands. She has been taught how to treat fevers and common ailments and how to clean and dress many types of wounds. You should rest more easily now the fever's left you.' Without more ado he left them.

'Now you're awake I'll fetch you something to eat when I've dressed your leg,' the young woman said. 'You must be hungry.'

When she talked Charles realised the depth of her charm. Her voice was low and beautifully modulated. 'My horse? Do you know what happened to my horse?'

'You will have to ask the man who was with you to tell you that. I believe he is being accommodated in the military encampment on the edge of town. I came upon you by chance and was concerned with getting you to the hospital at the time. Now please be quiet while I dress your wound. It will cause you some discomfort which, I am afraid, is unavoidable. Please remain still.'

Charles watched her as she worked, clenching his teeth when the pain almost overwhelmed him. In an attempt to overcome the agony, he concentrated on the young woman. Her body was lean and sleek as a grey-hound's. There was a natural grace about her, almost stately, and a quiet dignity. He'd noted as she walked towards his bed that she moved like a dancer.

An abundance of silky pale blonde hair drawn back from her face was plaited and wrapped in a coil at the nape of her neck. Her cheekbones were high, her features perfect, her eyes huge and the colour being a dark green flecked with gold lights that hinted at hidden depths, reminding him of a tiger he had seen on a hunt when he had first come to India.

The sun had tanned her skin to a golden colour and her mouth was rosy and full. Despite his pain he took pleasure in looking at her. Her face was alluring yet imperious, that told the world that she wasn't to be trifled with. Everything about her fascinated him, drew him to her, and he felt a stirring of interest as he looked into the glowing dark eyes. A large soiled apron covered her grey dress.

Her allure was tangible and he saw the danger of getting to know her too well. She was as exquisite and dangerous as the cobra he had seen emerge from the basket of a man in the bazaar in Madras.

Sitting on the floor cross-legged, the man had removed the lid of his basket and started to play his pipe. Soon the head of a cobra with its spreading hood had appeared, drawn by the mystical sound of the pipe. Its eyes were cold, mesmerising and deadly. Charles had stood and watched, transfixed. His companion had laughed at him when he had stepped back.

'Impressive, is it not, Charles? But be assured that its venom could fell an elephant should its fangs pierce its skin.'

Why Charles should think of that when he looked at Miss Quinn, a woman he suspected was in possession of an intelligent mind as well as beauty, he had no idea. On her part her attention was born of an inclination to minister to his wounds, but in a strange way her attention excited him.

'The doctor referred to you as Miss Quinn. Are you Jeremiah Quinn's daughter by any chance?'

'He is my father. You know him?'

'We have never met but his name is familiar to me. He was a Company factor I believe.'

'He was a Company Resident in Puna and a collector of land revenues. Ill health forced him to retire three years ago.'

'Yet he remains here—in Nandra.'

'He says he is too old to move on. He loves India and Nandra has become his home. It is where his friends are. I am Lucy Quinn. I brought you to this small infirmary. It was fortunate Dr Jessop was here to attend your injury.'

'For which I shall be eternally grateful. Hopefully my recovery will be swift and I will be on my way.'

'You used to work for the Company, did you not, Mr Anderson?'

He nodded. 'Once.'

'But you no longer do so.'

'You—have heard of me?'

'Oh, yes. You are well known. Your reputation has preceded you. Are you as wicked and dangerous as your reputation would lead one to believe?'

He laughed. 'Miss Quinn, I beg you not to destroy my reputation. I have worked very hard at it.' Was that a smile he saw twitching her lips?

'I imagine it wasn't too difficult. However,' she said, on a more serious note, 'I have heard you are a man of attainment, of exceptional courage and resourcefulness, that when you worked for the Company you took your duties beyond what was expected of you. Indeed, such is your prowess with lance and musket that I am surprised you did not make soldiering your career.'

Her remark was a statement of fact, without any form of sarcasm from which he would have taken offence. 'I happen to like what I do now and leave soldiering to the professionals. As for the Honourable Company, it did not take me long to realise the corporate greed of the Company's reign of supremacy, with the most dire consequences for the Indians.'

'Is that why you left?' she asked, curious.

His stare did not waver from her face and he did not immediately answer. All the years of his adult life, working at East India House in London, the only thing he had invested with real importance had been the Company. It had always given a meaning to his life, to everything he did. But all that had changed when he had arrived in India. With no sense of achievement he had left the Company with only the leaden sickness of disillusionment.

When he spoke, his voice was distant, as though all emotion had been carefully erased from it. 'Yes. What I saw about how the Company was run I found unacceptable. I was suspicious of the corruption of British politics by the money and influence that the Company's men have gained in India, which was why I resigned.'

'I see you are a man of principle, Mr Anderson.'

'I know the difference between right and wrong, Miss Quinn, and by continuing to work for the Company it could be seen that I was furthering its corruption. I now work for the British Foreign Office and diplomatic service—which is why I have come to see the Rajah of Guntal at his palace in Kassam. Guntal is an independent state and the Rajah, Naveen Madan, intends it to remain that way. He is not so well disposed to the East India Company and he will not be moved on the issue of Guntal being taken over by it.'

'You have been to Guntal in the past?'

He nodded. 'Once. I was appointed envoy to the court of the Rajah. While no major trading privileges have been conceded by him, I hope the result of my mission will be the beginning of a satisfactory relationship between the state of Guntal and Britain. It is my duty as a diplomat to build up Indo-British relations wherever I am sent.'

'Then I wish you every success.' Her work finished, Miss Quinn collected the soiled linen and the bowl and looked at him, balancing the bowl on her hip. 'You must try to rest now, Mr Anderson. I'll have some food brought to you. You should sleep more easily tonight.'

Charles watched her walk away. Above the smell of antiseptic, the faint scent of rosewater wafted around her, along with an air of hushed calm.

Closing his eyes, he rested more easily in his bed, determined not to be confined for longer than was necessary. He cursed his injury and was impatient to be about his business. India was made up of many territories ruled by different governments. Those not owned by the British and the Dutch separately were ruled by the Princes and Maharajas of the Hindu. As Charles worked for the British Foreign Office, it was his policy to seek better relations with these powers, but before he could further these relations he had to return to England.

Lucy lived with other British residents in the cantonment on the outskirts of the small town of Nandra. It formed a self-contained community, having expanded over the years. Set in smooth lawns dotted with well-tended flowerbeds and shaded with peepul trees, the simple one-storey buildings, wrapped round with deep verandas, were washed in white.

The cool, high-ceilinged house where Lucy lived

with her father was more spacious than most, the rooms still filled with her mother's bric-a-brac. The sweet smell of tobacco from her father's pipe hung in the air in his office, where his work of revenue records and land surveys had once been scattered on the desk. They had a small complement of servants needed to ensure their domestic comfort and Kasim, a man to tend her father now he was confined to bed.

Taking a cool drink on to the veranda, she sat and gazed into the night. Stretching out her legs and supporting her feet on a low foot stool, she sipped the cool lime juice, sitting back in her chair as two mynah birds squabbled raucously. Her thoughts turned to Mr Anderson. Almost everyone had heard of him and his exploits and how he had single-handedly held off a band of raiders when he had worked for the Company. In fact, the ladies of Madras where he had been stationed, married or single, found him quite irresistible apparently. There was no accounting for taste, but Lucy was confident that she would have no difficulty resisting Mr Anderson.

She thought back to the moment she had seen him on the ground, seriously wounded. His eyes were closed. There was blood in his hair from a head wound and blood had pooled on the ground from his injured right leg. His eyes, the colour dark blue, flickered open and then closed. A weak pulse throbbed in his neck. It was clear his life hung by a fragile thread. From the experience she had gained assisting Dr Jessop at the infirmary, she knew if his wound was not properly treated, he could have died of blood poisoning.

She'd assisted Dr Jessop as he'd operated on the leg.

She saw that Mr Anderson, stretched out on the table, had been endowed with a beautiful male body, tautly muscled and toned by years of exercise and partaking in the rigours of training along with the military to keep himself fit for every eventuality.

He was lean of waist and belly, and strong, muscled shoulders rippled beneath his shirt. His hair was thick and a rich dark brown, curling gently into the nape of his neck. His amber skin was clean shaven. It was obvious at a mere glance that he was an arrogant man, bold and self-assured—the kind of man she had learned to avoid.

A shudder ran through her as the memory of what had been done to her seven years ago returned as sickeningly as ever. Tears pricked her eyes. It was no good. She had tried in vain, day after day, to escape from that dreadful day which had destroyed her life, when she had been assaulted by a virtual stranger, a stranger who had brutally stollen her virtue. She had been just eighteen years old at the time, but in worldly experience she was still a child. Then, she'd had such high hopes for the future, her head filled with the kind of dreams every girl dreamed.

Mercilessly, inexorably, the horror of what had been forced on her came back to haunt her again and again. The man had taken his pleasure where he found it, for instant gratification, to be discarded and forgotten soon afterwards. Not so for Lucy, who had felt dirtied and corrupted and beyond redemption.

The warm sunlight bathed the small infirmary in soft light. Miss Quinn had just arrived and Charles leaned back on his pillows, watching her with interest, amazed by the gracious ease with which she tended the patients. He studied her profile, tracing with his gaze the classical lines of her face. She was quite extraordinarily lovely. He had never seen the like of her. She had an untamed quality running in dangerous undercurrents, a wild freedom of spirit just below the surface. For Charles Anderson, she represented everything most desirable in a woman. There was also something quite regal about her and she possessed a single-minded determination and a quiet will which he admired.

There was no doubting the sincerity of her tone whenever she spoke to him and he had begun to feel drawn to her, watching for the moment when she would appear and he could feast his eyes on her—and he didn't like the feeling. His present mode of life as a diplomatic envoy suited him. No ties. No regrets as he moved from town to town. And, most importantly, no emotional involvements.

Unbidden, a familiar ache returned to his heart, one he had long since buried. Sucking in his breath, he sternly dismissed the memories that threatened to overwhelm him, memories of Amelia, the woman he had thought was the love of his life, a woman to share his home and bear his children, a woman who was beautiful, gifted, only to discover she was also a callous and ambitious schemer with a highly refined sense of survival, who had betrayed his trust when she had left him for a man of wealth and superior rank.

That experience had left him wary of women. There was nothing to be gained from dredging up the past, or to waste time on what might have been. He knew the folly of placing his trust in womankind. But this did not stop his eyes searching for Miss Quinn when she did her daily rounds of those afflicted with illness and injury.

When she came to dress his wound, he stared at her bent head as her hands diligently removed the dressing. The sunlight shining in through the open window brought out all the glorious shades of her hair, from pale gold to silver. His experiences of life had conditioned him to react to any situation with lightning reflexes, yet now he didn't move, didn't think—and damn if his traitorous heart didn't beat faster and a spear of lust pass through him. The sensations spreading through him were like nothing he'd ever experienced before. They came in waves, each faster and stronger than the last.

There was something deep within Miss Quinn that made her sparkle and glow like a precious gem, a gem that needed only the proper place and setting to complement her exquisite features and alluring body. Suddenly the old, abandoned dream of having a wife to light up his life with warmth and laughter, to banish the emptiness inside him, returned.

He quickly caught himself up short, disgusted with his youthful dreams and unfulfilled yearnings, dreams and yearnings he had carried with him into adulthood, stupidly believing Amelia was the woman to make them come true, only to have them dashed like a storm-tossed sea breaking against the rocks. Suddenly pain shot through him when Miss Quinn began to redress the wound and he scowled as he realised she was bringing all those old yearnings back to torment him.

Aware of his sudden tension, Miss Quinn raised her head and looked at him, her eyes large and intense in her flushed face. 'I apologise if I hurt you. The wound is still raw, but knitting together nicely. You will be up and about in no time.'

'That's good to know,' he replied tightly, dreading the moment when he would have to test his leg's ability to carry his weight. 'How is your father?' he asked when she paused and handed him some water.

'No better, I'm afraid.'

'And your mother?'

'She is no longer with us. She has been dead two years now.'

'You miss her?'

'Yes, daily. We were close. Father is a quiet man, a clever man, who took his work with the Company seriously, even though, like yourself, he did not always agree with how things were run.'

'What has life been like for you in the cantonment?'

'Pleasant enough. People entertain at each other's houses. Father would entertain his friends and drink too much, but then most of the men in the cantonment drink too much and many suffer from damaged livers.'

Charles smiled at the seriousness of her expression. 'I can see you love your father, Miss Quinn.'

'I do—passionately. He is the only person in the world I do love. His love of India he has passed on to me,' she told him as she began to wrap a clean bandage around his leg, 'educating me with the enthusiasm which comes of real affection for one's subject so that I quickly accumulated a fair knowledge of India's complex history. I learned to appreciate and respect the traditions and customs of what to many will always remain a land of mystery, with its unique culture, beliefs and super-stitions and its ancient gods.'

'If he is up to it, I would like to meet him when I am back on my feet. I am surprised that you work in the hospital,' he said as she put the finished touches to his dressing. He was curious to know more about her. 'Is it not frowned upon by the ladies here in Nandra?'

'Absolutely, but I don't let it concern me. I help in the hospital when I am needed. There are always wounds needing attention and Dr Jessop values my assistance.'

'And I imagine all the patients fall in love with you, Miss Quinn,' he remarked with a desire to know how she interacted with other patients in her care.

Her face hardened. 'I sincerely hope not, Mr Ander-son. If that were to occur, then they would be disap-pointed and learn to stifle their amours. I have neither the time nor the inclination for such dalliance.'

Charles lifted a brow to regard her with some amuse-ment. 'You have an uncommon honesty about such matters—unlike most women.'

There was a gleam of battle in her eyes as she held his gaze. 'Many men see my independence as a threat. I protect my honour,' Miss Quinn countered.

'And to add to your accomplishments you speak flu-ent Urdu.'

'How do you know that?'

'I heard you speak to my servant before I lost con-sciousness. There are few people of my acquaintance who make any concession to learning local languages or customs. You are an exception.'

'I have been in India long enough to know these things. When I came here with my parents, knowing that I was to be here for a long time because of my father's work encouraged me to speak the languages. Some people who know this think it peculiar and are amused by it. I find it amusing for different reasons. If I were in France or Spain for any length of time and failed to learn to converse in French or Spanish, it would be regarded as neglectful. Urdu is a serviceable language to begin with.'

'You think that, do you, Miss Quinn?'

She looked at him, ready to argue, but found him regarding her seriously and with some interest. 'You don't find it peculiar?'

'Why on earth would I do that? I am impressed.'

'Do you speak it—or any of the other languages of India?'

'A little—I am determined to be more conversant. So you see, you, Miss Quinn, have me at a disadvantage—which is a first for me. You are also a forthright young lady—and your eyes are quite remarkable—unusual—as dark a green as I have seen before.'

Miss Quinn stiffened and averted her eyes. 'I have never thought there to be anything remarkable about my eyes—apart from the necessary fact that I can see through them very well. I don't like empty flattery, Mr Anderson, so please do not insult my intelligence by using it on me. I *do* have a truly direct nature.' He raised an eyebrow at her reproach. She imagined he was not used to a woman questioning a compliment.

'And you, Miss Quinn, insult my honour. I never say what I don't mean.' His tone was serious.

'You are very sure of yourself.'

'Not so sure as you might think. Accept the compliment for what it is. You are a lovely young woman and, for the time I am indisposed, I look forward to getting to know you better. My instinct tells me that you are a woman with spirit, with the face of an angel. I truly believed when I opened my eyes that I had indeed died and gone to heaven.'

When Miss Quinn spoke her voice was cold. 'You are too forward by far, Mr Anderson. As for becoming better acquainted with me, you are Dr Jessop's patient and will be treated as such and no differently from any of the other patients. Have you a wife waiting for you at home?'

Apart from a darkening to his eyes, his features remained impassive. 'I do not have a wife, Miss Quinn. I doubt a woman would be happy to share the life of a nomad and I'm never in one place long enough to put down roots and settle down. That is just one of the reasons I have yet to take a wife.'

He spoke quietly with a placid indifference to his bachelor state. He possessed a natural desire for a beautiful woman, but never for more than a passing affair. Yet Miss Quinn appeared to capture the very essence of the perfect woman who could tempt a man to bind his very soul to own her. He quickly recollected himself as he was beset with self-reproach. The bang on the head must have been more serious than he had thought to allow his thoughts such meanderings.

* * *

'I apologise if I have offended you, Miss Quinn,' Mr Anderson said as she finished her task. 'It was not my intention to scare you away, but for us to become better acquainted.'

He was watching her intently and Lucy tried to ignore the shiver that ran down her spine, which put her on her guard. She had felt something she had rarely experienced before when she had listened to his compliments— embarrassment. She was dishevelled and her hair was all mussed up, yet this man found her attractive.

Nobody had been so wholeheartedly complimentary before and she felt a small tingle of excitement. She was disturbed by Mr Anderson. He evoked feelings and conflicting emotions she did not welcome. He emanated vitality and masculinity that was so potent it sent an involuntary tingle down her spine. And yet with just one infuriating lift of his brows, one mocking word from him, she lost all decorum and dignity and turned into a virago, prepared to say the most appalling things so as not to give him the upper hand.

Then she was angry at herself for allowing the weakness. Like all the men she knew he was predictable and she was disappointed. She despised his type, men who thought all women were theirs for the taking. Their handsome looks and soft words masked something else, something sinister. The light-hearted banter was meant to hoodwink and posed a persuasive threat.

Normally she found it easy to fall in with anyone's desire for conversation, but Mr Anderson kept his eyes on her face with a sort of frank, unsmiling curiosity that embarrassed her. But she would not weaken. She would not allow him to see her wounds.

His reputation having preceded him, she knew him to be a man of action, fearless and ruthless, a ladies' man and an adventurer. His eyes were as turbulent and as enticing as the winds that blew down on Puna from the vast snow-capped mountain peaks in the north, the beautiful and mysterious Himalayas, their colours ever changing in the light of day. Her instinct also told her he was a man of passion. The insight made her shudder. She realised the implications of his presence at the hospital. He was a man to avoid getting too close to, so, after much deliberation, she came to the simple conclusion to act towards him with private and stringent reservations.

Raising her chin, she gave him a haughty stare. 'It will take more than you to scare me, Mr Anderson. As for becoming better acquainted with me, I will not be coming here again—not for a while. I have other commitments that take up my time.' Recognising the obvious admiration she read in his eyes, she was acutely aware of the boldness of his body stretched out on the bed, his maleness. There was a vibrancy about him that was like no one she'd ever met before. Too bold, she thought. Turning on her heel, she walked away.

Chapter Two

When a man tried to get too familiar, without warning blurred shadows of the assault on her person several years ago forced bitter memories to return, intensifying pictures of her weeping mother holding her. Lucy had wept with her and, once she had started to cry, she couldn't stop. She'd cried for herself. She'd cried for the loss of her virtue.

She'd cried for the death of the man she would have married, his humour, his caring of her, his gentleness and his hopes for them. She'd blamed herself for his death, for, by her actions and his need to avenge what had been done to her, he had lost his life. She'd cried for the pain he must have suffered and she cried for the dreams she had lost and the future she'd so blindly believed in. Her mother had told her everything would be all right. But it wasn't. It never would be again—not for her.

Silence had followed in her household. It seemed there was an unspoken decision that it would be unwise to speak of it, to put what had happened out of her mind—out of all their minds—and in doing so all memories would die.

For a long time, she had been frozen with shame and outrage, retreating into herself, going through the motions of living day to day. When her father had asked the Company to move him to another district, they had come to Nandra. Here she had learned to live again—not happily, but her life went on. There had been no more wild crying of rage, only an icy calm, a new strength to face what was ahead of her.

In Nandra, it was easy to hide away from the society of her former life. Only Dr Jessop knew what had happened to her. He had been there as she had battled with her demons. She had been bruised and traumatised, dirty and sullied, and he had tried to put her back together again. In fact, along with her parents, he had been her salvation…when the worst of things that could happen to a woman had happened to her.

Physically he had succeeded, but the mental scars were for her to deal with. Logically she knew it had not been her fault and yet the feeling of blame that Johnathan, the man she would have married, had lost his life avenging her lingered, lurking in the darkest corners of her mind. She yearned to go back to how it had been between them. How he had made her heart sing with joy and she had felt such passion the like of which she had never known.

She recalled the moment she had dressed Mr Anderson's wound and touched his flesh and the way he had watched her through half-closed eyes. She had been under some kind of narcotic when that awful thing had been done to her, but she could imagine it. Would she ever know what it would be like to experience passionate, mutual bliss—or even to know if it existed at all? Lucy could not imagine there might be any pleasure in such a procedure. Although, she mused, had she not enjoyed Johnathan's kisses and caresses? They had been sweet and tender and left her wanting more.

She knew there would come a time when she must reconcile with her past or she would be lost for ever, a crucial part of her missing. Was it time to be brave and push herself to become strong, someone worthy of her parents and Johnathan, to do something she had thought she couldn't?

Charles watched Miss Quinn go, feeling a rush of anger including disappointment that her departure had been so abrupt. Then he laughed at himself, bemused as to why he should feel that way, why he should feel anything at all. The woman was nothing to him, yet he was certainly not indifferent to her, which could apply to many women he had known—women who had enjoyed his attentions and shared his bed for a while.

He couldn't think of anyone, male or female, who would have stood up to him the way she had done, verbally reproach him and walk away as regal as any queen. She had spirit, a fiery spirit that challenged him. Her arrogance was tantamount to disrespect, yet in spite of himself he admired her style. Nor was she afraid of him. That was the intriguing part about her. The primal rush of attraction he felt for her surprised him. She was a beautiful woman whose grace would have won her many beaus on the London social scene.

But what he felt for Miss Quinn wasn't lust. This

was different. The feel of her hands on his flesh had stirred in him a powerful sensation that was unwelcome. When her cheeks were flushed from her exertions she reminded him of a rose and she smelled just as sweet. The perfect comparison.

Then he smiled wryly, for the rose might have a delicate flower, but its barbs were sharp and could draw blood. Why did she have to appear and complicate his life? She disturbed him in a way that could be diverting and dangerous and he needed to crush those feelings. He had a job to do, but first he had to recover from this damned injury and get back on his feet. As if to remind him the pain intensified.

'With the amount of work to be done here at the hospital, you must find Miss Quinn an enormous help,' he uttered when Dr Jessop came to look at his wound.

'She surely is—she's also a distraction, I'll say that, but she takes no notice of the besotted young gentlemen who pass through the hospital. Some of her time she spends teaching the British children in the cantonment, but she comes to the infirmary to help when needed, like now, when I haven't enough assistants to take care of all those who come through the doors. Medicine and staff are a problem, with not enough assistants to tend the numerous wounded from battles fought both here and in other field hospitals. It's a problem.'

'Miss Quinn works tirelessly—I've noticed.'

Doctor Jessop nodded. 'I wish I had a dozen like her. She's an absolute treasure. She is also a law unto herself. Miss Quinn is a brisk, no-nonsense soul who, since the death of her mother, has devoted her time to her father.

She's strong willed and has butted a few heads among the community with the work she does here. She's efficient and useful and cares not a fig for convention. Not even her father can control her.'

'I admire her for what she's doing. It takes great courage to go against convention. She appears to be a serious young woman. She has never married?'

'No, she hasn't,' Dr Jessop replied, directing his gaze elsewhere. 'As much as the bachelors who pass through Nandra admire her looks and open manner and her excellent seat on a horse, they are shy of her—which suits her. Unlike other young ladies who come out to India, she has opinions on everything—from the education of the children the families place in her charge to the way the Company is run. In short, she makes gentlemen uneasy and is fast heading towards that sorriest of all fates—spinsterhood—which would be a tragedy in my opinion. I admire a woman with a clever mind.'

Alone once more, Charles tried to close his ears to the moans of a man who had been badly wounded in a street brawl. He lay back wearily, contemplating his future and hoping it wouldn't be too long before he could continue with his journey to see the Rajah of Guntal.

Miss Quinn had nursed him through the initial dangers and the long bouts of agony that followed his injury, so Charles was disappointed when he didn't see her at the hospital again. She had told him that she wouldn't be returning to the hospital, but he did wonder if her reason for not doing so was because she wanted to avoid him, and if so, why? Had he offended her in some way? He sincerely hoped not.

Once his wound began to heal and the pain was less severe, until he placed his weight on it, he decided he had wallowed in bed long enough. Gritting his teeth, he sat on the edge of the bed, prepared to endure the agony of forcing the injured muscles in his thigh to function. He drove himself on, walking with the aid of a stick, but Dr Jessop warned him his leg might never function as well as it had.

After one week he had recovered enough to move into more comfortable accommodation in the cantonment, procured for him by Dr Jessop, in a bungalow to himself and a seemingly endless supply of servants— a luxury he seldom enjoyed in any of the stations he visited. Considering the seriousness of his injury, he made a remarkable recovery, for which his constitution, as much as Dr Jessop's ministrations, could take the credit. The time he had taken exercising and trekking in the mountains had paid dividends, for they had toughened him as nothing else could have done. His leg pained him still and he returned daily to the hospital to have his dressing changed.

Unable to get Miss Quinn out of his mind, setting his jaw, he set out to find her. He was directed to the military encampment close to the cantonment, where Miss Quinn, who was a frequent rider, kept her horse. It was also where Captain Hugh Travis, already known to him and who had been appointed to accompany him on his journey to Guntal, was staying. Hugh had been to the hospital on several occasions to enquire after his health and was content to pass his time with other military men until Charles was sufficiently recovered to resume his journey into Guntal.

Charles arrived at the military encampment where rows of military tents stood in regimental lines. Servants cooked the midday meal over open fires and the soldiers not on duty lounged about, talking and laughing among themselves. A company of soldiers were about to be put through their drill, the company commander watching them. Captain Hugh Travis, standing at the side of the drill sergeant, told him to continue. The drill sergeant immediately began barking out a series of commands. The soldiers all marched as one in perfect synchronisation.

Seeing Charles, Hugh beckoned him over. Hugh was a fair-skinned robust man with a pleasant face that suggested a kind and genial disposition. Having spent a good deal of time together in India, the two men were good friends and he greeted Charles with a friendly slap on the back.

'Good to see you back on your feet, Charles. How's the leg?'

Charles grinned, leaning on the cane he used to aid his walking and swinging his injured leg as a point of defiance. 'Getting better by the day, Hugh—better by the day.'

Hugh laughed. 'I'll take your word for it. Come to check on your horse?'

Charles nodded. 'I'm keen to be back in the saddle, Hugh, and be on my way.'

Standing by the Captain's side and observing the sweating soldiers being put through the drill, Charles shook his head. 'I thank the Lord I'm attached to the Foreign Office and not a soldier having this kind of practice day in and day out. This heat at this time of day is enough to fell a man.'

Hugh laughed. 'The best way to help them is to make sure they're fighting fit and ready for action. They'll thank the drill sergeant for it in battle.'

'And when not in battle the curse of peace time is boredom when a soldier can indulge in his pleasures— drinking to excess.'

'When they've done here it's time for musket practice. How is the leg really, Charles?' Hugh asked as they sauntered away from the drill, slowing his walk to accommodate the invalid. 'It is healing all right?'

'If you want the truth, it's damned painful. The muscles of my thigh tighten like wet leather when I remain immobile too long. Doctor Jessop explained the healing process would be slow—that I'll have to be patient. As you know, Hugh, patience is not one of my virtues. Thought I might take a short ride—get used to being back in the saddle.'

'Your horse is in the pen but don't you think it's a bit soon?'

'I don't think so. Have you seen Miss Quinn by any chance—the young woman who helped nurse me back to health? I was told she keeps a horse in the encampment.'

'She does. In fact, I saw her riding out about half an hour since—in the direction of the river.'

In no time at all Charles had his horse saddled up and was riding at a careful pace away from the encampment.

She left her horse grazing close to the shallow river, which meandered its way through the valley, flowing sluggishly over a stretch of shallow stones. Strolling past a row of tamarind trees with bright green feathery foliage and down a steep bank, Lucy stopped at a place where she often came to sit and put her mind in order. Removing her hat and jacket, then unfastening the top buttons of her blouse, she dipped her handkerchief into the water and, turning her face up to the sun, she bathed her face and neck, some of the water trickling down between her breasts.

The water was cold and refreshing. How she would like to strip off her clothes, to lie in the river's shallow depths and let the water wash over her naked body. She dared not, but she did remove her riding boots and stockings and dangled her feet into the cool depths. Content to sit and dream and survey the mystery of the plains stretching out in all directions, she smiled broadly when she looked down and saw tiny silver fish swimming between her feet. Turning her head, she watched as a lizard scuttled across the ground.

When stones rolled down to where she sat, she looked up the bank to see Mr Anderson standing there, looking down at her. His powerful masculinity was an assault on her senses. As if he had reached out and touched her flesh, a tiny erotic trickle coiled through her, startling her, as if a switch had been thrown deep inside her. Impatiently she tried to shake off the effect he was having on her. She had tried not to think of him, wishing she could treat him with detachment, with indifference— but she was powerless to prevent him slipping through her guard, to force her into an awareness of him. Why had she allowed herself to be attracted by him?

Charles stood looking down to where Miss Quinn sat at the water's edge. On finding her he was content to simply look at her and was sorry he had disturbed her. She was the most baffling, beguiling woman he had ever come across and, for his sins, she fascinated him. Observing her day after day as he had lain in his hospital bed, he had become ensnared by her allure. Her profile was soft against the setting sun. She was beautiful, exquisite. Yet there was something else about her that intrigued him. It was not easily apparent.

Having one failed and painful love affair behind him, he had decided not to become caught up in another serious relationship, that his work would come above all else. He was now master of himself—he was sure of that—or perhaps not so sure when Miss Quinn suddenly turned her head and looked at him, a half-smile on her lips.

The effect on Charles was as potent as the full smile she had given him on coming out of his delirium. He felt the tingling in his neck and then down his spine, as intense as any he had ever known. He was bewitched, utterly enchanted by this new picture of Miss Quinn as she smiled, her lovely face suffused with pleasure and her soft lips parted and lifted with laugher. He was relieved to discover she had not lost her ability to smile after all.

Spellbound as he was, the tingling turned to heat, a curious, inflaming heat. The heat grew as she continued to look at him—he was aroused by that smile. For a moment he felt his resistance waver. It pulled him up short. It was a small warning, but a warning all the same. Too often for his peace of mind, Miss Quinn could get beneath his guard. He would have to keep a tighter rein on his attraction to her, but she was not an easy woman to ignore. Her manner and personality along with her beauty, of which she seemed unaware, remained unblemished by self-interest. Until that moment he had not fully realised the extent of the emotions she aroused in him, but, seeing her like this, immersed in her own thoughts, at ease and uninhibited, he knew it was going to be no simple matter leaving her behind when he left for Guntal.

When Lucy saw who it was who had come to disturb her peace, her smile was fleeting, vanishing from her lips. Immediately she withdrew her feet from the river, pulling down her skirt, no doubt feeling extremely vulnerable that he should find her with her bare legs dangling into the water.

'Mr Anderson!' she said, glancing to where he had left his horse, close to her own. 'You take me by surprise. I did not expect to see you back in the saddle quite so soon.'

'I'm impatient to regain the strength in my leg. The sooner I can continue with my journey into Guntal, the better. Do you often come down to the river?'

'When I can.' Grasping her boots and stockings, she scrambled back up the bank.

'I came to find you. I hope you don't mind.'

She seemed surprised. 'Did you? What on earth for?'

'To apologise for any offence I may have caused—which I hope was not the reason you haven't been to the hospital of late. I've come to make amends,' he told her, sitting on a convenient boulder and lounging back in an indolent manner.

She eyed him warily. The amazing eyes still focused on her as he waited for her to reply. She drew a deep breath. 'You have? You seem unsure.'

He raised one well-defined eyebrow, watching her, a half-smile playing on his lips. 'I'm quite sure. You are well, I trust.'

'As you see,' she replied evenly, 'I have survived our previous encounters without scars—and my absence from the hospital has nothing to do with you. I have other duties, teaching children here in the cantonment, which keeps me busy most days.'

Charles noted the softening of her expression that was currently replacing her normal hauteur. No man could not be moved by the lovely features of this woman, who possessed a spirit equal to his own. It really added to his admiration of her. He'd known it from the start by just looking into her eyes and realised the spirit of her there, the intelligence. 'Hasn't anyone told you it isn't advisable to go wandering off alone?' He looked down at her feet. 'I see you have removed your boots and stockings as well.'

'Clearly,' she replied, her sarcasm not lost on Charles. 'I couldn't resist the pull of the cool water.' Her look challenged him to argue.

'Now that I can understand. I have noted that since

our meeting at the hospital, things have been somewhat strained between us. If I have been at fault and offended you in any way, then I beg your pardon. I would dearly like us to promote a deeper understanding and friendship between ourselves—if you are in agreement, that is?'

Sitting on the ground and proceeding to pull on her boots, Lucy stiffened. 'No, of course not. But I think we understand each other well enough—and I was not aware that our friendship needs promoting. You will be leaving for Guntal as soon as your wound is healed enough to withstand the journey and we will never see each other again.'

'I did not intend to cause you any...puzzlement. When I came across you and took you to the hospital, to me you were no different to any other wounded man or sick child who needed care. If you find me quiet, that is because I am a private person. I have much on my mind.'

Perched on his boulder, he continued to watch her, his eyes dark and brooding. 'I have no wish to break into your privacy, but you have erected a barrier between us which puzzles me. You appear to have formed an adverse opinion of me and keep me at arm's length for some reason, which I find hard to understand. I believe I have expressed my gratitude with all sincerity for what you did for me when you found me wounded.'

'For which I thank you. I have never wished to be hurtful or unfriendly towards you, Mr Anderson,' she said, having pulled on her boots and standing up, 'and I do not believe I have been either. You misjudge me and my motives. I apologise if you find my manner and my character at all unfriendly. I do not mean to be. It is as I am and I cannot guess how else you would have me be. My father is very much on my mind at present. With that and the work I do, I can think of little else.'

'I can understand that. It cannot be an easy time for you.'

'It isn't. I appreciate your concern.'

'How long have you been in India, Miss Quinn?'

'Since I was ten years old. Father was born here. He didn't like England when he finally got to go there—he said it was too cold and always raining and he couldn't wait to get back to India. Sadly, my mother, who was an only child and was brought up in London, couldn't settle in India. She couldn't stand the dust, the humidity and the poverty she found here.'

'You still have relatives in England?'

'My maternal grandmother—whose health has deteriorated of late. My grandfather, who was in banking, died of a seizure several years ago. I correspond with my grandmother on a regular basis—although as you will know from your own experiences regarding any correspondence from England, by the time letters arrive here, it is old news.'

'That is true.'

'Grandmother hated it when Mother left for India. She missed her terribly and lived in hope that she would return home. Sadly, they never saw each other again.'

'And what is your opinion of India, Miss Quinn?'

'I like it very well. When I first came here, I found it a magical place to be and very exciting. I loved the vibrancy of it all. It all seemed very exotic to me. It quickly became my home.'

'And you are still unmarried.'

She nodded, turning her head away, but not before Charles had seen a dark shadow enter her eyes. 'Yes, and that suits me very well.'

There was some history there, Charles thought, and he was tempted to probe further. But it wasn't his business and he knew there was no point pressing her to reveal more than she wanted to reveal. If she felt like talking about it, she would.

'How unconventional you are, Miss Quinn.'

'I'm afraid I am,' she agreed with an unregretful sigh. 'The ladies in the cantonment, with nothing better to do, discuss me over their afternoon tea all the time, having already decided I am beyond redemption, that I have utter disregard for the rules that govern the conduct and outlook of other young ladies. And you, Mr Anderson?' she said, swinging the conversation around to the safer ground of asking him about himself. 'Are you as popular with the ladies in Madras as you are portrayed as being?'

'No one is ever quite what they seem, Miss Quinn,' he replied, sidestepping the question. 'Not even you. Besides, since leaving the Company I have not been to Madras. You know,' he said, his gaze never leaving hers, 'you have a unique distinction.'

'I have? What is that?'

'You have the distinction, apart from my sister, of being the only woman to have reminded me of my less than honourable reputation to my face.' His lips twitched with ill-suppressed amusement. 'I recall you accused me of being wicked and dangerous. Lying there in the hospital, I felt wounded to the quick and deflated, as though I'd been pricked all over with thorns.'

'You have a hide thicker than an oxen's, Mr Anderson,' Miss Quinn retorted drily. 'I'm sure you'll heal. Why did you come to India?'

'Because I wanted to. I was working for the Company in London and when the opportunity for me to come to India arose, I leapt at the chance—which was as well. It is only by being here—working for the Company—that my eyes were opened to the corruption that went on.'

'Which is why you left and became a diplomat—a much more honourable profession.'

'I think so.'

'And you get to go to wonderful places. The Rajah of Guntal's palace is renowned for its beauty.'

'You have been there?'

She shook her head. 'No, but I would love to. You can see it from here—see?—far in the distance.'

Shading her eyes, she looked across the shimmering expanse that separated Nandra from Guntal, to the blue mountains topped with snow. The pink walls of the Rajah's palace could just be made out over the miles, sleeping under the open blue sky, basking comfortably in the heat haze.

'There,' she said, pointing in the direction of the palace. 'That is where the Rajah of Guntal lives in fantastic splendour in the city of Kassam. You should get there in less than a day's ride.'

'Which is fortunate considering my injury.'

'Yes—you are so lucky to be going there.' Tearing her eyes away from the object of her dreams, she looked at Mr Anderson, who was watching her closely. 'You mentioned that you would like to meet my father.'

He nodded. 'I would—if it is convenient.'

'I told you he is unwell, but I know he would be pleased to meet you. Perhaps tomorrow evening.'

'Of course. I will look forward to it.'

'Then that's settled. You have family here?'

He shook his head. 'What family I have is back in England.'

'Who is Tilly?'

'Tilly? She is my sister. Why do you ask?'

'Because in your delirium when you were at the hospital, you kept repeating her name. You must be close, I think.'

'You think correctly. Tilly is younger than me—she married an earl and went to live in Devon before I left to come to India.' He looked at her sideways, squinting his eyes in the sun. 'You remind me of her,' he said suddenly.

'Do I? How?'

'It is a compliment, Miss Quinn. Believe me. Tilly is like a free spirit, but she is also a fierce individual.'

Miss Quinn smiled. 'So you are saying I am fierce—but I'll accept the compliment. You miss her, don't you?'

He was silent for a moment, his gaze shifting to a place beyond her. 'Yes, very much. I haven't talked about her in a long time.'

With the sun settling on them both, Miss Quinn waited for him to go on.

'I remember the joy of her, the way she had of teasing me mercilessly, the sound of her laughter—and the way her eyes would sparkle when she was happy.'

'I see the way you love her.' She felt his gaze steady and searching on her face, as if he wanted her to know his sister.

'I also have a half-brother—he's a marquess.'

Miss Quinn raised her eyebrows in mock surprise. 'A marquess? How very grand.'

He grinned. 'He is. He came out to India with the Company before leaving and going off on his own, before returning to England to take up his inheritance.'

'And where do you live, Mr Anderson, when you are in England?'

'In London—although I do have a house in Devon.'

'Devon is a long way from London.'

'It is—and I have yet to see the house, which is close to the coast. I inherited it on the death of an uncle. I did consider selling it, but Tilly lives close by—she lived in the house for a while and loves the place. She persuaded me not to sell it—not until I've seen it.'

'And will you go and see it?'

He shrugged. 'I have no idea. Probably—when I return to England.'

'Who lives there now?'

'At present my aunt is in residence—along with a couple of servants. She has fallen in love with the place, so I expect I shall have to please them both and hold on to it for the present.' He struggled to his feet when Miss Quinn began to walk towards the horses, bringing a scowl to his face. 'Do you have to walk so quickly? My wound forbids me to move at a faster pace,' he said when she glanced back at him with suspicion.

'You do not look to be in great pain, Mr Anderson, so

I am inclined to think your wound is healing.' Then she frowned at the guilty smile that flitted across his face. 'Although, it would seem you are not above playing on your infirmity to garner sympathy and to get your own way,' she said sweetly but pointedly.

His grin was disarming. 'You read me too well, Miss Quinn. I will not lose any opportunity to gain your attention in the hope that on better acquaintance you might get to like me a little better.

As they rode side by side back to the encampment, looking straight ahead Lucy thought of the strange conversation they had engaged in. Had she been too ready to judge, to believe the gossip she'd heard about him? Was he so different from what she had assumed? For the short time she had known him, she decided that none of it described him or did him justice. There was a powerful charisma about him that had nothing to do with his honed physique or mocking smile.

There was something else, too, something behind that lazy smile and unbreachable wall of aloof strength behind his dark blue eyes, that told her that Charles Anderson had done, seen and experienced all there was to do and see, that to know him properly would be exciting and dangerous, and therein lay his appeal—an appeal that frightened and unnerved her.

She told herself that he was nothing to her, just a spectacularly handsome man who happened to have entered her life when he had taken an unfortunate tumble from his horse. As soon as he was recovered, he would leave for Guntal and any association between her and the infamous Charles Anderson would cease.

Yet all the time Lucy rode beside him or followed him along narrow, winding paths, she was burningly aware of him in ways that she had never been with Johnathan. She was shaken to the core by the bewildering sensations racing through her body. She tried to turn her head away, but his extraordinary presence would draw her back. These feelings and emotions disconcerted her and made her feel strangely lightheaded. It was as if he invaded her very being.

Vaguely she realised that, despite what had happened to her and her youthful romance with Johnathan, she was an innocent when it came to physical desire. She had never experienced anything even vaguely resembling what she was experiencing now. All about them was the sweep of the landscape and a sky full of birds rising and wheeling in glittering formations against the puffs of cloud. Her increasing preoccupation with Mr Anderson troubled her. Better to keep him at arm's length, prudence whispered—but since when had she listened to prudence?

Chapter Three

Seated in her usual chair on the veranda awaiting the arrival of Mr Anderson, Lucy saw him coming towards her, his firmly marked eyebrows drawn together as he concentrated on placing one foot in front of the other, steadying himself with his cane. As her thoughts raced, he paused and looked at her, then carried on walking towards her.

In that moment she noticed the startling, intense blue of his eyes and again thought how extraordinarily attractive he was. Her heart seemed suddenly to leap into her throat in a ridiculous way and she chided herself for being so foolish.

She was lightly clad in a shimmering green and gold sari. A curling lock of gleaming blonde hair had come loose from its arrangement in the nape of her neck and curled over her shoulder, resting on her breast. Lucy knew instinctively that he was just as aware of her as she was of him and bent her head so that he should not see her confusion. After a moment, quite composed now, she lifted her eyes and rose and stood at the top of the steps to wait for him, flicking the lock of hair back over her shoulder. His direct masculine assurance disconcerted her, but she was determined not to show weakness.

'I trust it's still convenient to meet with your father?'

'Yes, of course. He's awake now and looking forward to meeting you. Excuse me while I go in and tell him you are here.'

Lucy paused in the doorway of her father's bedroom. The punkah, suspended over the large bed with its richly embroidered silk cover that stood in the centre of the room, swayed gently in the draught from the door. Seated in a curved-back armchair close to the window overlooking the garden at the back of the house, was her father. He was wearing a long, loose robe of saffron silk, with a pair of soft slippers on his feet. His eyes were closed as if asleep or in deep thought.

Lucy paused for a moment to take in the sight of him. His face was drawn and there were dark rings round his eyes. He looked so frail and elderly. He had lost weight and his skin was an unhealthy yellow.

As if sensing a presence, he opened his eyes. On seeing her a smile spread across his face.

'Mr Anderson has arrived, Father, and is eager to meet you.'

'And I him. Doctor Jessop speaks highly of him.' He squinted at his daughter. 'Tell me, what is this Mr Anderson like? Is he to your liking?'

Taken by surprise by his question, Lucy averted her eyes, but was unable to quell the flush that mantled her cheeks, which did not go unnoticed by her father and brought a frown to his brow.

'Yes—I mean—he is well liked and highly thought

of by those who know him—but I do not know him very well.'

'But well enough to have formed an opinion, surely.'

Lucy shrugged complacently. 'You will soon see for yourself what kind of man he is.'

He nodded, studying her closely. 'I dare say I will. It pleases me when visitors come to call. It provides me with the opportunity to talk about the old days in India.' Tilting his head to one side, he said, 'You look well, Lucy—more relaxed somehow—different. Happily, I believe I am beginning to see the old Lucy slowly emerge from her shell.'

'I'm trying, Father. Every day I try.'

'Of course you do. It's time to move on. It's been long enough—too long. Don't let what happened to you steal your future. I would not want that for you. You are too young to shut yourself away.'

'I know. I know. It's all I've thought about of late. But—it's hard, Father.'

'Of course it is.' He patted her hand affectionately. 'But knowing you, you'll get there. Now—we have a guest I am looking forward to meeting. You'd better show him in.'

Going out, Lucy thought of what her father had said about what had happened to her in the past and realised with shock that he was right. She was beginning to feel like her old self, an insight into how her life could be if she would let it and move on. It was up to her to take the initiative.

Mr Anderson turned to face her when she reappeared.

'We'll go in now…' She smiled. 'He has a habit of dropping off to sleep, I'm afraid. He is extremely poorly.

Doctor Jessop sees him on a regular basis, but there is little to be done.'

'I'll try not to tire him.'

Charles levelled a steady gaze at the silver-haired man, noting the unhealthy yellowing of his skin. Silently they took stock of each of each other before shaking hands.

'Mr Anderson.' Jeremiah Quinn spoke to him amiably because his daughter would not have lied about his character. 'I'm sorry I was not there to receive you, but as you see I am incapacitated just now. My health is not good. Jessop has ordered me not to overtax myself. It's more than my life is worth to defy him.' He looked at Lucy standing at the side of his chair. 'You've met my daughter.'

Charles's gaze passed warmly over her, bringing a slight flush to her face, which did not go unnoticed by her father. 'It has been my pleasure.'

'I'm proud of her. She's grown into a fine young woman.'

'Alas, I fear I'm not that, Father,' Lucy retorted. 'Mrs Marsh still thinks I'm a hopeless hoyden and her friend, Mrs Senior, says my manners are deplorable and I am a disgrace. I fear they are both right.'

Her father chuckled softly. 'They are just two old ladies with nothing to do with their time other than gossip.'

He fixed his attention on his visitor. 'I never did keep a tight rein on my daughter, which I have oft had reason to regret, but she has a single-minded determination and a will to match—in addition, she is a courageous young woman with a particular brand of quiet fortitude. You were injured, Mr Anderson—fell off your horse, Lucy tells me.'

'I did and I am grateful to your daughter and Dr Jessop for putting me back together. My wound still bothers me, but it's nothing I can't deal with. I hope to be on my way to Guntal shortly.'

'You must take care. Skirmishes both in Puna and Guntal occur on a regular basis.'

'Father is right,' Lucy said, looking at Charles. 'These raids happen all too often—by such wicked people, who seem to be a law unto themselves.'

'There are good and bad people everywhere.' Jeremiah looked at his visitor. 'You're no longer a Company man, Mr Anderson—not that I blame you. Your new position as a British envoy you must find rewarding. You have met the Rajah of Guntal, I believe. What is the nature of him?'

'I think you'd like him. He's a benevolent sort—but one shouldn't be fooled. He's as shrewd and cunning as an old fox and misses nothing. As you know, Guntal is an independent state and the Rajah intends it to remain that way. Thankfully the two of us get on reasonably well.'

After speaking of diplomatic issues a while longer, Jeremiah's eye lids began to droop. Tactfully Charles left.

Back on the veranda, Lucy indicated the cushioned wicker seat opposite. 'Please take a seat.'

Mr Anderson did as invited and sat opposite her, biting back a curse at the discomfort this caused him. He had turned white around the mouth, Lucy noted in dismay, while his hand rubbed his right thigh. After a moment his pain must have eased because he relaxed and stretched his legs out in front of him.

Recognising the obvious admiration she read in his eyes when he looked at her, she suddenly became aware of the boldness of his body, his maleness and the impropriety of entertaining a gentleman alone at this time of night. Mrs Marsh would consider such behaviour scandalous. Lucy smiled inwardly, uncaring what Mrs Marsh would say.

'You appear relaxed,' Mr Anderson said softly, his gaze appraising.

'I love this time of day, when smoke and dust hang over the town. I love the cool of the evening and often sit and look at the lazy meandering of the river below the sloping lawn and watch the colourful sunsets and the stars come out, which I used to do with my father before he became confined to his bed. We would sit and listen to the crickets and the night birds and the sound of unoiled wheels on the dusty road—all contributing to the murmur of the Indian night. It's a time for dreaming.' She fell silent for a moment as her gaze swept appreciatively over her surroundings.

Cool drinks appeared before them, offered by a young Indian serving girl dressed in a bright pink sari, her shining black hair plaited down her back. A broad smile stretched her lips and she dipped her gaze when she saw the imposing visitor.

'Thank you, Nisha,' Lucy said.

Nisha left as quietly as she had appeared. Accepting the drink Lucy handed to him, her visitor drank gratefully. After a moment's silence he managed to stand.

As he did so his expression was pained, betraying the effect of his exertions. He stood looking down at the river, his tall, lean body clearly delineated by the moonlit night. 'You are in a good position here, with no over-looking neighbours.'

'Don't you believe it,' Lucy said with irony. 'There are few secrets here. Everyone knows everyone else and what is happening. Your appearance in Nandra will have been seen and noted, and, come breakfast, everyone will be gossiping about it and speculating on the reason for your visit to the house.'

'And will be met with censure, I suppose.'

'You suppose correctly. The British and their an-tiquated ways of doing things—ways that dominate women's lives especially—needs reforming.'

'Forgive me, Miss Quinn, but you seem to have done that all by yourself.'

'Only because it suits me and because I don't give a fig for anyone's opinion. Boredom can set in if one is not careful, which is why I began teaching the children of the British community their lessons and helping Dr Jessop in the infirmary. Before my father's retirement, sometimes I would accompany him on official trips that were not too far away. At other times I ride out in the cool of the day, keeping to the confines of the town for my own safety.'

'You ride alone?'

'Maya, one of the house servants, loves to ride and often accompanies me.'

'And on occasion you even take to wearing Indian dress'

Lucy smiled. 'As you see. I find the light fabrics cooler

and more suitable to the Indian climate. They are also far more comfortable to wear than being trussed up in yards of cumbersome skirts and undergarments and whale bones that restrict the freedom of movement of a healthy female form.'

'Indian dress also shows the natural shape of a woman's body and brings out in her an innate femininity,' Charles said softly. 'I think you are the most unconventional young lady I have ever met, Miss Quinn. You are your own person. It is a relief to find a woman who has dispersed with ridiculous conventions.'

'Not all of them,' she denied indignantly. 'There are still some that I abide by—otherwise my life would not be worth living.'

Charles chuckled softly. 'I do believe you,' he said, his expression telling her he was not convinced.

Lucy smiled. 'I must confess that I find it hard to submit to the taboos and restrictions that govern the conduct of an unmarried English lady in a small station. My lack of convention at first shocked the English ladies of the community, especially one, who scrutinised me thoroughly through her lorgnette when she called on my father one day, and declared it was an outrage that I should flaunt myself so shamelessly. As if that weren't bad enough, another lady, Mrs Marsh, almost suffered an apoplectic fit when I began assisting Dr Jessop in the infirmary. As far as she and the other stiff, elderly ladies who make up the British community were concerned, I broke nearly every rule that dictates the lives of young ladies.'

'Is it not the opinion that a woman should not find herself independent?'

'What? And be governed by the fears and restrictions that blight so many women's lives? I do not share that opinion. I have a mind and will of my own and make my own decisions—for which I am condemned by the likes of Mrs Marsh.'

'How did you react to such condemnation?'

'I simply shrugged off the recriminations and ignore their censure, uncaring what others think of me.'

'And who exactly is Mrs Marsh?'

'She is the doyenne of the British community here. She believes she has the right to dispense orders and judgement like a queen. There are so many rules an English woman in India must abide by—most of which I have broken. A young lady must never voice her opinions in public or discuss politics, which should be left to the men, and she must never appear in public without a servant. In other words, all young ladies must show decorum, prudence and the virtues of sobriety at all times, both in public and in private. She has the young ladies quaking in their shoes.'

'But not you, Miss Quinn.'

'Absolutely not. I am no eighteen-year-old miss, but a woman with a mind and a will of my own. I will not be dictated to by women of Mrs Marsh's ilk.'

Mr Anderson laughed. 'Or anyone else who does not gain your good opinion. You are certainly no delicate, pampered young woman, that's for sure.'

'Precisely. Despite the likes of Mrs Marsh, if you are to remain in Nandra for some time, on the whole you will find a spirit of kindliness and hospitality among the British community. We've had to learn the value of society and don't be surprised when you begin receiving invitations to attend social functions and entertainments. As handsome as you are, Mr Anderson, you will have every lady buzzing round you and wanting to partner you in the dance.'

'Dancing is not one of my favourite pastimes.'

'No? Well, you have the perfect excuse not to—your wounded leg has put paid to that. I do have many friends here—we are all in the same boat, after all, and Mrs Wilson, who came to Nandra with her husband at the same time as my parents and has a married daughter living in Madras, takes me under her wing from time to time, for which I am grateful.

'But I often wonder if the English will ever realise that their customs and values cannot work here in India, where the old gods rule. Few make concession to local custom—beyond the gentlemen smoking hookahs. The fact that I go my own way and don't always listen to the dictates of my father has crystalised all my sins in Mrs Marsh's mind. My father says I am too wilful and unconventional—and I suppose I am. Which is why all the old ladies in Nandra are always complaining to him about me and giving him advice on the best way to deal with a wayward daughter. But he likes me the way I am and wouldn't like it if I were to change.'

'Your father is quite right. You are what you are. You can't please everybody. One's true character springs from the heart and dwells in the eyes. Unconventionality is an invitation to disaster in the world we inhabit.'

Lucy stared at him. 'How very profound.' Gazing into his unfathomable eyes, she saw cynicism lurking in their depths. She had the uneasy feeling that his indolent manner was nothing but a disguise to lull the unwary into believing he was civilised, when he wasn't civilised at all.

Hearing a lilting voice singing in the nether regions of the house, Mr Anderson rested his hips on the rail and folded his arms across his broad chest and cocked a curious brow. 'Someone sounds happy.'

'That's Nisha. She's a great help—although she is to be married shortly and will not be coming here when she is wed. All she's talked about for weeks is the wedding, what she is going to wear and the preparations.'

'It was arranged, I suppose.'

'Of course. It was arranged between the bridegroom's family and her own some time ago. It is the custom—and she is fortunate to have fallen in love with her future husband at first sight.'

'You think that, do you, Miss Quinn—that she is fortunate?'

'Of course I do. A marriage based on love is more likely to withstand the trials and tribulations of the future. Don't you agree? Although I imagine your opinions on that particular subject differs from mine.'

'I have told you previously that I have no time at present for marriage and affairs of the heart. A man who loves too well is vulnerable.'

'When has love anything to do with marriage?' Lucy returned, deriding his cynicism and going to stand beside him at the rail. 'Marriage is a contract based upon oneself for security and property, whereas true love must be free—uninhibited—and have the foundations of trust and fidelity.'

'Ah, but love is inconsistent,' Mr Anderson proclaimed. 'Desire is a more honest and recognisable emotion.'

Lucy lifted her chin as her eyes caught his flickering appreciatively over her from the top of her head to the slippers peeping from the hem of her sari. She shook her head. 'Desire is fleeting, while love is all-consuming.'

'And when love and passion burn themselves out, nothing is left but a shedload of bitterness.'

There was a deep blush on Lucy's cheekbones, as much to her gathering annoyance she found she did not mind his calm, unhurried appraisal of her. 'It doesn't always end like that.'

'Love is not the only side to a relationship.'

'I know. But it is the most important one. I realise that for some, money and gain in some way is the only consideration, but there is more to marriage than that. Two people should marry because they love each other, because there is a longing to be close to each other.'

'You really are a romantic, Miss Quinn.'

'I suppose I am. When I marry, I will settle for nothing less.' When he gave her a sceptical glance, she raised her brows in question. 'I see you find something wrong with that.'

Shaking his head slowly, he smiled thinly. 'In my opinion love is a common passion, in which chance and sensation take the place of choice and reason and draw the mind out of its accustomed state.'

'That is your opinion, but I will not under any circumstances reduce myself to living in wifely obedience in a loveless marriage.'

His gaze returned to her face. He gave her a long slow look, a twist of humour around his beautifully moulded lips. The smile building about his mouth creased the clear hardness of his jaw and made him appear in that moment as the most handsome man in the world. 'And there speaks a hopeless romantic,' he declared softly. 'Love is for the young and idealistic. It is magnificent while it lasts, but once it is appeased it is soon reduced to the boredom of familiarity.'

Lucy laughed despite herself. 'And those are the words of a rake and confirmed bachelor. You should have a care, Mr Anderson, for the day will come when you venture too close to love's flames and get burned. It will bring you more heartache than you can ever imagine.'

'I see that you are determined to think me some kind of reprobate,' he said coolly, 'which is quite untrue I hasten to add. But if so, does it not concern you that to be seen in such bad company might rebound on you?'

There was more than a hint of mockery in his eyes though he continued to smile.

'Not at all. I may be unconventional, but I am far too independent to be concerned whether the company I keep is good or bad. I run my own life.'

'Run it or ruin it, Miss Quinn?' He grinned, his eyes twinkling with mischief. 'Unconventional ladies are always the most exciting.'

A smile twitched the corners of Lucy's lips. 'You may be right. How can I argue with an experienced man of the world? The ladies appear to be enamoured of you. Enjoy your popularity while it lasts.'

'But you will never be one of them, will you, Miss Quinn?'

'Never.' She laughed to dispel the seriousness of the moment. His words were flippant, but Lucy heard an edge to his voice. Some woman in his past had caused that cynical note, she was sure. 'Your words and the seriousness of your expression tells me that whatever has befallen you in the past—perhaps an unrequited love affair—has left scars, as yet unhealed.' What had happened to harden his heart so? she wondered.

He turned away from her. His body was tense, the tendons of his neck corded. Lucy stifled an impulse to reach out to him. The content of their conversation had revived memories for him and she regretted that. She had bitter memories of her own she had no wish to discuss, so she knew exactly how he felt. She continued to stare at his profile, uneasy at the tension which lay between them.

His voice was mocking when he eventually spoke. 'You are right, Miss Quinn. Aren't you curious about her? Aren't you going to ask me who she was—what terrible deed she committed? You are a woman—is that not what all women want to know?'

'It has nothing to do with me. If you want to tell me, you will. You are well travelled, Mr Anderson, and must have been to some interesting places and seen much. You must also have made friends and enemies along the way. Your comments prompted me to draw a conclusion. I didn't mean to pry.'

Drawn by the sincerity of her words, he turned and looked at her. The intensity of his gaze was so profound that Lucy thought he was about to tell her more of the woman who must have got under his skin at some point.

'There are some things one prefers to forget.'

Lucy respected his privacy. She had her own demons to deal with. His gaze was drawn to the scoop of the low neckline of her bodice, which displayed the gentle, upper swell of her breasts. Seeing where his gaze had settled, she put a hand to cover her decolletage.

Suddenly, his direct masculine appearance disconcerted her. She was vividly conscious of his proximity to her. She felt the mad, unfamiliar rush of blood singing through her veins which she had never experienced before, not even with Johnathan. Immediately she felt resentful towards him. He had made too much of an impact on her and she was afraid that, if he looked at her much longer, he would read her thoughts with those brilliant eyes of his.

Clearly amused by her haste to defend her modesty, he chuckled softly. 'Devil take it, Miss Quinn. How am I ever going to regard the woman who nursed me back to health in the same light again?'

She laughed. 'Don't they say restraint is good for the soul?' she challenged.

'I believe they do, but I have yet to find it so. Why do you remain unmarried?'

Lucy turned her head away, having no wish to tell him how she had wrapped the pain and the grief of Johnathan's loss about her like a blanket. 'I—I lost someone—we were betrothed. It—was difficult. He was killed,' she said quietly, a faraway look in her eyes. 'There was an—an incident that led to his death.'

A shadow crossed her face and, for a moment, her companion knew she was recalling the pain that was inflicted on her of her betrothed's death. An incident, she said. She wasn't telling him everything. There was some history there, he thought, and he was tempted to probe further. But it wasn't his business and he knew there was no point pressing her to reveal more than she wanted. He set it aside, for now. There was a desperation about her that he had not witnessed before. She was usually so composed.

'My father always said I hid my feelings and he was right. It has become a habit with me and perhaps a form of defence, too.'

'A defence against what?' The bravado fell away from her, like a cloak, and she transformed before his eyes into someone much more vulnerable.

'Becoming hurt again. At the time it seemed so unfathomable to me that someone whom one had strong feelings for could die so suddenly.' Mr Anderson reached out and touched her arm. Their eyes met and something passed between them. She half smiled. 'To lose someone you love in such a brutal manner is the worst thing that can happen. It's made me more determined never to experience the pain—such distress— like that again. So you see, I have relegated myself to the proverbial shelf for ever.'

He nodded, looking at her from beneath hooded lids. 'Until someone comes along to pluck you off that shelf.'

Again, there was that flirtatious touch in his words

Miss Quinn so distrusted. 'It's a very broad shelf, Mr Anderson. I very much doubt anyone will do that.'

'You are very sure of yourself, Miss Quinn.'

'Not as sure as you might think. I have my weaknesses just like everyone else.'

'You accused me of being a libertine—are you not afraid to be seen in the company of a man with an unsavoury reputation?'

Although Lucy could feel her pulses racing, she somehow managed to maintain her calm expression. 'I haven't thought about it. Should I?'

He arched an eyebrow. 'No. You are quite safe.'

'As you said yourself, Mr Anderson, no one is what they seem. Perhaps you are a scoundrel with a sudden urge to reform.'

A low chuckle preceded his reply. 'Heaven forbid! I confess that I find this unfortunate development a nuisance, but one good thing has come out of it.'

'It has? And what is that, pray?'

'I get to spend time getting to know you better.'

'Why? Do you find my company pleasant?'

'When you're not being stubborn and temperamental.'

'I am never temperamental.'

'I disagree. There's no question about it.'

'Only if I'm driven to it.'

'You know, Miss Quinn, despite what you say about living on a very broad shelf, a lovely young woman like you should be surrounded by doting swains.'

She looked away. 'Why on earth would I want that? I wouldn't know what to do with them. I have my work at the school, which I enjoy, and helping Dr Jessop, which is important to me—and now, perhaps, my father to take care of. I will allow nothing to interfere with that.'

'Not even love,' he murmured softly, his gaze capturing hers.

'No.'

'Are you afraid of love, Miss Quinn?'

'No, of course I'm not.'

'I don't believe you.'

'Believe what you like. It's true,' she retorted.

'Then if you are not afraid of love, why do you hide behind your work at the school and the hospital?'

'I am not hiding—and it is not my school. I just happen to teach there.'

'Now you are prevaricating, Miss Quinn. I think if you didn't have to mix with others on the cantonment, you would be quite happy to make yourself invisible—to fade into obscurity.' He smiled at her sudden look of indignation that his words had provoked.

'I apologise if my opinion is unkind, but you must admit that it does have the ring of truth about it.' She appeared to think about what he had said for a moment. He hoped there was something in his face that would invite her confidence, but it was not forthcoming.

'Whether it is true or not, I would not admit such a thing to you. The man I loved and would have married was killed. I am no longer interested in forming any kind of relationship.'

His eyes narrowed on her face and he spoke softly. 'Then as a woman you are truly unique.'

She looked at him warily, swallowing nervously. 'You

are not trying to seduce me by any chance, are you, Mr Anderson?'

'Would you allow me to seduce you, Miss Quinn?'

Something stirred deep within her—the need for this man that increased with every moment she spent with him. And she had to stop this, needed to remember that he was soon to leave for Guntal. In spite of the fact that his eyes were touching her in a way she hadn't been touched in a long time, she gave him a defiant look. 'Now you're mocking me.'

'I wouldn't dream of doing that. You are far too adorable to mock.'

Her lips curved in a reluctant smile. 'And you really are a complete rogue, Mr Anderson, arrogant and overbearing.'

He grinned. 'I am. I admit it. What I need,' he said, moving closer to her, 'is a lovely, patient and extremely tolerant young woman to take me in hand, to make me see the error of my ways and reform me.'

'Then I wish you luck.' Turning her back on him, she clutched the rail with her hands. 'Intolerance and impatience have always been two of my failings, but there must be a female somewhere who will fall for a silken tongue and an accomplished womaniser, who will be willing to expend so much energy, time and effort on such an unenviable task.'

He laughed softly. 'Maybe there is, but she will never be bored, I promise you that.'

'So, you admit it—what they say about you is true after all.'

When she fell silent, his hands clenched and his eyes

hardened. 'Let me assure you that what you have just accused me of being—a philanderer of the worst possible kind, I believe—is exceedingly exaggerated and I would like to set the record straight. I am a man of pride and honour and with a strong sense of responsibility. You really shouldn't listen to gossip. I am sorry to disappoint you and shatter the illusion you appear to have of me, but I must tell you that it is with some regret that I find I have little time for the kind of pleasures you speak of. Much of my time is taken up with the more important matter of furthering British relations with India.'

Her expression became serious and she nodded slightly. 'I apologise if I have wrongly maligned you. Despite what I have said to the contrary in our short acquaintance, I have never been one to listen to gossip, only facts.'

He moved to stand closer to her. 'You are a lovely young woman, Lucy Quinn—a temptress—a dangerous temptress I am finding increasingly impossible to resist.'

Suddenly Lucy sensed danger. Her spine prickled. The air between them was alive with tension. She felt every moment with such heightened sensuality that she knew if he were to continue speaking to her in this manner, she was in danger of releasing all the tensions and worries she'd been carrying for so long. The need to be away from him was strong and frightening in its intensity.

She hesitated. Reaching out, he took her arm and drew her closer to his side. Should she let him prevail in his hunger, his desire? No, she didn't want it—or did she? Her confusion, her passion and her pain rose to a pinnacle as she stood trembling against him. To be this close to Mr Anderson felt as though she was suffocating. She didn't think she could survive it. But she would survive it. Her instinct told her that this man wouldn't hurt her. She trusted him. Could he be the one to lead her back to normality, to a normal life, to take away her fear of what to expect from any man who encroached too close?

Tentatively turning to face him, her slender jaw hardening with resolution, she met his gaze directly. 'Mr Anderson,' she said very clearly, 'I would like you to kiss me.'

Chapter Four

Mr Anderson stared at her, clearly wondering if he had heard her correctly. 'What did you say?'

'I want you to kiss me,' Lucy repeated quite clearly. From the way he was looking at her, Lucy realised that he could see she was in the grip of some powerful emotion, for he must be able to feel her trembling.

Involuntarily, he dropped his gaze to her mouth. It was a tantalising mouth, made to be kissed, generous, that begged for a man's caress. 'You don't know what you're asking.'

'I know very well what I'm asking. And it isn't particularly flattering for me to have to plead with you—and if you refuse my request then such will be my embarrassment that I shall have to ask you to leave and will never be able to look at you ever again.'

The roguish glint that must surely be what had charmed half the females he had ever met made his blue eyes dance with an inner light. 'Then I should hate to disappoint and cause you any embarrassment.'

Lucy stood there, gazing at him, shocked to the core by her own audacity. But she had done it now. There was no going back. Suddenly everything seemed to happen in slow motion. Taking her arms, he drew her close, his hands gentle and controlled, yet unyielding. She did not have time to change her mind before he lowered his head and found her generous mouth with his own.

The kiss was brief, little more than a meeting of lips, yet before it ended, she felt him stiffen slightly, as if he had found something surprising. And when he raised his head, she could see that he was frowning down at her, his heavy brows drawn together as if in puzzlement. Momentarily stunned, Lucy returned his gaze, shock holding her motionless. He didn't release her, but continued to stand there, appraising her.

'I'm surprised,' he said huskily. 'It's the first time a lady has invited me to kiss her. It's usually me who does the asking.'

'I expect it is—but—well, I suppose there's a first time for everything—even for you.'

'Having tasted your offering, it has left me dissatisfied and craving more.'

She smiled softly, her eyes warm and glowing as they settled on his lips. 'Oh, dear me—then to avoid any kind of discomfort you are experiencing, I think you should kiss me again, don't you?'

Their lips met again. His mouth was pure and sweet, gentle and tender. Her breasts were flattened against his broad chest, her legs pressed intimately against his muscled thighs. Her senses were dazed—perhaps it was the scent rising from the damp earth and greenery in the garden—or perhaps it was the distinctively clean scent of his skin.

She could not remember Johnathan affecting her in

such a manner—leaving her breathless and trembling. Nor had he ever kissed her the way Charles Anderson was doing now. His strong hands moved up her arms to her slender shoulders as he kissed her in an almost leisurely way—deeply, thoroughly, gliding his long fingers along her delicate jawline to tangle them in the silken tresses of her hair.

Lucy felt the wildest urge to respond to his overpowering maleness, to the warm animal magnetism that radiated from him. His mouth was warm and exciting. How very different this kiss was from what she had expected, she reflected with one part of her brain. The other had been full of trepidation and more than a little pain, but this kiss was the kind of kiss she had dreamed of and helplessly she responded to it. Sensations coursed through her.

When the kiss ended and he raised his head, she stared up at him, her composure shattered, wondering at the amazement she saw on his handsome face. Then, like an animal shedding water, he shook his head, as if to clear his muddled senses.

The movement brought Lucy to her own senses. She felt a slow, painful blush rising to her face as she realised she had allowed—asked—him to kiss her. With quiet deliberation she drew back. Terrified of making an overestimation of her ability to carry out the course she had chosen for herself, somehow she managed to take a step away from him.

'This is a mistake,' she whispered, knowing that if she allowed some tenderness between them, she would be lost. 'I think I must have taken leave of my senses. I cannot believe I did that—and that I—I actually asked you to kiss me. Why didn't you refuse?'

'Because you asked me—and because I didn't want to.'

'It's been a long time since I was kissed—not since…' She sighed, unwilling to discuss her relationship with Johnathan or what had occurred that had led up to his death lest he thought her flawed in some way.

'Not since the man you would have married,' he said with quiet understanding.

She nodded, stepping round him and moving away. Folding her arms, she stood on the veranda and looked into the distance, towards Guntal, where Charles Anderson would soon be, Charles Anderson who radiated sensual hunger in every glance, every move and every touch, but she could not deny that something had passed between them that would change their relationship for ever.

And yet, she thought, why shouldn't she want to feel such things? Johnathan wouldn't have wanted her to wallow in grief for ever. The bitterness that had consumed her for so long helped no one, least of all herself. Despite what had happened to her at the hands of the monster who had molested her, Johnathan would have wanted her to wade through the sea of sorrow and pull herself out of the quagmire of shame and loss and grief she had been floundering in for far too long.

What she and Johnathan had shared had been a wonderful, very special thing, but he was gone now—and she would not allow the man who had violated her to undermine her. He was not worth remembering. Yet the blame for depriving Johnathan of his life and the happiness that should have been his was still with her, denying her happiness for herself.

Charles moved to stand by her side, taking her shoulders and turning her to face him, then looking down at her upturned face. The colour on her cheeks was gloriously high. Her eyes were sparkling. They were the most brilliant eyes Charles had ever seen, their golden flecks so bright they seemed to be lit from within.

He was not a man of such iron control that he could resist looking down at her feminine form, which she held before him like a talisman. Noticing things like how her sari clung to her round curves so provocatively, concealing the beautiful treasures beneath, gave him a clear sense of pleasurable torture. Being so close to her, he could feel her warmth, smell the sweet scent of her body, all in such close proximity, and the memory of her responsiveness to his kiss sent heat searing into his loins.

Why did this explosion of passion happen every time he was near her? Why could this one young woman make him forget the treacherous woman who had gone before? It dawned on him as he looked down into her face that he wanted her more now than he had ever wanted any woman, if that were possible. He couldn't bear the thought that when he rode away from Nandra and into the state of Guntal, he would never see her again.

He was unprepared for the moment when she raised her head and looked at him, her eyes filled with curious longing. He was also unprepared for the question that sprang to her lips.

'Who was she, Mr Anderson? Who was it that hurt you, that made you speak so scathingly of love? Did you fall in love with her?'

Charles stared at her hard, his body tense, unwilling to answer her question, but knowing he must if he didn't want to lose her just yet. He would face that when they had to part, but for now he wanted to keep her with him for as long as possible. He thought of Amelia and the type of woman she was—self-confident, sexually alluring to every man she came into contact with, never for a moment doubting her power over the opposite sex and her ability to control and manipulate them to her advantage.

After a moment he said, 'Her name was Amelia. She was the daughter of a colonel in a Company regiment. In the beginning she appeared innocent and shy—she was also beautiful and I fell in love with her. To my deep regret I later found out that I didn't really know her at all, so blinded had I been by her beauty. Then I began to realise how ambitious she was, how she thrived on duplicity and deception. I didn't know how treacherous she could be until I told her I was to leave the Company.

'We were to have been married—but to Amelia the Company and all the pleasures it provided—the society, the balls, the admiration she needed to thrive—were too important, too much a part of her life to give up. She had no wish to become the wife of an envoy, constantly travelling the length and breadth of India. In no time at all she became attached to a titled, high-ranking officer.' His voice hardened. 'All we had shared, every word she had uttered, were meaningless.'

'I see. I'm so sorry.' Miss Quinn's eyes were large and misty with regret. They mirrored his own sense of loss. 'That must have hurt your feelings terribly. I can understand your cynicism—that it is why, because of what she did to you, you despise what romantics call love?'

He nodded. 'Something like that. Until I met Amelia there always had to be the ideal. Not only must I love the woman who captured my heart, I must be loved by her with equal measure. Anything else was unacceptable.' He paused and stared down at her.

Raising her head, she looked at him. It was a special look just for him. It seemed to beckon with strange energies. It seduced him absolutely and left him bewildered in the most sensual way. He was intrigued by the enigma of this young woman, whose naive personality concealed a mysterious core of which Miss Quinn herself was perhaps not aware.

On the spur of the moment, he said, 'Come with me. Come with me when I go to Guntal. I'm not ready to be separated from you just yet. Come and see the palace in Kassam, the palace you have dreamed of seeing for so long.'

He was close once more, his head lowered, his warm breath caressing her cheek. She didn't move. After a moment's thought, she said, 'I can't. I can't leave my father.'

'Four days, Miss Quinn. Four days is all it will take—two days for the journey and two for you to spend in the palace before you make the journey back to Nandra. I will stay on to conduct my affairs with the Rajah before I have to leave for Madras where I will have to take ship for England. We can ride to Kassam together. I'll arrange for a small military escort so you will be quite safe.'

He moved away. 'I'll leave you to think about it, to speak to your father. I'll come and see you in the morning.' Going down the steps, he followed the path to the gate where he turned and looked back at her. 'My name is Charles, by the way. After what we have just shared, for you to continue addressing me as Mr Anderson is too formal. Will you allow me to address you as Lucy?'

'Yes,' she murmured. 'Yes, I would like that.'

Lucy stood on the veranda and watched him walk away, trying to come to terms with her emotions. She thought of what he had told her, and what had been between him and the woman called Amelia, and wondered if a man ever recovered from such a love. Her eyes were narrowed as her thoughts swirled about inside her head and she wanted to reach out her arms and draw him back, knowing she was as foolish as all the other women who had fallen prey to his allure.

Her attraction to Charles was scaring her, yet boosting her. It felt so good being with him and she wasn't ready to be separated from him either. His charm was his ability to make every woman fall for his attraction, to make her feel that she was the only woman important to him.

Going to her room, she crossed to her dressing table and sat before the mirror, contemplating her features as she had done so often in the past. She was deeply dis-

turbed by what Charles had said as she tried to see what
he saw in her. He had said she was a temptress. Was
she? Somehow the wide, lustrous eyes staring back at
her looked alien to her, but determinedly she plunged
her gaze into their depths.

And suddenly, like a will-o'-the-wisp, it seemed that
someone else gazed out at her, someone almost child-
like in her innocence, but at the same time seductive—
a temptress, who seemed to grow from a tiny seed in a
recess of her personality, a seed that had lain dormant
in fertile soil until this moment. But she vanished as
quickly as she'd appeared, too shy, too coy, to be caught,
but far too real to deny.

She sighed wistfully, continuing to study her face.
Charles Anderson had cast some magical enchantment
over her. His dominance was accomplished by tenderness rather than by force and she instinctively sensed
that if she were to succumb to the mesmeric force of his
personality, she would then be at his mercy.

The opportunity to see inside the Rajah's palace was
a great temptation. She wanted to go. She wanted to be
with Charles until they had to go their separate ways—
he to return to England, she to return to Nandra and her
ailing father. She would never see him again and, while
he was still here, she wanted to see as much of him as
was possible, to absorb every part of him. Her mind
made up, she went to inform her father.

It was decided that Lucy would go with Charles when
he left for Guntal, leaving her father in the care of his
loyal servant, Kasim. Indeed, he encouraged her to go,

trusting that she would be well taken care of by Mr Anderson and with Maya as chaperon.

Two days later, the night before they were to leave, Lucy had been too excited to sleep. The morning found her up early and dressed. A chattering Maya was more than happy to accompany her, her excitement to see the Rajah of Guntal's palace as great as Lucy's. She saw to it that their tough little ponies were saddled, with bags containing their needs for the short time they would be in Kassam, the city where the Rajah had his magnificent palace. In the early light, with a thin mist trailing over the land, the mountains on the horizon were jagged crests of moving shadows, sharp edged against the northern sky.

Captain Travis and a small escort, all mounted and armed, gathered in the military encampment to begin their short journey to the town of Kassam. Lucy slanted a look at Charles as he approached on his mount. He wore a tan riding coat, a pair of buckskin breeches and highly polished brown boots. A broad-brimmed hat covered his dark hair. He dismounted, his eyes darting to Lucy. The final preparations made, after making sure Maya was settled on her mount, Lucy led her horse to where Charles and Captain Travis waited.

'You are ready, Miss Quinn?' Captain Travis asked.

'Yes, I am impatient for us to be on our way,' she replied. Lifting her head, she met Charles's gaze squarely, her face now bright with anticipation of the journey.

Hoisting herself into the saddle with an agility that both astonished and impressed both men, Lucy prepared herself for the ride ahead. The journey would take up most of the day. She loved travelling anywhere and the idea of travelling across India's vast landscape always excited her. The sun had already risen behind the hills in the distance, staining the sky red and pink with streaks of gold.

Lucy rode a small grey mare—it was unusual to see a woman riding astride. Charles's gaze took in her buff-coloured breeches and riding boots beneath the skirts of her dark brown riding habit spread out over the horse's rump. He wore a look of scarcely concealed appreciation on his handsome face as he surveyed her. Her stout-hearted mount matched the other horses stride for stride as they headed in the direction of the border with Guntal.

They spoke little as they left Nandra behind. The horses were frisky and eager to exercise their legs. Their route had been carefully worked out. They rode across the hot, parched land, the heat somewhat lessened by a light wind that blew down from the hills. Lucy was gripped by the excitement of the journey. Nothing could detract from this exotic land of mystery and beauty.

They passed abandoned homes and temples, the vegetation intense with rampant vines clinging to the crumbling walls. Entering Guntal, they rode over plains and pastures and thickly wooded countryside. Towards midday the heat was relentless. It rose in waves from the rocky ground. Lucy dabbed at her face with a handkerchief. They finally stopped beneath the shade of some trees on the edge of a small village to take refreshment and to rest the horses.

* * *

As the day drew on the ride began to take its toll on Lucy. She tried not to let her companions see it, but she was exhausted with fatigue and her inner thighs were so sore that she felt as if she would never be able to ride again. She could hardly remember the girl who would ride almost daily, cantering on her horse. That girl was a lifetime ago. She glanced at Charles who was riding alongside Captain Travis, allowing her gaze to linger, wondering what went on behind those dark blue eyes.

She noted that he absently kneaded his aching leg. He had removed his hat and the sunlight glinted on his hair, giving it a lighter touch and accentuating the nobility of his features. If not for the shadow of pain in his eyes that gave him an air of vulnerability, she might have been intimidated by him. When he looked at her, the keen blue eyes seemed to see much more than she wanted him to see.

All the while Lucy had kept her eyes on the distant horizon as they got closer to Kassam and the Rajah's palace. It was early evening when they reached the outskirts of the town. Coming to a river, they crossed over an arched stone bridge. Along the banks mahouts were bathing their elephants and children splashed about while mothers busied themselves with piles of washing. They entered the town through one of the gates. Charles halted and looked about him, careful to keep Lucy close by while he took in the layout, memorising what he saw.

A wide street acted as the main bazaar, where food

vendors cooked on open fires and every sort of produce seemed to spill in profusion from the colourful stalls on either side. Lucy inhaled the heavy air, bursting with spices and other beguiling scents. Eventually they came to the main arched gateway to the palace—sprawling and vast. It was wide enough to allow four elephants to pass through at once. They paused and looked ahead. Guards stood on either side.

Lucy was infected by a heady mixture of anxiety and excitement and the tension mounted the closer they got to the guards. 'I do so hope we won't be sent away,' she whispered.

'My arrival is expected,' Charles replied, without taking his eyes off the guards.

They were met by a minor official who had been informed of Charles's imminent arrival. He was to take him to the Rajah directly. Dismounting, Hugh Travis and the escort left them to set up camp outside the walls, while Charles, Lucy and Maya went deeper into the palace.

As they moved along wide, cool marble corridors bristling with armed men, the grandiose interior did nothing to settle Lucy's nerves. Turbaned servants and people walked by in both directions, deep in conversation, lending what they saw an air of intrigue and conspiracy. They emerged now and then into internal courtyards. Cascades of brilliant coloured plants hung from galleries and latticed balconies.

At one point there was a huge marble tiger spouting water from its mouth into a crystal-clear pool. Orange and lemon trees rose out of huge terracotta pots and the scent of flowers was heavy on the air. Lucy and Maya kept stopping to look around in wonder. Charles took Lucy's arm, pulling her along, as the official marched quickly ahead of them. Lucy had to run to keep up with his long strides.

'What a glorious place this is,' she whispered as her feet passed over glittering mosaic floors. The palace was exactly as she had imagined it to be. 'I can hardly believe I am here and what I am seeing.' To be allowed inside the Rajah's palace was a great honour, even she knew that, and to be taken to his presence was doubly so.

Coming to the inner sanctum of the palace, they were ushered into the Hall of Public Audience. Here the air was heavy with the aroma of almonds and spices, of jasmine and musk, along with an air of tradition and history. Magnificently attired councillors and courtiers were milling about. Everyone turned briefly as they walked in, eyes darting towards these English strangers. Lucy could not tear her eyes away from the Rajah, Naveen Madan, as she bobbed a respectful curtsy. Never had she seen the like.

Charles bowed with respect. The warmth of the Rajah's welcome was sincere. Maya hung back when Charles drew Lucy forward. The Rajah's eyes passed over her and he smiled broadly.

'I am delighted that you spare the time to visit Guntal again, Mr Anderson, and I am happy to receive you, Miss Quinn,' he said in a light sing-song voice. 'You are most welcome. I trust you had a safe journey?'

Lucy was impressed by his fluency in English. He was decked out in splendid clothes studded with precious gems that reflected the light. His robe, which fell straight from his shoulders, was made of silk dyed deep blue and edged with gold and was extremely beautiful. A blue sash encircled his large waist, exposing the jewel-studded hilt of his imperial dagger. On his feet he wore turquoise slippers and his fingers were heavily weighted with spectacular jewelled rings. She placed his age somewhere between forty and fifty years and his dark hair shone lustrously. His features were fine cut and his eyes dark and glowing.

Surrounded by a small army of servants and officials on a raised dais, he sat cross-legged on a low divan spread with bright rugs and surrounded by a heap of brightly coloured silk cushions.

'We did, Your Highness,' Charles replied in answer to his question. 'I compliment you on your English. It is much improved since last we met.'

The Rajah laughed good humouredly. 'I have been working hard to improve it every day. With the rise of the East India Company, my father made sure I was taught to converse in English and understand the language from an early age, telling me it is a skill I need when entertaining the English. I also have a good memory. I value your coming here to see me. We had some interesting discussions on your previous visit—I hope we can do the same this time—about your King George and England—and I will show you some more of Guntal. You will remember how I enjoy hunting with hawks for game and wild boar when I have the time. Tomorrow is to be such a day. You might like to join me—and

Miss Quinn, too. You are a competent horsewoman, Miss Quinn?'

'Yes—and thank you. I would love to join you.'

'We have an early start. You may not care to be woken at that hour.'

'I will be there,' she assured him, smiling. 'I will look forward to it.'

While Charles continued to converse with the Rajah, Lucy's face burned as she felt those in the Rajah's privy circle scrutinising her. The Rajah's easy manner put Lucy at ease, giving her an insight into the man behind his position and all his finery. He was a man who had the weight of ruling his province upon his shoulders, but was still someone with a heart and, she sensed, a capacity to show pleasure.

A woman entered, drawing Lucy's attention. She seemed to appear from nowhere, gliding across the floor, her bare feet making no sound on the black marble floor and, save for the silvery tinkle that accompanied her movement, Lucy might have imagined her an apparition. Her skin glowed between the yards of pink and orange silk in which she was draped and dozens of gold bracelets jangled on her arms and legs. Her skirts were so fine they floated around her as she walked. She was blessed with womanly curves and she walked with grace and was light of foot.

Her features were sultry and unlined and showed humour and kindness. Her dark eyes crinkled as she smiled and her black hair hung in a thick glossy plait to her waist. Above her soft almond-shaped eyes, strands of fine beads and precious stones hung over her forehead and around her neck. Lucy suspected she was the Rani, the Rajah's wife, her suspicions confirmed when Charles bowed to her with respect.

She was accompanied by a group of ladies who hovered around her. A dazzling smile broke out on the Rani's red lips. 'You honour us with your presence,' she said in broken English, her voice rich and deep. Her eyes slipped to Lucy. 'And I see you have brought with you a companion, Mr Anderson? How delightful. You will by hungry after your journey. We will eat and then you will relax.'

In an atmosphere that was pleasantly friendly and informal, the food was served by an army of servants in white robes and blue silk turbans. It was carried on large silver trays—fish and meats and sweetmeats dripping in honey. It was spicy and delicious and washed down with spiced wines. The Rajah was the perfect host while his eyes constantly watched those about him like a hunting hawk noticing everything. Lucy was quick to compliment him on the food that set her tastebuds tingling.

The talk was of political matters, small skirmishes and rebellions and the need to crush them, and how the Rajah continued to keep the East India Company out of Guntal. As the meal progressed, the conversation went on more slowly for, comfortably settled with good food and the wine's sweetness, Charles was in no haste to move. In fact, it might have gone on all night long had Lucy not voiced her desire for sleep. But the Rani, who insisted on being addressed as Ananya, had other ideas.

'You must come with me. I have just the thing for

you after the journey you have made today. Afterwards you will sleep the sleep of the gods.'

Intrigued and with a nod and a smile from Charles, Lucy went with Ananya and her giggling ladies who floated in her wake, all moving at the same time. She was taken to a gold and blue mosaic chamber that she soon discovered was a luxurious bath house. The ceiling was domed and in the centre of the floor, surrounded by slender pillars, was a tiled, large sunken bath in which water was steaming.

Lucy gasped, her eyes alight with excitement. She had heard about these bath houses in the princely palaces but had never imagined them as being so luxurious. Thick, fluffy towels were to hand, while all around were vials of oils and soaps.

'Why, I have never seen the like,' she exclaimed, delighted. 'I never imagined anything that looks so tempting and pleasurable.'

Ananya laughed, pleased with Lucy's reaction. 'There is enough luxury for a person to wallow in for as long as they wish. Now come—don't be shy. There is no need for that. We are all ladies together.' She led Lucy to the edge of the tub.

Her ladies were chattering excitedly and, before Lucy could protest, they were undressing her as if it were the most natural thing to do. There was a great deal of giggling as her clothes were partially removed, but before they could remove them entirely, alarmed, Lucy put up her hands to stop them, trying to hold on to her modesty, but the more she protested the louder they laughed. Standing back, they began to undress themselves to show it was quite natural in the world they inhabited to bathe together in the nude.

They slipped into the scented water, beckoning for her to join them. Unable to resist the temptation of joining them, deciding to throw caution and all her inhibitions to the wind and to give herself up to the slow tempo of this life, Lucy began to relax and finished undressing swiftly. Squeals and gasps of admiration were drawn from the beautiful ladies when her pale slender body was revealed and her glorious mane of pale blonde hair, freed from its pins, snaked down her spine.

'You really are the loveliest woman,' Ananya enthused. 'Such a pretty face—and such milky skin—with hair like the purest silk and the colour of desert sand. You are quite perfect, Miss Quinn. Mr Anderson must find it difficult being close to you and not touching you.'

Lucy gasped, shocked that she should think that. 'Mr Anderson and I are not…not together,' she said, in an attempt to explain their relationship, but it was clear from the expression of disbelief on Ananya's face and her intelligent, all-seeing eyes that she did not believe her. Deciding not to dig herself in any deeper, Lucy slipped gracefully into the pool where she readily abandoned herself quite passively to the ministering of two of the young ladies' gentle hands.

A smile on her lips, Ananya sat on a low stool at the side of the pool, content to watch as Lucy's hair was washed and she was soaped all over.

Wallowing pleasurably, feeling the water about her like a caress, Lucy was astonished at the strange sense of well-being that spread through every part of her body.

Some of the ladies were chattering away in their own language, their laughter and cries echoing off the tiled walls. The abandon of these women and their brazen and unashamed nakedness shocked her, but after a while as she began to relax and she ceased to think about it.

When she stepped out, one of the ladies was waiting with a thick cotton towel to dry her, before taking her to a divan where she began to massage her body with hands that were amazingly gentle, rubbing in a strangely pungent oil that relaxed her muscles and gave her skin a soft patina.

While most of the ladies lounged about indulging in idle gossip, she relaxed and, spreading her arms, opened her eyes and gazed at the ceiling, at the colourful designs with a picture in the centre, of stars and a moon representing the heavens, and a golden sun in the middle. Pressing her eyes shut, she held her breath to hold on to the pleasurable sensation. Her body seemed to have broken all its earthly moorings. She was like a marionette, moving to the strings that pulled her, only her brain functioning slowly as her body was ministered to as never before and in ways she could never have imagined.

Beneath the massaging boldness of the woman's hands, a woman who had the air of a priestess carrying out some ancient ritual, she was honest enough to admit her treacherous woman's body was coming breathlessly alive, not even against her will. She sighed with contentment.

'You use such wonderful scents,' she murmured, as the woman proceeded to apply more oil to her skin. The air in the bathing chamber was warm and thick and redolent of perfume, not flower-like, but compounded of ambergris and musk—intoxicating and languid, artful weapons to entrap a man. That she should think such things just then did not surprise her, for Charles occupied her mind.

'Where did you learn to speak English?' Lucy liked Ananya. She was sure she'd met someone who, in different circumstances, could be a good friend.

Ananya's full lips stretched in a broad smile. 'My husband. He taught me. He said it was important that I learn to speak the language of the English should we find ourselves entertaining them in the future. And here you are,' she said with tinkling laughter, 'so you see, it is fortunate for me and you that I learned the language of the English.'

Bathed and scented, Lucy's body was soft and supple, her skin bloomed. They draped her in a flowing gorgeous white robe, the fabric so fine as to be almost shockingly transparent. Feeling more feminine than she had ever felt in her life before, Lucy stood back for the ladies to inspect their handiwork.

Ananya beamed broadly, well satisfied. 'You are very beautiful, Miss Quinn. Mr Anderson will not be able to resist you when he sees you out of those unflattering English clothes, which are too restricting and not at all suitable for the Indian climate. I suspect he is like my own husband in many ways—honourable and noble, as well as very handsome—all the things I cherish in a man. I have observed how he looks at you—how protective of you he is. You are a long way from England

and have plenty of time to be together, so it will be interesting to see what happens between the two of you while you are here in Kassam.'

Having no intention of remaining in Kassam for more than two days at the most, Lucy merely smiled and let the matter rest for the present. She suspected Ananya could ferret out secrets the owner had no notion of.

She spent the rest of the evening lounging on a divan in conversation with Ananya and nibbling on delicious sweetmeats. Eventually she was shown to a room of sumptuous luxury where she was to sleep. She still wore the robe and went barefoot, luxuriating in the feel of the soles of her feet against the cool marble floors. After making sure Lucy was comfortable and she was unlikely to need her, Maya left her to explore the environs of the palace and chat with the other servants.

With Lucy being taken care of by the Rani and her ladies, Charles went to join Hugh encamped outside the palace walls. Hidden by the darkness, Charles lounged on the ground, staring across the starlit plains. The night wind smelt of woodsmoke from the campfire and a hundred other scents that drifted from the town on the night air.

Hugh and the rest of the escort sat around the fire, talking quietly among themselves. He could envisage the Rani introducing Lucy to the bathing chamber and he knew how she would look, her naked body glistening with fragrant oils and with her white-blonde hair combed out—in fact, he was aware of every single thing about her. Too aware, he thought disgustedly, his eyes narrowing.

He'd hoped that upon closer association his interest and preoccupation with her would fade. The opposite had happened. If anything, he was more fascinated by her than he had been when they had left Nandra and he was thoroughly annoyed by the fact and beginning to think that perhaps he should not have invited her to accompany him into Guntal.

During the journey he had expected to see her at her worst, but even covered in dust and with her hair in disarray beneath her hat, her long legs beneath her skirts astride her horse and urging it on with an energy that confounded him, she still managed to look appealing. She had made no unnecessary demands, had not complained or made a nuisance of herself—except to disrupt his peace of mind, he admitted grimly.

Chapter Five

In the cool freshness of dawn, the Rajah of Guntal's hunting party patiently waited for the signal to depart. Excitement prevailed, beaters assembled, restless horses whinnied and champed at their bits, eager to be off.

Lucy stood in the shadow of an overhanging tree, enjoying the rich confusion going on all around her. She slanted a look at Charles as he approached on his mount. He wore a riding coat, a pair of buckskin breeches and highly polished brown boots. A broad-brimmed hat covered his dark hair.

'After our ride yesterday, I thought you might have had a change of mind and stayed beneath the covers.'

'Not a bit of it,' she said. 'I woke this morning and it was so fresh and beautiful that the thought of riding out with the hunt was too tempting to resist.'

'Then stay close at all times.'

Lucy galloped along with the rest, jungle fowl rising, fluttering from the long grass and screeching as they thundered by. They came to a place where there was little sign of habitation. Lucy was aware of the remoteness of it all. When the party began hunting game birds, she found the sport not to her liking and had no wish to be in on the kill.

Seeing a river in the distance, its gleaming waters beckoning as it meandered its way leisurely across the landscape, Lucy rode off, enjoying her own leisurely pace. Becoming lost in the beauty of the distant hills and the vast expanse of the plains, she felt at peace, without any sense of how far she had ridden. That was when the rain came and a fierce wind rose so suddenly, she was taken completely by surprise. It blew about her with a viciousness that almost unseated her from her horse.

Within just a few minutes it was coming down in sheets. After such a long spell of dry weather, the ground quickly soaked it up. Lucy could smell the rich scent of earth as the rain quenched its thirst. Normally when the monsoons came, her inner self would feel at one with nature, but she didn't any more. This deluge couldn't have come at a worse time and in no time at all she was soaked to the skin. In danger of losing her hat she removed it and attached it to the saddle. Her hair was soaked, hanging down her back in sodden strands.

With the rain pouring down and the hunting party looking for shelter, Charles rode around looking for Lucy, hoping she'd had the sense to find shelter herself. Searching frantically, he soon realised she was missing, but forced himself to stay calm. Reason flooded back and his sense of anger and frustration was subdued beneath a firm grip of will as his concern for her safety increased. His gaze was drawn to the river in the distance. Dear Lord, don't let her have ridden as far as that. He knew how easy it was for a person to get swept away when monsoon rains poured down.

The landscape became almost invisible. Straining his eyes, he could just make out the shape of an animal in the distance—a horse, he was sure of it—it had to be.

'My God! The little fool—' he gasped, urging his mount into a gallop, his mindless terror giving way to blind panic as he went after her, sliding and skidding over the now sodden ground.

Lucy scolded herself for riding on ahead of the rest. Charles had specifically told her not to become separated from the party. Oh, Lord, why hadn't she listened to him? She glanced back, hoping to see the others following closely, but if they were the rain obscured them. Seeing a dark shape ahead of her that looked like the rocks she had seen earlier, with a renewed spurt of energy she urged her horse on.

On reaching the rocks, she threw herself out of the saddle and, taking the reins of her terrified horse, dragged the animal into the shelter. Wiping the water from her eyes, seeing a gap that looked like a cave in the rocks some yards ahead, where peepul trees had conspired to form a canopy over the entrance, almost hiding it from the world, she struggled to reach it, holding on to the reins.

Suddenly two strong arms were around her, helping her to remain on her feet and hauling her into the dank interior of the cave. Once there she fell to her knees coughing the water out of her mouth. When she finally managed to speak, she staggered to her feet and faced her rescuer—Charles.

'You little fool,' he chided, furiously, glaring at her, elbows akimbo. 'What the devil do you think you were doing riding off like that? I told you not to leave the hunting party—but would you listen? If you had gone anywhere near the river, you could have drowned. Didn't you see the clouds gathering overhead? No. You always think you know best.'

Undismayed Lucy glared at him with stubborn, unyielding pride. 'When it happens to concern me then, yes, I do. I wasn't in any danger,' she retorted, trying to ignore the enraged glitter in his eyes. 'Were—were you worried about me?'

'Of course I was worried. Anything could have happened to you. Thank God I saw you come in here, otherwise I wouldn't have known where to look.'

'As you see, I am still in one piece,' she said, trying to remain calm. Her chest rose and fell in agitation, but she tried desperately to appeal to his reason. 'You need not have worried. I do ride extremely well, you know, and I will not be dictated to by you or anyone else,' she retorted, seeing the fury her defiance ignited in his features.

'Now why doesn't that surprise me? You're too stubborn to listen to sound advice. You should have known better,' he chided crossly. Moving towards her, he leaned forward deliberately until blue eyes stared into dark green from little more than a foot apart. His eyes grew hard and flintlike, yet when it came his voice was soft and slow. Almost gently he warned, 'Before you consider going off again on your own, pause to consider there are tigers in these parts—man-eating tigers. Unless you want to provide a banquet for them, you'd do well to heed my words.'

Lucy felt the colour drain from her face. Charles's presence filled the small cave. He looked like a dark, invincible god, formidable, intimidating and yet strangely compelling. With his hair a cluster of dark wet curls, all she could do was stare with a bemused intensity. But then, his arrogance to assume he knew what was best for her raised her indignation and, highly incensed by his words, a feral light gleamed in the depths of her eyes. She was like a kitten showing its claws to a full-grown panther.

'Oh, I will. I didn't realise I had ridden so far. I didn't think the rain would come just yet—or so fast and hard.'

'You were wrong—and just look at you. You're soaking wet.'

'I am not the only one. You're as wet as I am.'

She was about to move away, only to find herself halted when he came up behind her with the sure-footed skill of an animal on the scent of its prey. She stood there, frozen, his strong hands on her shoulders. Unable to turn, she could feel his closeness, the muscular hardness of him, the vibrant heat of his body pressed close against her back and his warm breath on her neck.

'For God's sake, Lucy. I was scared out of my wits when I couldn't find you. I was afraid something might have happened to you. I'd no idea in which direction you'd ridden—not until I saw your horse.'

Lucy swallowed and wet her lips, her anger subsiding. 'I didn't mean to frighten you,' she whispered, her voice shaking with emotion as she tried to maintain the friendly relationship that had existed between them since they had left Nandra. 'I'm sorry, but I didn't think I was in any danger at the time. Truly. Don't be angry.'

'I'm not—at least not any longer. But I was concerned. When the rains came and I couldn't find you, thinking you might have gone to the river, I was beginning to fear the worst.'

Lucy thought he was going to chastise her some more, but suddenly all his anger seemed to disappear. She was touched by his obvious concern for her safety and deeply sorry and mortified for not having listened to his advice about becoming separated from the hunting party. Charles was right. She should not have ridden off on her own.

His hands on her arms were soothing, caressing her. She jerked her head slightly when she felt his hand on her head, but his fingers only threaded through her wet hair, freeing the strands, careful not to tug and hurt her, patient as he took several long strands at a time, all the while holding her with the other hand against his chest, easing her closer. The unconscious gentleness of the gesture touched and warmed something deep inside her.

Captivated by the heat of his breath on her neck, she trembled when he drew the heavy, wet mass of her hair to one side, feeling defeated, afraid when she felt his mouth gently touch the soft warm flesh on the back of her neck. But instead of stepping away, she leaned into him, the action encouraging him to continue to hold her. On a gasp she sucked in her breath when he parted his lips and touched her skin with the fiery tip of his tongue. Her heart was pounding when his voice spoke very quietly into her ear.

'Shall I tell you what I think when I look at you, Lucy?'

'I—if you like,' she said, trying to answer lightly, but her voice was low and husky.

'I see an extremely beautiful young woman with lovely hair like a shimmering cloth of gold.'

Lucy wanted to step away from him, but an answering quiver that was a combination of fright and excitement was tingling up her spine.

'Would you like me to stop now, Lucy, or would you like me to continue to hold you close?' he murmured.

Charles's closeness and his physical presence scorched through her and she could not move away if she tried. 'H-hold me a while—I would like that.'

She lowered her head, the floor of the cave becoming the focal point of her concentration, a misshapen image tugging at the heart of her memory, conjuring indistinct, cloudy visions in her mind. They blended in a confused jumble of events that took her back to another time, another place, when other hands had touched her, when she had wanted to flee before darkness had mercifully engulfed her, rendering her helpless and unable to escape the brutality of what was being done to her.

She fought a welter of unwelcome emotions that threatened to drag her down to a new depth of despair. But she was not immune to Charles standing behind her, of the hard rack of his chest pressed against her back, making her feel things that added to her confusion. He remained close, so close she could feel the heat of his body scorching through the clothes on her back to her flesh, along with an alarming, treacherous warmth creeping through her body, a melting sensation unlike anything she had felt in a long time.

For one mad moment she wanted to relax back against him, to feel his arm close around her, but because she could still feel those powerful emotions that seemed to have been drawn into her heart and soul from that day when she thought her life had ended, she could not bring herself to make that move.

The moment was oddly intimate. Maybe it was the way Charles was holding her, or maybe it was the way his closeness made her feel. She was nervous, but what did it matter? Yes, she was afraid—but it wasn't like before. While she didn't doubt for a moment that she was safe with Charles, that she was in control of this situation, she was afraid of the things she felt when he looked at her, afraid of the feelings he had awakened in her when he'd kissed her on the veranda of her home in Nandra.

She had concealed everything for so long, tried to stamp it out. She thought she might succeed with time, but this man made her think of the past and the uncertainty she was still living in. Since he had appeared in her life, she found she was returning more frequently to her memories of that dark day she wished she could forget—yet their shared kiss had been so sublime she was curious to experience the same again. A warm trickle of a familiar sensation ran through her, overwhelming her anxiety. It was that same stirring she had felt when he had kissed her.

With desire crashing over him in tidal waves, Charles

looked down at Lucy's bent head, his lips brushing her shining wet hair. Having no concept of her thoughts, he slipped an arm about her waist and drew her tightly against him, feeling a shimmering tremor in her slender body.

'You are as irresistible to me now as you were when we kissed, Lucy—which I am sorely tempted to repeat.'

Slowly she turned to face him, meeting his gaze, seeing the desire he felt for her in his eyes. Without warning his hand lifted and curved tenderly round her cheek. Gazing into those fathomless eyes, she felt a curious sharp thrill run through her as the force between them seemed to ignite. She was entranced, hardly breathing, wet strands of hair drifting over her face, and she thought his face bent over her was more beautiful than she had ever known. She saw the deepening light in his eyes and the thick defined brows and wanted to touch him as one touches the soft flesh of a newborn babe.

'Then kiss me again, Charles—it might be better this time.'

When she fell silent, his hands tightened on her arms and once again he drew her close, his lips settling on hers. They were cool and surprisingly smooth as they brushed lightly against her closed mouth. A jolt slammed through her as they began to move on hers, thoroughly and possessively exploring every tender contour. She found herself imprisoned in a grip of steel, pressed against his hard, muscular length, her breasts coming to rest against his chest and there was little she could do to escape. Alternate waves seemed to run through her body, but there was also another far more disturbing sensation.

His lips increased their pressure, becoming coaxing as he slipped the tip of his tongue into the warm sweetness of her mouth. She gasped, totally innocent of the sort of warmth, the passion he was skilfully arousing in her, that poured through her veins with a shattering explosion of delight. It was a kiss of exquisite restraint and, unable to think of anything but the exciting urgency of his mouth and the warmth of his breath, she felt herself falling slowly into a dizzying abyss of sensuality. His hands glided restlessly, possessively up and down her spine and the nape of her neck, pressing her tightly to his hardened body.

Trailing her hands up the muscles of his chest and shoulders and sliding her fingers into the crisp curly hair at his nape, with a quiet moan of helpless surrender she clung to him, devastated by what he was doing to her, by the raw hunger of his passion. Inside her an emotion she had never experienced before began to sweetly unfold, before vibrantly bursting with a fierceness that made her tremble. His kiss became more demanding, ardent, persuasive, a slow erotic seduction, and Lucy, lost in a wild and beautiful madness and with blood beating in her throat and temples that wiped out all reason and will, responded with equal passion.

When at last he lifted his mouth from hers, his breathing was harsh and rapid, and gazing up at him Lucy felt as if she would melt beneath his scorching eyes. Slowly she brought one of her hands from behind his neck and her fingers gently traced the outline of his cheek, following its angular line down to his jaw and neck.

'Well?' Charles asked, his voice low and husky, recovering more quickly than Lucy. Her face was bemused, her eyes unfocused, her soft pink mouth partly open. 'Do you like being kissed?' When she did not reply immediately, he grinned and murmured, 'Surely I cannot have rendered you speechless.'

'It certainly took my breath, and, yes, I like it very well,' she confessed, still drifting between total peace and a strong, delirious joy, while at the same time a feeling of disquiet was creeping over her as her mind came together from the nether regions of the universe where it had fled. Slowly she disentangled herself from his arms, stepping round him and moving away.

'I—I can't believe I kissed you like that,' she murmured. 'I—I don't usually…'

In a daze of suspended yearning and confusion, she hesitated as his eyes held hers in one long, compelling look, hiding all her frustrated longing and unfulfilled desires. That one kiss had been too much and too little, arousing deep feelings she did not fully understand. What had happened between them had been a sudden overwhelming passion, heightened by the intensity of the knowledge that it shouldn't be happening.

Turning abruptly, she started to walk away from him, her feet driven by panic. She stepped outside and took hold of her horse, vaguely aware that Charles was following her. She didn't look at him, but she sensed he was bewildered by her behaviour. It didn't matter. Nothing did just then. Let him rant and rail and chastise her to his heart's content if he wanted to—anything. Just let him never look at her as he had just then, or touch her with such tender intimacy. She would not let herself be at the mercy of a man like Charles Anderson, who radiated sensual hunger in every glance, every move and every touch.

As she was about to mount her horse, Charles steadied her by placing his hand over hers. 'Do not hurry away. Give me a moment, Lucy.'

'Why? Have you not said all you have to say?'

'Not quite.'

'Is it that you want to kiss me again?'

'Yes, I do, very much, as it happens, but I'm not going to. I enjoyed kissing you, but there will be no repeat of it. When—if, I kiss you again, I will do the asking.' He turned her round to face him, frowning when he saw the look on her face. 'And don't look like that. You're like a disgruntled hedgehog and just as prickly.'

Lucy continued to glower at him, her fingers slipping away from his face. It was taut, his eyes fixed squarely on hers. Now the rain had ceased, the light behind him made an aureole around his dark head. He regarded her in silence. She was profoundly aware of him and the wet state she was in. There were too many feelings struggling to come to the fore to resurrect feelings and emotions, which was disconcerting.

Trying not to let any of those emotions show on her face, she folded her arms. 'Just what does a disgruntled hedgehog look like? I really have no idea.'

'Had I a mirror to hand, I would show you.'

'I think I get the picture. I see there's no danger of my head swelling from any compliments from you.'

'I apologise,' he said simply.

'There is nothing to apologise for,' she answered quietly.

For a long moment Charles's gaze held hers with penetrating intensity. It was as enigmatic as it was challenging and unexpectedly Lucy felt an answering frisson of excitement. The darkening in his eyes warned her that he was aware of that brief response. Something in his expression made the breath catch in her throat and the warmly intimate look in his eyes was vibrantly, alarmingly alive. Not for the first time since he had come into her life, she found herself at a loss to understand him.

'You really should not go riding off like that, Lucy. You gave me one hell of a fright.'

'I'm sorry. I didn't think.'

'There are so many dangers when it rains like that,' he said quietly. 'I just want to keep you safe.'

'No one can promise that.'

'I can be very determined,' he answered with a half-smile. 'I am not perfect. Far from it in fact. But I will do all in my power to see that you come to no harm.'

'Thank you for your concern, Charles, but I can do that perfectly well myself. I am not helpless.'

'I'm not saying you are. You are accomplished in many things. You are also wise enough to know a fool when you see one. You have confidence, too, as well as a sense of humour—although I have seen very little of that of late. And your compassion for others compels my admiration and respect.'

Lucy trembled, staring at him.

'You are also brave,' he continued as she turned her

head away. 'The fact that you have worked your way through adversity in life and your profession as a teacher and the care you take of your father is commendable and bespeaks your courage and good sense. It makes me feel that I can trust you in your integrity, which is a rarity for me. It is not often I come across a person I can trust.'

She looked at him, listening like a doe in the woods, but poised to flee from him. She was rendered helpless by his words. It was difficult to argue with a man who praised her not for superficial things, but for the very qualities that she valued in herself. Mounting her horse, she looked down at his upturned face and half smiled.

'I'm an ungrateful wretch. I don't think it even occurred to me to thank you for your concern.'

He smiled back at her, happy to see a softening and friendliness in her eyes. 'You're welcome. Now I think we should get back to the others before they send out a search party.'

Lucy cantered on, Charles loping easily in her wake. A disturbed fowl rose with a flutter and a squark. Bent low over her mount's neck, Lucy's response was to urge it into a faster pace, its hooves kicking up the wet earth.

Looking straight ahead and uncomfortable in her saturated clothes, she knew something was happening within her, something overwhelming over which she seemed to have no control. How could it have come to this—finding herself fascinated, angered and beguiled by Charles Anderson? A man whose mere touch and the sound of his voice woke turbulent emotions she hadn't known she possessed.

Yet an inexplicable heaviness weighed on her heart—probably, she thought, because she hadn't yet determined how the kiss had affected Charles. It didn't help, either, that her own thoughts kept returning to it. Perhaps he hadn't been as affected by it as she had been. Perhaps Charles Anderson was the kind of man to whom kisses meant little, the kind of adventurer with a woman in every town. Maybe by now he would have forgotten about it entirely. Yet she couldn't forget. Sensations she had not felt in a long time, and never as strong as this, coursed through her. It was a new kind of madness she was unable to resist.

She suddenly wanted to feel Charles's arms around her again for reasons she could not understand, but had everything to do with his hard frame pressed against hers, to feel his breath on her neck. It startled her, this reaction to his nearness. It would not go away and she was left with the insane desire to taste that kiss again. But these new feelings Charles had aroused in her frightened her—she was aware that he was far more dangerous to her now, now that her own body was betraying her.

Her heart beat rapidly when she thought about him. He had stirred an excitement that had been lacking for a long time. She fought the battle within her, but something stronger pulled at her senses and with a groan of defeat she left whatever it was to have its way.

For too long, she now realised, she had avoided anything other than the daily routine at the school and assisting Dr Jessop, too afraid to feel happy or excited. Her father, with his wise old head, had told her time and again not to worry, that it would all work out, that time healed all wounds. But could she move on? Her life didn't have to stop because of what had happened to her, she told herself.

Growing up, she'd had so many dreams, like most girls dream, of marrying the man you fall in love with, having children, watching them grow up happy and carefree, just as she had. Except it didn't happen that way. When Johnathan had died all her dreams lay in tatters. But there was no reason why she couldn't have children, although they would never be Johnathan's.

As an innocent, naive girl, before the assault on her person, she had seen no wrong in the man who had violated her. But because of her actions she had deprived Johnathan of any chance of happiness as well as his life and, for as long as she lived, she would never forgive herself. She did want a child of her own, she couldn't deny that. But it couldn't happen unless it was with someone else.

Riding a horse length behind Lucy, Charles looked ahead in deep reflection. With frustration he attacked his sentimental thoughts until they cowered in meek submission, but they refused to lie down. When he had found Lucy missing, in the space of a heartbeat, a fury had replaced his calm composure. He was furious that she'd worried him with her recklessness, furious that she was able to evoke any kind of emotion in him at all, but he had been more concerned by her disappearance than he'd cared to reveal. He'd known instinctively that she must have ridden off alone.

Panic had beset him. With the torrent of rain unleashed on them he knew she was in danger, immediate and terrible, and with every instinct in him, he had ridden after her, ready to berate her—or hold her close in relief, to comfort her.

His growing attraction to Lucy was disquieting—in fact, it was damned annoying. If he wanted an affair or diversion of any kind, he had a string of some of the most beautiful women back in Madras to choose from—so why should he feel this insanely wild attraction for a woman he hardly knew? Only Lucy Quinn would have done something so outrageous as to ask a man to kiss her and then dared to confront him so magnificently.

A reluctant smile touched his lips when he remembered her standing valiantly against him when he had come upon her in the cave. She had been soaked to the skin, her hair hanging about her face and down her back in wet profusion, but he thought she had never looked so heartbreakingly lovely or so young, with those mutinous dark eyes flashing fire, seeing nothing wrong in what she had done.

Something in his heart moved and softened, then something stabbed him in the centre of his chest. What the hell was wrong with him? Her behaviour had made him angry, and at the same time he had been overwhelmed by the realisation that if he didn't take care, she would come to mean something to him.

Lucy Quinn was an unusual female, intelligent, opinionated and full of surprises. She was also the epitome of stubborn, prideful woman. Yet for all her fire and spirit, there was no underlying viciousness. She was so very different from the sophisticated, worldly women he took to bed—experienced, sensual women, knowl-edgeable in the ways of love, women who knew how to please him.

No, Lucy was different, a phenomenon. She had a touching self-belief. He sensed a goodness in her, some-thing special, sensitive—something worth pursuing. There was also something untapped inside her that not even she was aware of—passion buried deep.

Reaching the hunting party, the unseasonable storm had created a stir among the men, which had been so severe that there had been no time to spare a thought for the missing Miss Quinn or that Charles had ridden off to find her, for everyone had been frantically seek-ing shelter and securing the animals before the worst of the storm was upon them.

Returning to the palace, Lucy paid another visit to the bathing chamber, hoping the pampering and min-istrations of Ananya's ladies would relax her. But sleep evaded her that night. It was impossible to sleep after such a day. She stood on the latticed balcony, where anyone could look down on life below without being seen. The night was glorious—an Indian night, the sky indigo blue and rich with stars that glittered softly. The walled garden was filled with mango trees and pine-apple bushes, the air heavy with the sweet fragrance of frangipani. From somewhere, a peacock sounded its melancholy cry above the buzz of cicadas. There were thousands of them all around, but they kept out of sight.

Looking down, she saw a figure standing alone. She could see at once it was Charles. He was leaning against a bench, relaxed, as if he belonged there. She took a moment to observe him, admiring the fine figure he made. A white shirt, opened at the throat and ruffled at the cuffs, contrasted sharply with his bronze skin, and his lean, muscular build was accentuated by the close-fitting breeches and white stockings. As if sensing her watching him, he looked up. An amused smile twitched at the corners of his mouth.

His presence lightened her heart. Encouraged by the sudden startling wish for something different, something new, she saw a star shoot across the sky. Something *new*. Was it really possible? Charles Anderson disturbed her in ways that surprised her. The more time she spent in his presence, the more she wanted to be. How could she equate this truth with the awful thing that had happened to her when she had resolved never to be drawn to a man as she had been to Johnathan ever again, that she would never speak of it, to keep it inside her head.

She continued to look down at him, resolute, all the more determined to make changes to her life. She would not let what had happened to her determine her life, the person that she was. For too long she had kept a part of her mind closed even to herself. If, after years of pushing it away, she embraced it, perhaps the pain and the shame that had plagued her since that time would ease and she would be able to live her life without feeling tormented. She refused to spend her life feeling frustrated and angry, her only outlet the children that she taught and her work at the hospital. It was time she put an end to this tedious monotony that had dominated her everyday existence for far too long and had become her fate.

She watched Charles shrug himself away from the bench and cross the courtyard, moving with a sensuous grace and a sureness in his stride, as if he carefully planned where each foot would fall. He appeared relaxed and at ease.

After several moments there was a soft tapping on her door. Knowing with a certainty who it was and that she should not answer, ignoring her own advice and knowing she shouldn't be alone with him at this time of night, she opened it. Unbeknown to her, she was between Charles and the light, so that her slender form was outlined through her thin robe. His admiring gaze took in her fashionable *toilette*, lingering on the gentle swell of her breasts beneath the thin fabric. Lucy felt herself grow hot with embarrassment.

'Charles—can't you sleep either?' The dark liquid of his eyes deepened as he became caught in the warmth of her presence and she read in his face such evident desire that heat flamed for a moment in her belly.

'Can I come in?'

Lucy hesitated. His stance was casual, but his eyes were intense, penetrating. Again she experienced the depth to which her mind and body stirred whenever she was in his presence. Then a feeling of carelessness took over and she opened the door wider. He stepped inside. Closing the door, she stood perfectly still as he came closer. There was an aura of calm authority about him. His expression was now blank and impervious and he looked unbearably handsome. The sight of his chiselled features and bold blue eyes never failed to stir her heart.

Taking her hand, he raised her fingers to his lips, enjoying the scent and taste of her. When he looked at her there was a twinkle in his eyes. 'Are you happy being here, Lucy? No regrets?'

'I am glad I came—I have no regrets.' And she meant it. With every moment she spent in this gorgeous palace with Charles Anderson she grew more comfortable with him and more intrigued by him. And felt more free.

'I can't believe the change in you. You look like some eastern princess and very lovely.'

'And you, Mr Anderson, are extremely handsome,' she said with a teasing glint in her eyes.

He grinned wickedly, sauntering over to the balcony. Perching his hips on the balustrade, he folded his arms across his chest. 'As a lady you're not supposed to say that to a gentleman—but, I have to admit to having known a lady or two who have admired my charms.'

She laughed, joining him on the balcony, sitting in a cushioned chair and looking at him candidly. 'As to that I don't doubt, but I'm sure you always behave like a perfect gentleman.'

'Always.'

Perhaps it was the magic of the night, the warmth and subtle floral scents, or her need to be close to him, but whatever the cause, Lucy's heart doubled its pace.

In a voice like rough velvet, he said, 'I meant it when I said you are a lovely young woman, Lucy. Where has the woman I met in Nandra gone?'

Mesmerised, she stared into his fathomless dark eyes, while his deep, husky voice caressed her, pulling her further under his spell. 'Nowhere. She is still here.'

'The robe suits you. Ananya told me of your visit to the bathing chamber after we had eaten.'

'I was quite ravenous when we got back to the palace.'

'I noticed.'

'You did?' She recalled how he had watched her with some amusement as she ate her way through dish after dish of the delicious food set before them, as if she had eaten nothing for days.

'For a young woman of such sender build, you have a remarkably robust appetite.' His eyes narrowed and one dark eyebrow rose in amusement.

'After a long day with the Rajah's hunt and having eaten nothing all day, I was starving.'

'So it would seem. And to put the finishing touch to the day, you were once again bathed and pampered by the Rani's ladies.'

'And what is wrong with that?'

'Nothing at all, for I must admit to finding the end result very pleasant. There is a glow about you and you smell quite divine.'

Acknowledging the compliment, Lucy smiled sweetly. 'Why, thank you, Charles. You do say the most charming things, although you say it with a curl to your lips which makes me not quite sure how to take your compliments. It's as if it gives you immense enjoyment to tease me.'

But it was not malicious or hurtful, for there was a wicked gleam in his eyes which she could not interpret. He was a complex man who allowed no one to see the hidden depths of himself.

'No doubt you enjoyed the pampering?'

'It was delightful. It is one of the things I shall miss

when I leave here. It's so far removed from anything I have ever known or could have imagined. I have been bathed, scented and oiled so much that should anyone try to get hold of me, I will slip out of their fingers.'

Relinquishing his perch and stepping forward, he winced suddenly. Thinking of his wounded leg and the rigours he had endured on the journey, Lucy said, 'Your leg still pains you, I see.'

Charles ran a distracted hand through his hair. 'It does somewhat, but I am also weary after the hunt. It has been a long day.'

'And yet, like me, you can't sleep.'

'It would appear so.'

'So—what should we do about it? What do you suggest?'

His eyes were partly hooded as they fastened on her face, his voice soft and seductive when he spoke. 'My night is free. You have me all to yourself—if you want me.'

Chapter Six

Unable to ignore his suggestive remark—Charles knew how to use his potent charm to lethal effect—Lucy couldn't help but catch her breath.

He was gazing at her hard, looking like a man in the throes of some internal struggle. 'Is it possible that you are even more lovely now than when I first saw you?' he said in a lazy, sensual drawl that made Lucy's heart melt.

She laughed uneasily, getting to her feet. 'Fancy waiting until I'm in the Rajah's palace with nowhere to run, to tell me that—dressed in nothing but a robe and my hair unbound. It puts a woman at a disadvantage.'

'I like you in your robe and your hair unbound,' he breathed.

Lucy realised just how perceptive this man was. She was disturbingly aware of those warm blue eyes delving into hers as if he were intent on searching out her innermost thoughts. Placing his hands on her shoulders, he held her at arm's length, his eyes, full of intensity, refusing to relinquish their hold on hers. For an instant she thought he was angry, but then she saw a troubled, almost tortured look enter his eyes.

'I've known many women, Lucy, and ventured far

and wide, but no woman—not even Amelia—has provoked my imagination to such a degree as you do. You are a temptress, dangerous in your innocence. It's hard for me seeing you on the occasions we've been together, knowing you are almost within my arm's reach and not touching you as I want to do.'

His voice had softened to the timbre of rough velvet and made Lucy's senses jolt almost as much as the strange way he was looking at her. Suddenly her sense of security began to disintegrate. 'Did you really bring me all the way to Kassam to say that?' she asked quietly, feeling a treacherous warmth slowly beginning to seep beneath her flesh.

'I wanted to be alone with you. Because we are soon to part, I wanted to prolong our relationship. Can you understand that? Does it alarm you?'

'And—and why should you think I want to be alone with you?' she whispered shakily.

His relentless gaze locked with hers. 'Neither of us has anything to gain by pretending the other doesn't exist—that the kisses we have shared never happened. I remember them and I know damn well you remember them, too.'

'I haven't forgotten them. How could I?' she added defensively.

'So far, I have managed to convince myself that my memory of how sweet it was is exaggerated. Now I'm curious to know if it really was that good and ardently wish it might be repeated—and to finish what we began.'

'Are you telling me you want to make love to me?'

The sweetness of her question was almost Charles's undoing. 'It is my fervent desire. It is not just a question of wanting you, but of wanting you too much. The mere fact of being alone with you now is torture for me. But worry not, Lucy. I am not in the habit of seducing gently reared, virginal young ladies. I have developed a high regard for you—no, more than that—an attraction and a strong and passionate desire for you. I will not dishonour you. I came to your room to spend a pleasant hour in your company. Nothing more than that.'

He spoke in that soft, cajoling tone that charmed Lucy. She shivered when she recalled the touch of his lips, which she was consciously yearning for. Breathing deeply, she savoured it once more, feeling the hour of her defeat approaching. She became thoughtful, observing him with earnest attention. Remembering the ugliness of what had happened to her in the past, she shuddered.

Charles noticed. 'Is something wrong?'

'No. Just a memory.'

'An unpleasant memory?'

She looked at him and he stared into the depths of the dark green eyes, open so wide, so filled with fear and at the same time with trust. 'Yes, but it doesn't matter now.' By some hidden force she became gripped by some powerful emotion. Having removed his hands from her shoulders, she moved a little closer to him and lifted her eyes to his, holding his gaze with her own. This was the moment. Unbeknown to him, he had just presented her with the opportunity she had been waiting for.

'There is something I want to tell you,' she said, trying to keep the nervousness out of her voice and failing completely. 'I didn't intend to—but now I think I must.'

'What is it?' he asked, watching her closely.

She took a deep breath. 'It—it's about the time when Johnathan died—about what happened to me—that made me who I am today—why the way people see me is not always…pleasant. I cannot believe that I have spent all the years since he died living in the shadows.'

'Why? What are you trying to tell me, Lucy?'

'When I met Johnathan I was an ordinary girl. I wanted all the things girls want—parties and balls and excitement—to share it all with the man who was to be my husband. I wanted romance—to be held and kissed…' She sighed. 'I had all that, but then…'

His dark brows almost joined in a frown. 'Then? What happened, Lucy?'

His voice was softer, more tender than she'd ever heard it. Her heartbeat quickened to a frantic rhythm and time stood still. Once again, she was back there, all that time ago. She wet her lips and tried to speak, but the words stuck in her throat. She swallowed and gathered her courage.

'Something unpleasant happened to me. I was having supper with my parents at the residency in Bhopal— that was where we were living at the time. Having finished my meal and leaving my parents to chat over their coffee and brandy, feeling stifled and in need of air, I wandered out on to the veranda. I remember how quiet it was with just one young man lounging at a table. He invited me to join him.

'Already acquainted with him, but knowing nothing

of his character and unable to see anything wrong with sitting with him until my parents were ready to leave, I accepted. He ordered me some coffee. We exchanged pleasantries. I remember feeling sleepy and then, apart from being manhandled and seeing a shadowy face looming over me, I knew nothing else until I woke in the hospital.

'That was when I met Dr Jessop. With my mother present, he told me what had been done to me—but I already knew. One cannot be raped and not know. I wanted to die, but I had to go on living. I blotted it from my mind, only to suffer further trauma when Johnathan, intent on revenge, sought out the perpetrator, only to lose his own life by the hand of the man who had violated me.'

'Dear God!'

Charles stared at her, his shock so plain for her to see. She wanted nothing more than for the earth to swallow her up. All her courage fled and painful embarrassment took its place. 'I can see how shocked you are—and I cannot blame you. What happened to me cannot be erased or changed. I have to accept it, live with it and get on with my life.'

She spoke with a tired resignation, without anger or resentment. Charles understood all too well what she was saying. With their disparate lives, their completely different experiences, they had something in common. He reached out and placed his hand on her cheek in a comforting gesture that surprised him. It surprised her, too. Reaching up, she placed her hand over his.

'Thank you,' she said.

'For what?'

'Listening to me. I've never told anyone about what happened to me. I couldn't. I have never spoken of it. It was too difficult.'

Lowering her eyes, she turned her face half away from his penetrating gaze, still unable to tell him of her guilt—the deep and terrible abiding guilt that still consumed her—that by her actions of allowing her abuser into her life, she had unwittingly signed Johnathan's death warrant. Had she not sat with a virtual stranger and invited conversation and drank the coffee he'd placed before her, Johnathan would not have died. A terrible despair had engulfed her and with it the shame. She still felt trapped by her guilt, knowing her impulsive action had endangered not only her future, but had led to Johnathan's death.

'I was too ashamed,' she whispered. 'I couldn't speak of it—not to anyone.'

'And yet you have told me.'

'Yes. You see—since meeting you I began to realise all that I have missed, to experience all the things once more that I so enjoyed before…before Johnathan lost his life avenging what had been done to me.'

'Tell me how it was—to help me understand—and about the man who committed the crime.'

'He was a Company employee. What he did to me was in retaliation for Johnathan reporting him to the Company for embezzlement. As a consequence, he was dismissed.'

'Was it proved that he killed Johnathan?'

'No, but a close friend of Johnathan's at the time,

who knew others who were there when the attack on Johnathan took place and intimated the fact, was in no doubt. Before that, when I went missing, I was found in quite a state, wandering in a disreputable district. I was disorientated and, mercifully, with no idea where I was or what had happened to me at that point. I—I had been drugged and raped. Demented with anger and anguish, in an act of vengeance Johnathan went looking for the perpetrator. Unfortunately, he lost his life in the fracas that ensued.'

'And the man responsible?'

'Was found in an opium den. As I recovered from my ordeal there was pain and misery and the dark and unmistakable bruises—a legacy of the violence inflicted on me. It was ugly.'

Charles stared at her as he tried to take in what she had told him. He was entirely unprepared for what she had disclosed. He was incapable of any kind of rational thought. What he felt at that moment was raw, red-hot anger. He was horrified—horrified at what that monster had put Lucy through. Where there was rage at what had been done to her, there was tenderness and sorrow, and he felt a surge of deep compassion as he realised how distraught and anguished she must have been at the time.

He could not bear to think of the pain Lucy must have experienced because of that horrendous act. The pictures thrust through his brain like knives. Lucy had been bound up in the secrets of the past for far too long. Clearly it was too private, too painful, something she was locked into, for her to speak about. Not that he could blame her. No doubt she felt that to confess she would be punished without mercy and she had learned to keep her secret so well that she hardly knew her motives for doing so. He could well imagine how her betrothed must have felt and understood his need to avenge Lucy.

His heart ached with the enormity of it all. The thought of Lucy knowing a moment's terror was too agonising for him to deal with just then. Had the rape left such an indelible scar on her that it went deeper than the surface? That was the moment he realised he didn't know her mind, what went off inside her head. She wouldn't admit him into it. She was an enigma.

'After what he was guilty of? Was he not appre-hended for that?'

Lucy shook her head. 'You must understand that it was a highly charged, sensitive situation at the time. Apart from my parents, and a couple of Johnathan's close friends, no one knew of it. Had it become known my violation would have fuelled vicious tongues and tarnished me for ever. My parents and Dr Jessop, who put me back together, thought I had suffered enough. My father wanted the whole affair hushed up. For my sake they wanted to escape a scandal. Afterwards I re-treated into myself, refusing to speak of it, but I was deeply traumatised by what had been done to me. When my father was moved to Nandra, I threw myself into working with the children and helping at the hospital in an attempt to forget.'

'Why have you decided to tell me this now, Lucy?'

'I want to experience what I missed because of what

happened to me.' Her jaw hardened with resolution and she said very clearly, 'You kissed me—showed me how it could be. I want you to show me again—I want you to make love to me.'

Charles stared at her, clearly wondering if he had heard her correctly. He could not believe what she had asked him to do, the enormity of the responsibility she was placing on him. Touching her cheek tenderly with the tip of his finger, he shook his head. 'I don't know if you are being serious or just teasing me, Lucy.' Seeing the courage she had mustered to expose her inner self disintegrate, like a flower wilting in the hot sun and how she moved away, he watched her turn her back on him, her shoulders drooping.

'I—I'm sorry if this is not what you want.' She kept her face averted, not wanting him to see how it hurt. 'After what I have told you, knowing what you do now, if you find the whole idea of making love to a woman who has been raped abhorrent, then we will stop now and never speak of it again. I will understand absolutely and apologise for any embarrassment I have caused.'

Charles moved to stand behind her. Though he wasn't touching her, she felt the heat of his body behind her as if it were a touch. His warm breath fanned her cheek as he bent his head.

'Nothing about you is abhorrent, Lucy—or the fact that another man took from you that most precious thing a woman has to give to the man she loves.' Placing his hands on her shoulders, he turned her to face him, tenderly wiping away the strands of hair fanning her cheeks and tucking them behind her ears. 'Since that time, what you have done, the way you have dealt with it, has been no more than an act of personal survival—something anyone with the same kind of courage would have done, faced with the same situation.'

Having emptied her heart, Lucy almost broke into a sea of tears and emotion. The pull of Charles's gaze was too strong for her to resist. It was as though he were looking into the very depths of her heart and soul. She felt the touch of his empathy like healing fingers touching and soothing her pain like a balm. She had seen in his eyes the reflection of her torment and now, as though he were God's own advocate, he was offering her redemption.

'Thank you, Charles. Your words mean a lot to me.'

'I hope you realise what you're really asking for,' he murmured.

'I was not joking, Charles,' she said quietly. 'I was being serious. My feelings are comparable with yours, but that is all. I will not expect any kind of commitment from you. I do not want it. That would only complicate things.' She met his intense blue gaze squarely, searching his eyes to guess his mood. They were dark with desire and a hunger.

'No one need know of this but us. I have no inhibitions and no pretences. I am doing this for myself. I am twenty-five years old and I don't have my virtue to worry about. I *want* you to make love to me. I ask nothing from you other than that—no commitments. I know your views on what you consider to be a debilitating emotion called love—you told me in no uncertain terms. I know the rules and I expect nothing from you that you are not prepared to give. Afterwards we will go our separate ways—no recriminations and no regrets.'

In the warm intimacy of the room, Charles was beginning to see another side to Lucy emerge, pushing the old one away, a Lucy without conscience, without shame, as if she were feeling something that was completely physical, hinting at joys that could be hers, telling herself this was a moment not to be missed—a night of the kind of pleasure she had never experienced before.

Involuntarily, he dropped his gaze to her mouth, a mouth lush and generous, a mouth that tantalised, a mouth made to be kissed. He remembered how soft and warm and inviting those lips had felt when he had kissed them before. It had surprised him. He never would have expected the fierce desire that had shot through him. Lucy Quinn was a lovely young woman, with her light fair hair spilling down her spine like a waterfall, and the exotic scent of her recently pampered body intoxicating. She had a mysterious allure he found hard to ignore.

'I think the palace and the attention showered on you by the Rani and her ladies has affected you more than you realise, Lucy. You don't know what you are asking of me—the responsibility you place on me. You tell me you were raped—that no man has touched you since that time. How do I know you won't run screaming from my arms?'

'I promise you I won't do that. I know very well what I am asking—and it is not particularly flattering for me to have to ask you. After the kisses we have shared, I wouldn't have thought you reluctant to carry on where we left off.'

'And I recall telling you that if there was to be a next time we kissed, then I would do the asking.'

'Then ask me.'

Seeing the determination on Lucy's lovely face, Charles frowned. He couldn't believe she was offering herself. It had been quite some time since a woman had warmed his bed and he was more than tempted by the slender body beneath the almost transparent robe before him.

When he didn't reply Lucy moved even closer. 'Why do you hesitate? Don't you want me, Charles? What must I do to persuade you?'

He studied her bathed in the glow of the moon and the lamps. Her large dark eyes were wide and wary. She looked completely vulnerable. Which was exactly what she was. Vulnerable and still innocent, despite what had been done to her, and without any idea of what she was asking for. He could show her. He wanted to show her, more than he had ever wanted anything before. His desire for her was driving him mad.

But now, when she had asked him to make love to her, when all he had to do was take her to bed, he was unable to move. It was no easy matter. He didn't want to hurt her. He respected her too much. He had never made love to a woman who wasn't willing. She only had to say no and he would stop.

'Lucy—what you are asking me to do is a huge undertaking on my part. The last thing I want is for you to hate me afterwards should you have any regrets.'

'I could never hate you, Charles—and I think I'm perfectly capable of deciding what I want.'

'At this moment, perhaps. But not when I leave Kassam—when I leave you and move on.'

'I'm not asking for tomorrow,' she murmured. 'I told you—no commitments. All I'm asking for is tonight. Help me move on from the past.'

Seeing the way she was looking at him—the softness in her eyes—he knew he should leave now, tell her no, but instead, taking her face between the palms of his hands he lowered his head and kissed her lips. 'Then that is what you will have,' he murmured against her mouth. 'Tonight.'

His arms went round her with infinite care, bringing her in close contact with his lean, hard frame, savouring the warmth of her body against his. His mouth came down on hers. Her lips parted freely and, with that instant response from her, the taste of her, Charles knew there was no turning back.

Sliding his fingers through her hair, revelling in the silken feel of it, he kissed her long and deeply. Her voluptuous bloom of womanhood evoked in him a strong stirring of desire. He could not believe how much he wanted her, that the body his own had so fiercely craved from the moment he had first laid eyes on her was in his arms.

Sensitive to her vulnerability, he knew that if he was to dispel the memory of the terrible thing that had been done to her, then he had to take it slowly, to be patient, to wait until she was ready. He tore his lips from hers and buried his head in the curve of her neck, his hands sliding down to her slender waist and drawing her close.

His fingers caressed the small of her back, pressing her body closer still.

Scooping her up into his arms, he carried her to the bed, settling her on the cool covers. With her hair spread about her in lustrous waves, he had never seen her look lovelier. He looked down at her face. 'Is this what you want, Lucy? Are you sure?'

She nodded, taking his hand and placing her lips on his open palm. 'I do—more than anything. Just the two of us, here, in this room.'

He smiled. 'Two lonely people finding solace in each other arms.'

'I would like to think it is more than that,' she murmured, losing herself in those blue eyes gazing down at her, now hazy with desire.

Slowly Charles's hand slipped about her waist as he drew her body against his and kissed her gently, amazed and intrigued by the mixture of innocence, boldness and fear which fired this woman. He would like to make her body sing before they were done, to shatter her demureness and reserve and lay bare the woman of passion.

He kissed her again and again, lost in the heady beauty of her. By God, she was lovely, and he wanted her with a fierceness that took his breath away. An uncontrollable compulsion to make love to her overwhelmed him and he kissed her until she was moaning and writhing in his arms and desire was pouring through him like hot tidal waves, but he had to contain himself, to be patient, to wait until she was ready.

Slowly he shoved aside her robe, exposing the softness, the curves of her naked body. He bent his head, again covering her mouth with his, his hand gently caressing her neck. Her eyes darkened and she tried to cover her breasts with her arms, Charles gently caught her hands and pulled them away. He knew he must be gentle lest her fear destroyed the moment.

'No, Lucy. Open your eyes and look at me.' Slowly, she met his gaze and his heart sank on seeing the apprehension and fear in their dark depths. Leaning up on his elbow, reaching out he tenderly smoothed the wayward strands of hair from her face. Pride surged through him at her courage. The beautiful, brave young woman was prepared to give herself to him, and him alone. He wanted to make up to her all that she had suffered in the past, when her virginity had been taken with brutal swiftness.

'I don't know what you're thinking,' he said softly, 'but you look terrified. Don't be afraid. I'm not going to hurt you, I promise,' he said reassuringly. 'I want to please you.'

Lucy swallowed, lowering her hands, but she continued to clasp the edges of the robe to her body. He wondered if she was going to change her mind. He wanted her, wanted to continue kissing those soft lips, to span that invitingly narrow waist with his hands and draw her hips beneath him. The fierceness of his wanting startled him, but he would not force her. Hearing her faint inhalation, he held back, looking down at her.

'What's wrong, Lucy? Keep your robe on if you like. But if this is not what you want, then it is not too late. We can stop now.'

'No—don't stop, it's just—I—I don't know what I'm supposed to do.'

'Then I'll show you—slowly—every step of the way. Any time you want me to stop, just say the words and we will go no further. You have my word.'

His hands stroked downwards, over the curve of her hip, and then upwards along the velvet softness of her inner thighs. She gasped, reflexively tensing her muscles and clamping her legs together. Once more, Charles stopped what he was doing.

'Lucy,' he said huskily. 'You don't have to do this.'

Above her, Lucy could see his face was tense, his eyes dark with passion, yet there was so much tenderness in their depths that her heart ached. 'Yes,' she murmured, 'I do.' The pull of his gaze was too strong for her to resist. It was as though he were looking into the very depths of her heart and soul. It was as if he knew her fear that twisted within her chest, as if she were so transparent, he could see all she had kept hidden laid bare. She felt the touch of his empathy like healing fingers soothing her apprehension like a balm.

Like a celestial being she raised her arms and wrapped them about his neck. Charles gathered her to him in reverence. Her fear was like a cutting edge and yet sublime, and when it left her and she felt the warmth of his lips, she was wide open in a flood of wondrous new emotions.

He took her soft lips she was offering in a long, sweet kiss that was almost beyond bearing, then, releasing her, he divested himself of his clothes and slipped his naked body on to the bed beside her.

Tentatively she moved her fingers over the furring of dark hair on his chest and felt the slight increase in the steady thudding of his heart. Very slowly he began to kiss her, long and lingeringly, with all the aching tenderness in his heart and she, after a few moments of tense passivity, began to kiss him back. Her slender arms slid up his chest and went around his neck and she pressed herself to the full length of his hard, unyielding contours.

Charles groaned, his mouth opening passionately over hers. Gently moving her robe aside, his hand slid to her midriff, then moved upwards, cupping the ripeness of her breast. She trembled beneath his touch, but instead of pulling away, as Charles expected her to do, the stiffness flowed out of her body and she relaxed, surrendering to his gentle, insistent persuasion.

She moved closer to him, fitting her body against his, her heartbeat increasing with a mixture of pulsing pleasure and fear when she felt the demanding heat of his maleness pressing against her thigh. Instead of pulling away, she gave herself up to his caresses until there was no more fear, only an exquisite, aching need to have him inside her. His hand continued to caress her, glorying in the softness of her flesh, and when he shifted her on to her back and leaned over her, what Lucy was feeling was drugging, delirious and quite wonderful.

She looked up at him, her eyes enormous and unblinking in her small, flushed face, and her mouth was rosy, as though waiting for further instructions on how to proceed, as if she wanted to take a more active part in what was slowly becoming a pleasant pastime, but was not sure how to go about it. It was as though what Charles was doing to her unlocked her heart.

She could sense the need in him, the need he had of

her and her body, and she gloried in it, but when his fingers reached that part of her that was totally private, she stiffened and bit her lip, briefly recalling he was not the first to touch her like this. Even though she could not remember what had happened to her at that time, she doubted that other man had treated her as lovingly and gently as Charles was doing. Immediately she thrust the unpleasant thoughts away and concentrated on what he was doing. She had to. She owed this to herself and would not let what that monster had done to her take away her capacity for loving.

The sensations Charles was arousing in her were utterly erotic, burning her flesh to a compelling, melting, quivering need, to go on until the very core of her ignited and inflamed every part of her body. Nothing else in the world mattered. They were completely absorbed with each other.

Leaning on his forearms, Charles gazed down at her lovely face. 'I want you, Lucy,' he whispered against her parted lips, his voice hoarse with tenderness. 'I want you very badly. Are you ready for this?'

Lucy nodded. 'Yes,' she whispered. 'Please—don't stop now.'

A fierce exhilaration swept through her as he slowly, tenderly entered her, filling every vein with liquid fire. She wrapped her arms around him, lost in incoherent yearnings. With his lips devouring hers, more eloquent, more demanding than before, he moved inside her, his eyes never leaving her face.

Some essential part of her that Lucy had not been aware of until now awoke and she ceased to think at all.

She felt something unfold inside her, spreading and filling her with warmth, with colour and light and reaching every nerve in her body, when suddenly a shudder rocked him and he let out a gasp as he thrust against her one last time.

A shimmering ecstasy pierced Lucy's entire body, sending sparks of pleasure curling through her that increased until they became a flame inside her and they lay together in sweet oblivion.

They lay for a long time, not speaking, reluctant to shatter the tranquillity and completeness of what they had found with one another during this magical night. After a moment when their bodies ceased to tremble, with an overpowering wave of tenderness, Charles rolled on to his side, taking her with him, cradling her in his arms, reluctant to let go of her. With her face resting in the curve of his jaw, Lucy experienced a joyous contentment, a languorous peace—and exultation, that the terrible thing that had been done to her had not taken away her capacity for loving.

'Are you all right, Lucy?'

Hearing the concern in his voice, Lucy felt an overpowering wave of tenderness wash over her. 'Yes—at least—I think so.'

'What are you thinking?'

'That now I am indeed a fallen woman—and I feel no shame, no regrets, just an incredible joy that has opened like a flower inside me—and I have you to thank for the way I feel now and I shall be forever grateful. For the first time since...' She faltered. 'I won't speak of that. I have no wish to tarnish the exquisite joy I feel now with the past. I feel vibrant, alive, and I want nothing more than for this moment to go on for ever—even though I know it must soon end.' Closing her eyes, she pressed her cheek against his chest and sighed, listening to his heartbeat.

'It must—when the time comes for you to return to Nandra.'

'Don't,' she whispered. 'Don't say it, Charles—not now. We'll deal with that when the time comes.' She nestled closer to him. She would allow nothing to steal the joy, the quiet glow of absolute bliss, which was with her now.

The room had become a magical place, their own private heaven. Sighing now, she placed tantalising little kisses on his chest, their naked bodies fitting together in sweet perfection. Lucy could smell him now she had her senses back, smell his skin, the scent of his cologne and a musky odour she could not identify, not an unpleasant odour—an odour of sensuality, one she knew she would always associate with this moment. She heard him sigh with contentment.

'You were a delight, Lucy. Something truly special.'

'And I am delighted to hear it,' she murmured.

'Do you realise how desirable you are?'

'Am I?' she whispered curiously. 'I'm amazed you can say that, for I never thought you felt anything for me but irritation—at least that's the impression you gave me when we first met.'

He chuckled softly. 'Was I that bad? I suppose you were irritating at times—and I was in a great deal of pain, don't forget,' he teased, tightening his hold on her.

'There you are. I was right.'

'Call it self-defence.'

Laughing delightedly, she wriggled away from him and stretched her body for him to inspect. 'I don't think I care for that remark. I think I'm going to have to punish you.'

'And how do you intend to do that?' he asked, devouring her with his eyes, his fingers tweaking a lock of her hair.

'By insisting that you make love to me again.'

'You call that punishment? I call it pleasure.'

And to prove his point, leaning over her he took her hands and held them above her while he carefully inspected her breasts, her waist, the curve of her hips. He knew her now, every part of her, knowing the true nature of her.

His senses were alive to every inch of her form languorously stretched out before him and, desire pouring like boiling lava through his veins, he kissed and nuzzled and caressed her until she felt the heat return to the pit of her belly. She sighed with absolute delight as he took her again with a lovely languor, consumed in a passion infinitely more powerful than before.

Afterwards, Lucy felt sleepy with contentment and her eyes fluttered closed. For a long time, she had been like a captive bird and now Charles had opened the cage and let her fly free.

The golden glow of the night washed over them as they lay clasped together, their moist skin cooling in the night air. They were breathing heavily as they waited for the slow and powerful beating of their hearts that follows climax to return to normal and to preserve the moment of their union a moment longer, as though afraid to disturb their fragile link by moving.

Gazing at the incredibly lovely young woman resting in the crook of his arm, her satiated body aglow from the force of her passion, Charles felt strangely humble and possessive. The enchanting temptress who had yielded to him without reservation, who had writhed beneath him as he had made love to her, was gentleness and goodness personified. He revelled in the sweetness of her as he stroked her spine, trying not to think and to hold on to the fading euphoria. He had been surprisingly enchanted with her and her body's responses to his own, and recognised the needs of the flesh without the complications of the heart.

Lucy asked for no more of him than he did of her. So why did it bother him that they were to go their separate ways? The answer was a mystery. He admired her tenacity and resolve. She had the ability to amuse him and he liked being with her. She was also honest and kept her word, which was somewhat rare in the women he had known previously. She was exciting to be with and he enjoyed her company, but it was time to put a stop to it before she began to expect more of him than he was prepared to give.

Besides, she was not free. She was still caught up in a web from which she could not escape—a web which the man she had been betrothed to and the man who had ruined her had woven round her. She could lead a happy and dignified life—but always her thoughts would turn to Johnathan. For the first time in his life Charles experienced a real, bitter jealousy. It was a cruel emotion; one he was not accustomed to.

With the dawn came the reminder that he had promised to accompany the Rajah on another hunt. Lucy wasn't aware when he reluctantly slipped away from her, kissing her bare shoulder before pulling on his clothes and leaving her to slumber.

When Lucy awoke, little remained of the girl who had been a victim of a rapist. She was a creature of the past. The mysterious alchemy of her inner self, mixed with elements inside Charles, had worked the miracle of transformation. The change in her was clear, and for the first time in years she felt at peace with herself.

A great burden had been lifted from her and she felt so happy it was like walking on air. It was as if she was waking up after a long dark sleep and what her soul had craved for the past seven years. She realised that she had turned a corner in coming to terms with the events of what had been done to her and it was Charles that had helped her to do that.

Her mind was filled with images of Charles and she held the memory of their loving as it wrapped itself about her like a warm blanket. Her mind and her very soul had been possessed by that perfect body, a body without flaw. It was no use hiding from the fact that they had been attracted to each other from the beginning, despite her initial show of indifference, but she must not mistake the kindness and tenderness he hàd shown her for something deeper.

Charles had the infuriating ability to pluck at the worst of her nature, to see what no man had ever seen before. But, she thought, on a warm tide of feelings, he also had the ability to tease, to cajole, to delight her senses in a way no other man had succeeded in doing before. He had created yearnings inside her she was a stranger to, yearnings she wanted to satisfy, and only Charles could do that.

Yet no matter how intense her feelings were for Charles, how constant, dominating her every thought, the burden of guilt she still carried in her heart over Johnathan's death, that he would still be alive if not for her, continued to plague her and she felt undeserving of any kind of happiness.

Throwing back the shutters, she noticed the flush of rose and apricot in the sky, along with a tinge of lilac and orange. A flock of small birds came and settled in the trees. She glanced at the sun rising behind the low hills, now the colour of ochre and gold. It enchanted her. It seemed as if they were living things, changing colour depending on the sun and the time of day. This was the colour of India in all its magical glory, she thought.

Chapter Seven

Lucy was in the garden along with Ananya and several of her ladies. This was where Charles found her. She was seated alone on a bench, watching the colourful scene of the ladies happily lounging on the grass, laughing and talking among themselves. Drinking in the fragrant tranquillity, he took a moment to observe her, admiring the fine figure she made. For a moment he felt as if she had reached into his chest and squeezed his heart. And then he blinked and shook off his strange abstractions.

Looking up from where she was seated on a wooden bench, she smiled on seeing him. 'Charles? Are you looking for me by any chance? I was wondering when you would show yourself.'

Her familiar voice rose above the sounds of the chattering ladies. Charles did not realise how much he had missed her until he heard it, or how the sight of her warmed his heart—and it had not been twelve hours since he had left her. He ached for her—to touch her, to gaze on her lovely face, to hear the sweet, soft sound of her voice. When they had made love, she had touched a tenderness and protectiveness within him he hadn't known existed.

He stood before her and his eyes glowed, complimenting her appearance, and a smile hovered on his mouth. The dark liquid of his eyes deepened as he became caught up in the warmth of her presence. Outwardly she appeared composed and very calm, making it impossible to determine her feelings and emotions generated in her following their night together.

'Here you are. I've been impatient to see you again, Lucy.'

'Oh? I missed you when I woke and found you gone,' she said, getting to her feet. 'Although perhaps it was as well. Maya is an early riser and would have scolded me severely had she found us together at that hour.'

'I'd arranged to go hunting again with the Rajah this morning and he wanted to make an early start. I've just returned. Later on today he is eager to show me his domain—and to spend the night with some of his friends at a hunting lodge. We will be back before you have to return to Nandra.'

'I see. Well,' she said, beginning to saunter away from the chattering ladies in the direction of a fountain spouting water high into the air, 'that is the reason why you are here, to spend time with the Rajah to promote better relations between Britain and India.'

'Our talks have been favourable so far.' He looked sideways at her as he fell into step beside her. 'Did you sleep well?' he asked quietly.

'Like a babe after you left me.'

Her tone, her very posture, were cool and aloof. Charles

peered at her, trying to read her expression. He wasn't sure what he had expected. An acknowledgement of what had passed between them, he supposed. His appraising gaze swept slowly over her once more, as if he couldn't get enough of looking at her. 'You look adorable. The sari suits you. I imagine you will be reluctant to get back to wearing English garb.'

'Indeed, I will,' she said as they continued to stroll along the quiet paths. 'I took advantage of another session in the bathing chamber earlier. In fact, I find myself remarkably transformed. The comfortable, indolent life at the palace, the rich food, the leisurely strolls in the flower-filled courtyards and gardens, and all the dexterous attention of Ananya's ladies have worked wonders. I have spent a good deal of time resting. I'm just not used to having so much time on my hands with nothing to do. I shall find it hard readjusting to the many duties that occupy my time in Nandra.'

'I have enjoyed our time together. I shall miss you, Lucy.' He looked down at her. 'Will you miss me?'

'I dare say I shall—although I expect you will soon find another diversion.'

'Diversion? Is that how you think of yourself?'

'No, of course not. It is what I intend not to be.'

Charles stopped walking and looked down at her, his expression serious, searching. 'You were never that. Do you regret it, Lucy—what we did?'

Her wide-eyed look was one of complete innocence. 'No, of course not. It is right that you should know how I feel. When I gave myself to you I did so gladly—without shame or remorse. In fact, it was quite wonderful—the most wonderful thing that has ever happened to me,' she confessed.

'I am relieved to hear it. You know how I feel about you.'

'Do I, Charles? Do I really?' Tilting her head to one side, she gave him a teasing look. 'I do hope you are not saying that you love me, Charles?'

'Love?' He slowly shook his head. 'I despise the idea of what the romantics call love. How does one define love? I've told you before that I no longer know what the word means. I care for you—a great deal, as it happens—but don't confuse physical desire with love. I have lived through one disastrous relationship, which taught me that it is an unpleasant experience I have no desire to repeat. The woman in question wrung almost every emotion out of me.'

'And so you judge every woman to be the same,' Lucy said quietly.

'No, not all of them, but I realised a long time ago that poets may write about love and balladeers may sing about it. It exists for others—but not for me. Despite the feelings and emotions we aroused in each other, do not fool yourself into believing it had anything to do with love.'

'Don't worry, Charles, I don't and I thank you for being honest with me. But I would have imagined you would have too much common sense to attribute to all women what you have experienced in one.'

'You would say that. You, who showed me so much vulnerability, so much generous passion.' He looked at her, wondering what the change in her attitude was all about. Was she ashamed of what they'd done? He didn't think so. On recalling the passionate, irresistible tempt-ress he had aroused in her bed, of the pure bliss they had each felt in their union, he believed her when she said she had no regrets.

'But what of you, Charles? Do you have regrets?'

He shook his head slowly. 'I refuse to regret or apol-ogise for what happened. We wanted each other—we were attracted to each other. It was as simple as that. I well remember what your body looks like, Lucy.' His eyelids were lowered over his eyes as he looked down at her upturned face, gently flushed a delicate pink by his remark. 'I remember everything about it—every curve, every hollow and every inviting, secret place.' He smiled at the shock that registered in her eyes.

Lucy's attempt to chastise him for his forward re-mark, when Ananya and her ladies had fallen silent and were watching them with curiosity, failed. 'Please be quiet, Charles, lest we are overheard.'

'Worry not, Lucy. Apart from the Rani and perhaps an odd one of her ladies, our exchange will not be un-derstood.'

His voice was deceptively soft and Lucy cast her eyes away, registering her unease. 'Nevertheless, I think you should leave. I will see you in the morning before I de-part for Nandra—if you get back in time, that is.'

'I will make a point of it. But there is something I would like to say before we part.'

'Oh?'

'I hope you find someone who will show you a way to a new life. Someone who will bring you out of the past. Someone who will give you a chance to put all that happened behind you. Do you intend to mourn Johnathan for ever?'

His words seemed to take her off guard. Clearly she had not expected this. He saw the hurt and despair in her eyes. He felt something inside him, some strange emotion that was unrecognisable to him just then, and unconsciously his hand went out to her. His expression became one of mixed emotions, strangely gentle, and his eyes softened and were filled with sorrow and compassion, telling her of his regret that his words should give her pain.

'You are right. I have lived too long in the past. I might have been Johnathan's wife now. I would have been happy with him.'

'You were in love with him.'

'Yes, I was. How could I not be? He was handsome, kind—a gentleman and highly thought of by everyone.' She looked at him gravely. 'There are some things in my life I cannot set aside, Charles. Johnathan is one of them.'

Charles paused to collect his thoughts and marshal the facts, for that was the moment he realised her betrothed's loss remained a gaping wound. There was nothing in Lucy's attitude to give him any encouragement and he had no intention of trying to compete with a dead man.

In some way, he was reminded of his own situation. With his instinct for self-preservation, he was suddenly furious with himself for having succumbed so easily and foolishly to a woman's charms once more. Tentatively he made a move towards her, but he could almost feel the alert tension of all her muscles. Her very stillness was like a positive force.

'I would have said more, Lucy, as I could now, but I do not have the right.'

'The right? No, Charles, you don't. It's best not to say anything else.'

'Just one thing. Johnathan has been dead these past seven years. It is time you accepted the fact.'

Lucy met his gaze. His blunt words were cruel and hit their mark. 'I do accept it, Charles, but that doesn't mean I can forget him—or the fact that it was my own actions that brought about his brutal death.' Drawing a deep breath, she stepped away from him, unwilling to discuss the matter further. 'Tomorrow I shall return to Nandra. I shall not forget our time together.'

'I sincerely hope not. I shall not forget it either and, whatever the future holds for you, Lucy, I sincerely wish only for your happiness.'

The attraction of his handsome face and deep blue eyes, which could be as stormy as India during a monsoon or warm with depths of tenderness, had been irresistible. Whenever they were together Lucy's feelings had intensified until they brought an ache of emptiness to her heart. He did not love her—not that she expected him to, but his consideration as a lover had brought her to a pleasure that Johnathan had never achieved.

That night had held a thousand unexceptionable and unexpected pleasures for them both, but she would not allow herself to become caught up in a romantic dream. Her emotions were torn asunder and she could find no solace in the depths of her thoughts. Knowing they must part had strengthened the barrier about her heart, but that barrier was not made of stones. Their first kiss had brought some of them tumbling down. Now, as he walked away, with an awful lump of desolation in her throat, her heart ached.

The following morning, having reverted to western dress, as though adopting armour for the journey back to Nandra, Lucy said her farewells to the Rajah and Ananya. She was sorry to be leaving her new friend.

'I will miss my English friend,' Ananya said. 'I will remember you always. But you are not far away and will be welcome any time at the palace. I have a gift for you to remember me by.' She clapped her hands and a servant rushed forward with a package.

'But I can't possibly accept it. I shall be for ever grateful to you and the Rajah for the kindness you have shown me.'

'It was our pleasure. Now open it. You will like it, I know.'

Lucy did as she asked and gasped when she saw the carefully folded sky-blue silk finely threaded with gold, so fine yet so delicate that if filtered through her fingers like liquid. She gasped. 'But—this is so beautiful. I—I cannot—'

'Yes, you can. It is my gift to you. You cannot refuse.'

'Thank you, Ananya. I will treasure it always.'

Accompanied by Maya, who had found so much wonder within the palace that she would speak of it for evermore to her children and grandchildren, Lucy found

Captain Travis and the small military escort waiting for them with the horses.

She had not seen Charles since they had parted in the garden the previous day. Now, as she was about to leave Kassam, he suddenly appeared, looking harassed in his haste to see her before she left. He came towards her, his expression grim. There was an unusually brooding expression in his eyes.

Taking her arm, he drew her away from the others, 'You are ready to leave?'

'Yes. It is time—although I am sorry to be saying goodbye to Ananya and all those who have shown me kindness.'

'Kassam is just a day's ride away. I am certain the Rani would welcome you again.'

'Yes, she had invited me to return. When do you leave for Madras?'

'A couple of days here and then I shall be on my way. I hope to obtain a passage quickly. I don't relish the thought of having to kick my heels in Madras for any length of time.'

'Then I wish you a safe voyage.'

He nodded, his brows drawn together in a frown. 'There is a matter you should give some thought to, Lucy, which must be considered seriously.'

'And what is that, pray?'

'It is possible that a child may be the result of the night we spent together. Has it crossed your mind?'

'A child? Yes, it has.' Unconsciously her hand went to her abdomen and for a moment she could think of nothing more wonderful than to give birth to his child. 'I will give the matter some thought if that should happen.'

'And if you are carrying my child? What then?'

'I will deal with it.'

His frown deepened. '*You* will deal with it?'

Lucy flinched at the bite of his tone. 'Yes, I will have to—although it is not a situation I wish to find myself in. But I suppose like everything that has gone before, I shall weather the storm and hope for the best.'

The flippancy of her remark provoked Charles's eyes to flare with anger. 'No, Lucy, you will not. *We* will deal with it. Should it happen, the child you will be carrying will be mine, too, don't forget. I *will* have a say in how it is raised. You will write and tell me?'

Lucy felt anger and frustration rising within her. 'Of course I will tell you—I would not deprive you of seeing your child. I know you to be an honourable man who would give support and provide for it. But I will not have what I do in the future and the destiny of my child—should there be one—dictated by circumstance,' she said, suddenly boldly audacious in her maturity. 'Really, Charles, I cannot see why we are having this conversation now when in all probability I have not conceived. You must understand that I have some control over this—which I shall have no choice since you will be hundreds of miles away in England.'

'I shall not be in England for ever. I intend to return to India at the earliest possible time.'

'Well, there you are then. But a baby is not on the agenda at this crucial part of my life,' and, she thought, certainly not with a man who would stand by her out of nothing but a sense of duty. 'What we did was a mutual decision—my feelings comparable with yours. We had a strong desire for each other, nothing more than that.'

'It was more than that and you damn well know it. If you find yourself with child, then I have a duty to both you and the child and I insist that you inform me.'

'If that is what you want, then so be it. If there is a child, then I promise you I will write and tell you of the fact.'

'I think you misunderstand me. If I do not hear from you, then I shall call on you when I return to India— however long it takes—to make quite sure there is no child.'

'I understand you very well, Charles, and you insult my integrity if you think I would keep such an important matter from you. But do not think you have a right or a responsibility to arrange my life because of what happened between us. Do not put yourself out on my account. It is over, Charles. I am a grown woman. I can take care of myself. I will not be any man's duty. I thank you for your consideration and, should I find myself with child, I will inform you. That is my final word on the matter.'

He was standing very close. She had to look up to him. Impatiently she tried to shake off the effect he was having on her, regretting the harshness of her words and reminding herself that if it had not been for Charles she would still be battling her nightmares.

Without relinquishing the hold he had on her eyes, he looked down into her face. 'Of all the women I have known, Lucy, none has possessed the fire of heart and mind as you do and I am going to miss you like hell. You are beautiful. A temptress. We are to part and may never see each other again, so there is nothing left for us to say other than to bid each other farewell.' His gaze settled on her lips. 'A parting kiss, Lucy, as a farewell gift?'

As he bent his head, his firmly chiselled lips began a slow, deliberate descent towards her. She did not draw away—in fact, she raised her face to his, too tempted to forbid him a kiss. At first, he kissed her lightly. She tried not to show surprise or emotion, but that first touch was exquisite. His lips were warm, his kiss soft, and he kissed her long and lingeringly, a compelling kiss that made her head swim.

That was the moment when Lucy's mind went blank as his sensual mouth seized hers in an endless, drugging kiss that quickly built to one of demanding insistence and shook her to the core of her being. The world began to tilt as he crushed her tighter to the hard length of his body, parting her lips and exploring the honeyed softness of her mouth. Whether from fear or desire, Lucy moaned softly. She clung tighter to him, raising her arms and sliding her fingers into the crisp hair above his collar.

By the time Charles finally raised his head, Lucy's weakened defences crumbled completely. She felt dazed and her body quivered with all the raw emotions and the mindless pleasure he had aroused in her in her bed.

He tipped her chin. 'Look at me, Lucy.'

That deep voice saying her name was capable of making her do anything. She dragged her wide, wary gaze up to his smouldering blue eyes. 'Please let me go, Charles. You go too far.'

He smiled lazily, his white teeth flashing from between parted lips. 'Come now, Lucy, you are being unreasonable.'

'Unreasonable? Because I don't want you to kiss me?'

'But you do. You wanted it just as you wanted me in your bed. Be honest with yourself and admit it.'

The amusement in his tone angered Lucy further. She faced him squarely, her eyes flashing. The memory of that burning kiss, and the dark, hidden pleasure it had stirred in her, roused her to fresh paroxysms of anger.

'You think I am so easy to manipulate, don't you?' she said, choosing her words with great care in the hope of preserving what little was left of her pride. 'You have got it all wrong. You have misunderstood me completely. I will not be bullied.'

One eyebrow lifted in sardonic, arrogant enquiry. Seeing fire flame hot and sure in her eyes, a smile curled his lips. 'Ah, I appear to have stirred your temper.'

Lucy could feel the anger begin somewhere in her breast, a hard knot just where her heart lay. She found his hostile manner and egotistical attitude outrageous. She also felt a dreadful resentment that he should feel he had the right to speak to her as though she were nothing at all. Stiffening her spine, she raised her head defiantly, proudly, her pride being her strength. 'I do lose my temper and I am hurt just as easily as anyone else.'

His expression softened. 'I know. We cannot leave things as they are between us.'

'We have to, Charles. You should concentrate on leaving for England.' She was glad that he could not see what an effort it was for her to be close to him. Why else would she be experiencing this painful yearning that was equal parts rejection and want? 'I think everything that needed to be said has been said. Talking about it will not change anything. I'm sorry if you feel you have wasted your time, but it is hardly a tragedy.'

His eyes darkened in his anger. 'Be careful what you say,' he said harshly. 'And don't be misled by the fact that I once showed myself indulgent in my dealings with you—'

'You might say more than indulgent,' Lucy snapped back. 'It infuriates me that I allowed such liberties to be taken by a man who thinks of me as no more than a moment's pleasure when you get me alone.'

'I don't recall you complaining at the time. You were the one who invited me in, don't forget.'

Something welled up in Lucy, a powerful surge of emotion to which she had no alternative but to give full rein. It was as if she had suddenly become someone else, someone bigger and much stronger than her own self. Her eyes flashed as cold fury drained her face of colour and added a steely edge to her voice.

'Which, if you are not careful, I will begin to regret. As a matter of fact it did mean something to me. To you, what happened may have seemed commonplace,' she upbraided him, her words reverberating around them, 'just another one of the many flirtations, romances and infidelities that give others something to gossip about. But I am not in the habit of sleeping with gentlemen who are relative strangers to me, or any other kind for that matter.'

'I was not accusing you of such.'

'You, Charles Anderson, may hold a lofty position with the British government and not for one minute would I aspire to wanting to get to know you better than I do now. But after saying that, there is nothing about you that intimidates me. You may be an envoy and mix in the highest circles when you are in London, but you are not the sun around which the world revolves. I know who I am and what I am and I do not need anyone to remind me. You will soon forget me when you return to your duties at the Foreign Office—forget that you ever came to Puna and met a woman called Lucy Quinn.'

'Your judgement of me is harsh to say the least. It is completely false and you know it. I think this journey—with you—will remain with me for a long time.'

'I am honoured that I have given you such food for thought.'

'Of course you have. It is quite natural when I consider that you are different from anyone I have ever known.'

'That is usually the case. No two people are alike.'

'Nevertheless, most of the people I meet arouse little interest in me.'

'Maybe that is because you are too self-absorbed.'

Her words angered him. He stood before her, tall and powerful, his face austere. His eyes focused on her with a clarity that seemed to gain strength from his anger, his eyes searching hers for the truth of her words. 'That is the last thing I want. I would not hurt you in any way.'

'I do not doubt it,' she uttered caustically, feeling more hurt than she cared to admit. In his expression there was no affection, only a resolute determination to have his way.

They looked at each other in a struggle that racked them both and Lucy clung to the sudden coldness between them as a shield. Drawing herself up proudly, she raised her chin. He would never know how much she was hurting.

'Very well,' he said, stepping back. 'What can I say except goodbye and please take care. But remember your promise and contact me at the Foreign Office if need be.'

'Yes, I will. Goodbye, Charles.'

He walked away without turning to see her. Her heart leaden, Lucy's eyes followed his tall figure helplessly. He looked so handsome with the sunlight casting a warm halo about his dark head. She wanted to go after him and tell him how sorry she was for all her harsh words, but her pride came forward, forbidding her that comfort.

Not for one moment did she regret having known him. Until then her heart and body had been dormant, waiting for the spark that would make it explode into life. And if Charles had not ignited it, she would have spent her whole existence not knowing what it felt like to have a fire inside her soul, would never have known that such a wild, sweet passion could exist. Better by far to experience that passion for such a short time than never to have known it at all, even if it brought such pain and heartache, or to die not knowing such joy was possible.

The thought that she would not be with Charles again tormented her and she could not bear to think of a day, a month, let alone an eternity beyond that, without him. The weight of it was almost more than she could bear. Her heart ached with the desolation of it and with the loss that must come next. Her mind was filled with thoughts of him, just as her eyes were filled with tears. The great black void of her parched existence threatened to swallow her up once more.

On her return to Nandra, Lucy was surprised to find Dr Jessop waiting for her. He looked tense. Clearly, he had something on his mind, something unpleasant to impart. Alerted by a quivering tension in the air, she became still.

'Doctor Jessop? What is it? Is something wrong?'

'I have some sad news, Lucy. You must prepare yourself.'

'For what? Is it Father? Is something wrong?' She looked around her, not understanding. Before he even uttered the words, she knew her father was dead.

He nodded. 'I deeply regret to inform you that your father passed away during the night. I am so sorry.'

Bright tears filled her eyes. She swallowed and held herself very erect. Without uttering a word, she went past him and hurried to her father's room. She stood close to the bed in which her father lay, still in his night attire, his eyes closed in his waxen face. Kasim, his loyal servant of many years who had been keeping vigil, appeared from the shadows, his elderly face etched with grief.

'Leave me for a moment, will you, Kasim?' Her voice

was broken with sorrow. 'Please,' she entreated. 'Leave us alone.' Mercifully he went.

Alone now, the silence settled around her like a shroud in the room with its elegant and colourful hangings. As she looked at the bed where her father lay so still, grief welled up within her. She was absolutely mortified that she had left him, that this had happened when she was away. So extreme were her thoughts that her brain retreated into some kind of limbo.

She waited until her breathing was normal before she let herself out of the room, but she had no clear recollection of leaving it, for the insensibility nature provides to protect the mind fell over her. She thought she would wake any moment and find that it had all been a hideous nightmare, not more than that, and that her father wasn't dead after all.

In the unforgiving heat it was necessary to inter Jeremiah Quinn without delay. It was a small, sorry company that gathered to witness his final interment. After a brief ceremony in the small church, he was laid to rest in the small cemetery outside the cantonment.

Lucy held herself in check as the coffin was lowered into the deep pit. It was laid next to that of her mother. A cleric who lived in the town intoned the final words of interment, reminding them all of where they had come from and where they would return to, then it was over.

Devoid of her father, the house no longer felt like home. Lucy was feeling lost and unusually tired and depressed. Even with all there was to do and think about, she could not help wondering what awaited her in the future.

Her days were consumed with packing up her life in Nandra—her life and her father's. She had almost finished when she received a letter from her father's lawyer, Mr Fleming, in Madras. He had written to inform her that he had heard from her grandmother's lawyers in London of the old lady's demise and that she had left Lucy a substantial legacy.

Lucy was deeply saddened to learn that her grandmother had died. She had been her only remaining relative. However, Lucy hadn't known her very well, being just a child when she had stayed with her. She had been ill for some time and at eighty-five years of age her demise was to be expected.

Her husband, Lucy's grandfather, had left her a wealthy woman. All that wealth, along with her grandmother's house, had now passed on to Lucy. Lucy had given little thought to such matters. Her parents had never spoken of such things to her. But with that and the substantial wealth her father had accrued over the years with the East India Company, to suddenly find that she was a wealthy young woman in her own right and that she need not fear for her future, was such a wonderful feeling and such a tremendous relief that she could not believe it at first.

Fixing her gaze on the distant horizon beyond the cantonment, she made her first decision about her future. Where could she go? What could she do? She had done nothing but help her father with his work. For the first time she began to wonder if there were other possibilities for her future besides teaching and looking after the sick. She decided it was time to stop believing she had no choices in her life. It was time to begin deciding her own destiny.

When Mrs Wilson went to stay with her daughter in Madras she would go with her—and maybe consider accompanying her when she left for England, even though it would break her heart to leave India. Mrs Wilson had two daughters: Celia, who lived in Madras, and Alice, who lived in London. Alice had recently been delivered of Mr and Mrs Wilson's first grandchild and Mrs Wilson was to go to England to see her. She was to spend twelve months with her before returning to India to be with her husband.

When the day came for Lucy to leave Nandra, tears flooded her eyes as she closed the door, realising that she was finally leaving the only place she had called home. She left Nandra with Mrs Wilson and others embarking on the week-long journey to Madras, with a regiment of soldiers making for Fort St George. One of the hardest things she had to do was to say farewell to Maya, who had been with her since she had come to Nandra.

Lucy would miss the life she'd led there and Dr Jessop, who had become a good friend to her and seen her through the darkest days of her life. She forced herself not to think about it. She couldn't afford to or she knew she would fall apart because of all she had lost. She couldn't allow herself to get sentimental now. She just had to keep going until she reached Madras and had found safe haven somewhere. A chapter of her life had closed, but the memories would linger.

Chapter Eight

Madras was all a bustle after the small parochial atmosphere of Nandra. White, colonnaded buildings of grace and proportion bespoke a dignified wealth. Lucy had stayed there with her parents when they had arrived in India. She had found it an agreeable town, where the English conducted themselves exactly as they would in London. The way they promenaded themselves in their fine equipages along Mount Road of an evening rivalled anything to be seen in London's Hyde Park.

Lucy was staying with Mrs Wilson's daughter and her husband in a house extensive and elegant along the shoreline and within sight of the massive walls of Fort St George, with its bastions, its Government House and gardens.

The days passed in a blur of activity as she assisted Celia in civic and church activities. Charles was never far from her thoughts. Despite the acrimony of their parting, she found it extraordinarily difficult, even after this considerable time, to think about much else. She saw his face, heard his voice, remembered him—oh, dear Lord, she remembered him, everywhere, all the time.

Mrs Wilson was a kindly soul and had been glad to

take Lucy under her wing. 'You have been to see your father's lawyer, Lucy,' she said over tea and cakes in the afternoon. 'Have you decided what you will do? Will you remain in India?'

'No. There is nothing here for me any more. Now I have been to see Mr Fleming I have decided to book a passage on the first available ship bound for England.'

'Then we will travel together. I would value your company on the journey. At least you have a house to go to, which must be a relief,' Mrs Wilson remarked, sipping her tea. 'And I must say, the way you have described it to me, it would be foolish of you not to take up residence.'

'Yes, it would. Although I know no one in London.'

'You will soon make some friends. Whenever I've been in England, I always found London such a delight. I loved seeing the sights and galleries and attending the many social events and the theatre my husband insisted upon.' She laughed, placing her cup and saucer on the table in front of her. 'I am so glad you will not be far away. And you must call on me and Alice. I look forward to introducing you to her.'

Lucy smiled across at her. 'And you and Alice must visit me, Mrs Wilson. I remember the house as being quite large, large enough to accommodate guests and central to the city's pleasure gardens and theatres.'

'We will visit, my dear, and how convenient to be close to all the city's pleasurable amenities.'

'You have always been very kind to me, Mrs Wilson— especially when my mother died. I am going to miss you when you return to India.'

'And I you, my dear. The cantonment won't be the same without you and your dear father. But I know you are going to love London.'

Lucy felt all was not as it should be with herself and there was a nagging fear in her that could not be discounted. She felt unwell and was often plagued by bouts of nausea. As the days progressed, disbelieving and shocked, the thought that another life grew within her crept in unbidden. It was a thought that could not be shaken. It filtered through her brain like some unwelcome shockwave.

She was unprepared for this sudden explosion in the quiet landscape of her life. It was a tenacious, terrifying reality. Charles loomed even larger in her thoughts. It was almost two months since they had made love. The pleasure and intensity she had experienced then was now too painful to contemplate. Her face became pale and drawn and there were dark circles beneath her eyes. She could not sleep, her predicament and her future causing her to lie awake night after night worrying, pondering over what she should do.

Mrs Wilson was not as shocked by Lucy's predicament as she had thought she would be, nor was she surprised on being told of the identity of the father. In fact, she was goodness and consideration personified and insisted on taking care of her. It was decided that they were to remain in Madras until the baby was born before leaving for England. And Lucy was eternally grateful, if a little guilt-laden that Mrs Wilson was to delay her own journey to England for so long.

Now, more than ever, Lucy needed the strength of her forceful personality to keep her sane in the days, weeks and the months to come. Charles had told her that this might happen and that if she found herself with child he wanted to know—Lucy would not dream of keeping something of such importance from him. Now that she was to have a child and feeling a love so powerful for that tiny being inside her and that she would do anything to keep it safe, to do what was right by it, it was her duty to inform Charles that he had fathered a child.

With the hope that he had not yet left Madras, enquiries were made. Unfortunately, he had sailed for England a month earlier. She did as he had told her and wrote to him at the Foreign Office, informing him that she was to bear his child and providing him the address in London where she could eventually be reached. If he did not receive it, she would have to wait until she arrived in London and make enquiries as to where he could be contacted.

Lucy was thankful that she now had enough money to care for herself and her child. The stigma of bearing a child out of wedlock would no doubt hit her eventually. Yet it gave her a strange, rather agonising joy to know that Charles's blood was at work somewhere deep inside her. Whatever he did now, he was bound to her by the ties of flesh and blood, so, now that the shock of the revelation of her condition had worn off, nothing could destroy her happiness in the knowledge that she bore his child.

Edward Charles Quinn smiled his wide, beaming, toothless smile and his dark blue eyes narrowed in his sweet face, before fastening his hungry mouth on his mother's breast. With a mop of dark curly hair, he was adorable, Lucy's pride and joy, and when she gazed down at him with a passion of love, she couldn't believe he belonged to her—to her and Charles. Her emotions for her son were so powerful that she shuddered at their strength. She loved him from the moment he was put in her arms.

The vessel on which Lucy and Mrs Wilson embarked from Madras took five long months to reach the Pool of London. It was a grey, miserable day in March when they finally put ashore and very cold. The contrast between it and the country they had left was astounding. And made her miss it all the more.

It had almost broken Lucy's heart to leave India. She would miss the colours of the sunset, the star-spangled night skies, the lilac and blue and soft pink of the dawn. She would miss the storm clouds that heralded the months of the monsoon, of mists and the curtains of rain. When they had set sail, the breeze carried the scent of Madras far out to sea, of flowers and spices and the ever-prevailing dust.

But she must forget about that now and focus on the future.

Lucy's grandmother's house in Kensington was an attractive manor house set in its own well-tended grounds. It was where her mother had been born and had lived until she had met and married her father. Inside it was just as Lucy remembered when she had been here as a child. It was warm and inviting. Fortunately, Mrs Yates, her grandmother's housekeeper of many years, was still in residence, along with two servants and a groom who lived above the stables to the rear of the house and looked after the two carriage horses.

Edward was soon ensconced in the nursery, where he was cooed over by an adoring nursemaid and Mrs Yates, who was delighted to have fresh life injected into the house regardless of Lucy's unmarried state.

Accompanied by her daughter Alice, Mrs Wilson was a frequent visitor. Alice was married to a Company employee who worked at East India House on Leadenhall Street. Their lives had been enriched by the birth of their daughter. Alice was a slender young woman and a brunette like her mother, with winged brows over friendly grey eyes. Learning of Lucy's troubled last days in India and the birth of her adorable son, not being one to judge, she had befriended Lucy from the start and was determined to introduce her to her circle of friends.

During the short time Lucy had lived in the house she had come to love it and soon began to look on it as her home. Whatever came about, she must be independent and do the best she could for Edward. She must become accustomed to the fact that she would never marry, for no man would take on a woman who had fallen so far from grace and given birth to an illegitimate child.

Lucy scarcely had time to catch her breath before Alice happily and enthusiastically transported her into a world of high fashion. They went to the most fashionable milliners, hosiers and glove makers to be found near the Exchange, then to the smartest drapers, where they purchased the finest linen petticoats and night-dresses, going on to the silk mercers on Ludgate Hill before finishing in New Bond Street, Alice advising and superintending the choice of colours and materials for her new gowns.

Having finished their shopping for the day, and feeling pleasantly exhausted, Alice suggested that, before going home, they drive through Hyde Park, which was an integral part of London's social life, one of the ways to see and be seen, to show off fine carriages and clothes. Leaving the carriage, they walked at a leisurely pace along the paths.

When Alice paused to speak to an acquaintance, two riders, a man and a woman entering the park, caught her attention. The woman was riding a chestnut mare and the man a grey stallion, a huge beast, a thoroughbred and no mistake. The pair made a handsome picture. She continued to watch in fascination. To her the perfectly groomed man was every inch an elegant, relaxed and poised gentleman. His dark blue jacket set off his broad shoulders and his snowy white neckcloth emphasised his dark hair and dark looks.

Suddenly Lucy felt the pull of those looks, her eyes drawn to them like a magnet, feeling her body freeze when she recognised those chiselled features printed indelibly on her heart. Like a stone statue, unflinching, her eyes unblinking, she watched him turn to the incredibly beautiful woman in an emerald-green habit. Leaning towards her, he bent his head to hear what she had to say and what Lucy took to be an affectionate gesture broke a hold in her emotional barricade. The woman's face was alight with laughter as they rode off at a cracking pace.

Lucy stared at the scene in ringing silence, filled with admiration for the woman's ability and daring. It was clear that she was utterly fearless. As she watched Charles, her face lost what little colour it had.

Alice, noticing her friend's strained profile beside her and sensing that she was not enjoying the park, leaned towards her. 'Lucy, are you all right? You're not ill, are you?' she enquired softly.

Pulling herself together, Lucy forced a laugh, turning to her friend. 'No. No—I'm quite well, Alice. I have a slight headache, that's all. I saw someone I thought I recognised. I was mistaken,' she said, watching as Charles disappeared among the trees.

In one fell swoop, all the hope and confidence, which had upheld her throughout her pregnancy and the voyage to England to the moment when she would behold Charles once more, crumbled to nothing. That glimpse of him with another woman had been like a dagger thrust to her heart. Never before in all her life had Lucy felt so agonisingly, unbearably jealous of another woman as she did of the one she had seen with Charles.

She gulped, swallowing down the tears that accumulated in her throat and threatened to choke her. She felt overpowered by an immense weariness and disappointment, born of the accumulated fatigue of the past months together with this shock she had just received. Disappointed, dazed and unable to form any coherent thought, wanting nothing more than to seek refuge, playing on her headache, she asked Alice to take her home. All she could see in her mind's eye was the touching scene she had witnessed between Charles and the beautiful woman.

One thing that Lucy was determined to do now she was in London was to visit Anna, Johnathan's sister. Before Johnathan had died, he had told her his sister would have to return to England to live with their Uncle Robert and Aunt Constance at Melcot Lodge in Kensington. It wasn't difficult to locate the house, but she was disappointed when told their niece had married and was now the Marchioness of Elvington. She and her husband, the Marquess, resided in Berkshire, but had a house in Mayfair.

Impressed by Johnathan's sister's high status, Lucy was apprehensive about meeting her, but, keen to do so all the same, she instructed the driver to take her to the address of the Marquess of Elvington.

The footman who admitted Lucy to the fashionable residence informed her that the Marchioness was at home and if she would care to wait in the drawing room he would see if she was available to see her.

With a lump in her throat, Lucy watched Johnathan's sister enter, not knowing what to expect. One thing she had not expected to find was that this was the woman she had seen in the park the previous day with Charles. Bewildered and curious at the same time, she decided not to mention this for the time being. They were strangers to each other and she didn't want to cause her any embarrassment should she feel the need to explain.

Lucy saw that the Marchioness moved with a regal grace not often met with. What she saw was a slender woman, slightly older than herself, assured and quite lovely in an understated way, her skin as white as milk, her eyes a warm shade of amber. She held her head high on its graceful neck, her golden hair exquisitely coiffed. There was an air of kindliness and generosity about her—she wouldn't have expected anything else from Johnathan's sister. Her resemblance to Johnathan was so striking that it brought back all Lucy's memories of the man she would have married.

Lucy stared at her. She could hardly breathe. Her chin trembled against her will and her eyes were awash with tears. She dashed them away as they began to fall and crossed her arms across her chest. So overcome was she with shock and heartbreak on meeting this woman whose connection to Johnathan reminded her of what might have been had he not died, that she couldn't trust herself to speak.

In her mind, Anna Harris was still the young sister of the man she had loved with all the innocence of her youth—which seemed so long ago now. How silly to think this was still that young girl who had written long letters to Johnathan. This was a woman—a beautiful woman, with eyes that were so incredibly like Johnathan's, so incredibly kind.

'Lucy?' Anna whispered, as overcome with emotion as she was. A deep sadness for the loss of her brother filled her eyes, but then a smile touched her lips and her eyes brightened a little when she said, 'I cannot believe it's really you.' Settling on the sofa, she indicated that Lucy should sit beside her. 'If only you knew how often I've thought of you over the years. I wanted to write to you, but I didn't know where to send the letter to. I never thought we would meet. I often wondered what had become of you. Did you remain in India after— after Johnathan…?'

'Yes—yes, I did,' Lucy replied, sinking down beside Anna, facing her. She wondered how much Anna knew about what had really happened to Johnathan—and the assault on herself. She prayed she didn't know, that Anna had left India unaware of the sordid details of the circumstances leading up to her brother's death. 'After what happened to Johnathan, my parents left Bhopal. My father was given a position in Puna. When my mother died, I remained with my father. When he passed away, with nothing to keep me in India and receiving a legacy from my grandmother, I came to England.'

'And were you sad to leave India?'

'Very much so. It had been my home for so long.'

'I didn't want to leave either, but I had no choice.' Anna lowered her eyes, her expression becoming grave. 'Lucy—I—know what happened to you in India,' she said softly, raising what Lucy had feared most.

Lucy swallowed, shaking her head slowly. 'You do?' she whispered.

Anna nodded. 'Yes, my husband told me.'

'Your husband? How—how would he know that— unless he was there.'

'My husband is William Lancaster. He was Johnathan's closest friend. Johnathan placed me in his care for the voyage when I returned to England.'

Lucy stared at her in shocked amazement. 'William? You married William?'

'Yes. As the heir of the Marquess of Elvington, he came back to England to take up residence at Cranford Park in Berkshire.'

'I remember William. He—he was very kind to me when it happened. I—I knew him as William Lancaster— although not all that well. I had no idea he was the Marquess of Elvington.'

Anna smiled. 'He wasn't then—not until his grandfather died when he returned to England.' She placed her hand on Lucy's arm. 'There is no shame, Lucy. None of it was your fault. I knew James Ryder, the man who—who…'

'Raped me,' Lucy managed to say bitterly. 'I was just eighteen years old, Anna, and he—he drugged me and raped me. How could he have done that—how could anyone?'

'I know. I met James Ryder on board ship. I didn't know what he was, who he was, what he was guilty of, until later. He—he tried to molest me also, Lucy. Fortunately, William found me in time—along with James Ryder's father, who banished him to America, and as far as I know he remains there to this day.'

'Good riddance, I say.'

'Precisely.'

'Poor Johnathan. He had good reason to despise him before that, but after what happened to me his hatred knew no bounds. But he shouldn't have gone looking

for him—to avenge what he had done to me. He would
not have died had he not done that. I blame myself to
this day for what happened. I was stupid and naive—
James Ryder was no stranger to me although I did not
know him well. He asked me to sit with him—brought
me some coffee. I stayed with him while I waited for
my parents—and I drank the coffee—which he must—
have...'

'Oh, Lucy, my dear,' Anna murmured, moved by her
distress. 'There is no blame attached to you. You cannot
continue letting this rule your life. Johnathan would not
want you to suffer and neither do I. Johnathan lived life
to the fullest and he would want you to do the same.'

'But I can't—even after all this time. Because of my
actions, I deprived him of his life—of happiness. I will
never forgive myself for that.'

'You are too hard on yourself, Lucy. Ours is a shared
loss—given that you lost the man you were to marry
and I lost a beloved brother. This is a tragedy that binds
us for ever. Like me you will carry on.'

Lucy gulped down her tears and nodded. She was
completely taken with the easy friendliness of this attractive woman and accepted the feeling as mutual
as Anna's fingers squeezed her own before releasing
them. 'I know—and I have tried, Anna—but it has been
hard—it is still hard.'

'Then we will help each other. I look forward to furthering our friendship—and to you meeting William.
He will be so delighted to meet you again—to know
you are here in London. He's still at Cranford at present, but I expect him in London any day.'

Hearing a child's happy laughter from somewhere in the upper echelons of the house, Anna smiled. 'That is one of my offspring.'

'You have children?'

'Two, and they are adorable. At four years old, Thomas is quite the young man, while Sophie is just beginning to walk.' She tipped her head to one side. 'And you, Lucy? Do you have any children?'

Lucy nodded, looking down at her hands. 'Yes—a son. He—he is seven months old now.'

'And—your husband? Is he here in London with you?'

Lucy shook her head, raising her head and looking directly at Anna. 'No. I am not married. My son's father and I—didn't see eye to eye, I'm afraid.'

Anna's expression was pained on hearing this. 'I'm sorry to hear that. It—must be difficult…'

'Being an unmarried mother?' Lucy sighed. 'Yes, I'm sure there will be many hurdles to overcome in the future, but that's the way it is. Since what happened to Johnathan I—I feel a great reluctance to place my well-being in another's hands—to have to rely on someone else.'

'Oh, Lucy, you shouldn't feel that way. I've told you, you were not to blame for any of it. You deserve happiness. Should you need any help and support, I will always be here for you.'

'Thank you. You are very kind, Anna.'

Anna smiled. 'I feel that you and I are kindred spirits, Lucy. Perhaps when you feel up to it you could share your stories of India—of your time with Johnathan, as memories are all that remain of him.'

'I should like that very much,' Lucy whispered. 'Johnathan was a good person—the best of men.'

'Praise indeed.' Anna smiled. 'Now I will have some refreshment brought in and you must tell me a little about India before you leave.'

This they did. When Lucy got up to leave, Anna walked with her to the door. Lucy turned to her as she stood on the steps. 'I—think I saw you yesterday, Anna—in the park. I didn't mention it at first because I wasn't sure it was you. You were riding a chestnut horse?'

Anna smiled with delight. 'Yes, it would have been me. I was with Charles—my brother-in-law. We often ride in the park. It's the only place one can have a good gallop here in London. He's due to leave for India shortly—works for the Foreign Office. You must meet him. I'll arrange for us all to get together when William gets here.'

Lucy's heart skipped a beat. How she managed not to reveal how shocking this pronouncement was to her she would never know. At times like this, her self-imposed training in outward control set in. She put an expression of interest on her face, kept her spine straight, but it was the thinnest of veneers. Beneath it her emotions were in turmoil.

'Yes—of course. I would like that.'

Relaxing against the upholstery in the carriage taking her back to Kensington, Lucy felt as though a huge weight had been lifted from her. She had been completely mistaken in thinking that Charles was in a relationship with the woman she had seen him with in the park, whom she now knew to be his sister-in-law. Nothing could be further from the truth, but his close ties to Anna and William Lancaster had come as a surprise to her and she wasn't sure how to deal with it right now, but at least she now knew how to contact Charles when she was ready.

Lucy sometimes went riding in the park with Alice and her husband, Henry, which she loved. Visits to the theatre and walks in the park with her new friends were also added to her agenda. When she was invited to accompany them to an exhibition of a prominent artist at the art gallery in Pall Mall, she accepted, even though she knew very little about the subject and did not have an educated eye for art.

The occasion was attended by the wealthy, artists, writers and journalists. Ladies and gentlemen were dressed in full splendour. It was an animated crowd, with laughing, gossiping and whispering faces. Never having seen anything quite like it, Lucy was all agog. There were no outsiders, everyone present having been issued with a gold-embossed invitation. Liveried footmen moved among them, bearing salvers of glasses brimming with champagne. The paintings on display drew a great deal of interest, although they did not appeal to Lucy.

Feeling out of her depth as she looked around at the animated throng, she glanced at Alice and Henry for reassurance. 'Goodness! I never imagined there would be so many people present.'

Henry's attractive face relaxed into a faint smile as

his eyes swept and absorbed the full length of the gallery. He was a great admirer of art and his eyes lit up, as always when he found himself surrounded by such illustrious company and fine works of art.

'These occasions are always well attended. If you will excuse me, there is someone I haven't seen in a while. I will go and have a quick word.'

Watching him thread his way through the throng to the other side of the room, Alice smiled, shaking her head. 'You must forgive my husband, Lucy. I always find myself neglected when he is surround by works of art and illustrious company. Come, let us circulate and I will introduce you to one or two people I know.'

This Alice did, but after a while of engaging in social chit-chat with friends and acquaintances of Alice, Lucy found it difficult to take it all in and the faces became a blur. Looking about her, hoping to catch the eye of one of the servants for a glass of champagne, Lucy focused on a couple of gentlemen who had just arrived.

Suddenly and inexplicably Lucy's heart gave a joyful leap at the sight of one of them and the familiar fine-boned, taut, bronzed face. Her whole being reached out to him across the distance that separated them. Being quite the tallest man there, Charles Anderson was a man who dominated his environment and his mere presence forced people to notice him. He and his companion were in deep conversation at the opposite end of the gallery, seemingly oblivious to the noise around them.

Lucy's feet became fastened to the floor as if they had roots as she looked at him across the room. The very air around him seemed to move forcefully, snapping with exhilaration and the restless intensity he seemed to discharge. He was splendid in a bottle-green frock coat that clung to his shoulders, which were broader and more muscular than she remembered. There was lace at his throat and his dove-grey waistcoat was embroidered with silver thread.

Suddenly Charles was looking down the length of the room, his gaze drawn to her. Their eyes met and she felt the strange shock of recognition shake her as it always had when he'd looked at her. Then he was striding towards her and she couldn't take her eyes off him. Her mind ranged through the evocative memories left over from the days they had spent together in Guntal at the Rajah's gorgeous palace. Though sorely lacking experience in the realm of desire, instinct assured her the wanton yearnings gnawing at the pit of her being were nothing less than the cravings that Charles had elicited during that lustful night they had spent together.

The vision that appeared in the room made Charles pause in his stride. The sure knowledge of Lucy's presence interrupted the conversation he was having with his friend, Sir David Henderson, a man of his own age and an extremely wealthy industrialist from the Midlands. David was saying something important, but Charles heard not a word. With her hair elegantly coiffed and her figure attired in a simple but fashionable gown of sky-blue satin, with her back to the open doorway, Lucy looked like a heavenly apparition, a radiant silhouette with the light shining from the adjoining room behind her.

The exultation he felt at the sight of her almost overwhelmed him. There was a new maturity about her, her figure more rounded. It suited her. She was beautiful, even more beautiful than she had looked when they had last met—a radiant sunburst in a city choked with darkness. My God, he had missed her.

In India they'd had no time to get to know each other. Yes, they had made wonderful and passionate love, but their deeper feelings had remained very much hidden. Seeing her now, he felt a world of feelings flash across his face—disbelief, surprise, happiness, but only fleeting. Unsure of how she would receive him, as he came closer his expression cooled.

Chapter Nine

Trying to ignore the treacherous leap her heart gave, Lucy stepped forward with a quaking reluctance, clutching her reticule in her gloved hands, her lips curved in an uncertain smile. Drop by precious drop she felt her confidence draining away, especially when the thoroughly piercing eyes locked on her and slowly appraised her.

She lifted her head and looked into his eyes, then wished she hadn't. She had forgotten what looking directly into those deep blue eyes was like. Rather weakened, she took a deep breath. In some strange way they seemed capable of seeing right inside her. It was all she could do to face Charles's unspoken challenge and not turn and flee.

'Lucy? It's been a long time. I did not expect to see you here.' His voice was soft, though his smile was knowingly chiding.

For an instant Lucy could not move. She felt herself relax, every limb slowly settling into its usual posture, her eyes still fastened on his, drifting on the enchantment of being in the same space as him. 'I did not expect to see you here either, Charles. I—I wondered if you might have returned to India.'

'I'm due to go back at any time soon. Why have you left India?'

'I had no reason to remain any longer. My father died—the night before I returned from Guntal—which came as a dreadful shock to me.'

'I'm very sorry to hear that,' he said sympathetically. 'I know how close you were. You will miss him.'

'There was nothing that could be done—but I wish I had been with him at the end.' She swallowed hard, but her voice was husky. 'It was a while before I accepted that he was gone. When my mother died, he became the centre of my world, so, yes, it was hard at the time but, as you will remember, his health had been deteriorating for a while.'

'Yes, I do. And now here you are, in London.'

Lucy managed a smile. 'Yes. When one door closes another opens—isn't that what they say? When I received a letter from my grandmother's lawyer informing me of her demise, as the only member of the family remaining, she left everything to me. Her legacy was substantial and gave me no choice but to come here.'

'Like you, there has been a death in my own family— my aunt—Aunt Charlotte. She went to live in Devon in the house left to me by my uncle, which was where she died.'

Lucy saw the pain slash its way across Charles's features and at that moment she knew he had loved his aunt with the same everlasting devotion she had felt for her father. 'This can't be easy for you either, Charles.'

'I loved her dearly. She will be sadly missed, particularly by my sister Tilly, who, as I told you, also lives in Devon. Aunt Charlotte left me her house in Chelsea, which is where I'm living.'

'So, you have acquired two houses.'

He nodded. His eyes softened. 'I've missed you, Lucy.'

Her heart was touched by his admission. 'You have?'

He nodded. 'More than you will ever know. How long have you been in London?'

'Just three weeks. I live in Kensington.'

'Then, if you will permit, I will call on you.'

For a moment she stared at him. There was so much she had to tell him, so much she wanted to explain.

'Yes—I would like that.'

'Are you glad to see me, Lucy?'

'Yes, of course I am,' she murmured with nervous apprehension. 'We knew each other for such a short time and I will always remember how it was between us.'

The sound of his warm, masculine voice never failed to bring her senses alive. Close to him at last, she was powerfully aware of everything that was masculine, primitive and demanding about him, which was always so strong it seemed to be an almost physical force. She was more aware of him now than she had ever been and here, with the whole world looking on, stood the man whose child she had given birth to, a child he didn't even know existed.

With so many people looking on, she wouldn't tell him now. She wanted to be alone with him to do that. Nor would she tell him about seeing him in the park or her visit to Anna. Clearly, he hadn't seen his sister-in-law since their ride in the park, because Lucy was certain Anna would have mentioned her visit to see her and, if she had mentioned Lucy's name, he would have known she was in London. Time enough for that later. Introducing Charles to his son was paramount at this time.

'When I think how easily you dismissed me from your life when we parted, I am encouraged by your reply.' A wicked twinkle sprung up in his eyes. 'Had you said otherwise, then I would probably have hotfooted it back to India without a by your leave.'

'Is what I feel so important to you, Charles?'

'Yes,' he replied on a serious note, his eyes holding hers. 'I'm afraid it is.'

'I didn't dismiss you from my life or my mind when you left India—quite the opposite, in fact. When I received my grandmother's legacy, I did write to you, telling you of my change in circumstances and where I could be reached here in London.'

'You did? I never received it. Where did you address it to?'

'The Foreign Office. I thought it would be passed on to you.'

A frown furrowed his brow in puzzlement. 'It should have been. I will make enquires—although the post between India and London is pretty poor at the best of times and mail does get mislaid.' He uttered a few words of quiet annoyance when a group of boisterous young men pushed their way through the throng, causing him to step aside to let them pass. Taking Lucy's elbow, he drew her out of the way. 'We have matters to discuss—things to say to each other that cannot be said here.'

'Then you can call on me tomorrow, Charles.' She looked past him to see Alice coming towards her. 'Here is my friend Alice. She is Mrs Wilson's daughter and has become a good friend to me since coming to London. Mrs Wilson and I travelled together on the voyage. She is to return to India very soon to be with her husband. Come. I will introduce you.'

When Lucy left the exhibition and returned to Kensington, there was a new lightness to her heart. Seeing Charles had everything to do with this and she was looking forward to introducing him to their son. She refused to think any further than that.

She would never forget Johnathan and their betrothal, which had ended so tragically, and since her feelings for Charles had not lessened since their parting, she had thought of him more and more. But that did not mean the guilt she still felt for the part she had played in Johnathan's death had lessened or that the pain had gone away. There were still chains around her heart. True happiness would continue to elude her until she could find forgiveness for herself.

The following morning Lucy awaited Charles's arrival with trepidation, although why she should feel this way she couldn't say because she had done no wrong. It was unfortunate that Charles had not received her letter informing him that she was to bear his child.

He appeared at eleven o'clock. Mrs Yates showed him into the sitting room where she waited. She stood up to receive him, watching the way he moved. For a man of such imposing stature, he had an elegant way of moving in his casual clothes. He wore a dark blue coat, his long legs encased in biscuit-coloured trousers and highly polished black riding boots. He had removed his tall hat and his hair was slightly dishevelled, brushing the edge of his collar.

She watched him raise his hand and, as he absently rubbed the muscles at the back of his neck, her treacherous mind suddenly recalled how skilfully those long fingers had caressed her own body and the exquisite pleasure he had made her feel. She could still taste that hungry mouth on hers, still feel his hands on her body, which had aroused such an intensity of desire within her. In her heart she yearned for him, as if he had put his own dark brand upon her soul.

And how he was here, coming towards her, smiling almost suavely, as if it were the most natural thing in the world that he should be there.

'Charles,' she said. 'Welcome to my home.'

'It's a charming house—so different from where you were living in India.'

'I think so. It's a different world to the one I knew there. Please sit down,' she said, indicating a chair opposite the one she sank into drawn up to the hearth— her manner was polite and proper when all the time she wanted to fling herself into his arms. 'I came here often when I was a child to visit my grandmother. I suppose, there being no one else for her to leave it to, I always knew I would inherit it one day, but I never gave it much thought.'

He sat across from her, his eyes settling on her face. 'And you intend to live here permanently?'

'Of course. I like the house and it serves all my needs. Why do you ask?'

He shrugged, crossing his long legs in front of him and steepling his fingers. 'No reason, although I could never imagine you living in a metropolis.'

'After India, you mean? I cannot go back. There is nothing for me there any more. Did you enjoy the art exhibition?'

'It was interesting—if one likes that sort of thing.' He paused, before continuing, 'I may be mistaken, Lucy, but when I saw you, I got the impression that there was something you wanted to speak to me about. Are there any secrets lurking in that pretty head of yours that I should know?'

She stared at him, a soft pink flush mantling her cheeks. With a raised brow he waited silently, expectantly, for her answer. She swallowed audibly, knowing the moment had come when she must tell him he had a son. 'Why—I—yes,' she said softly. 'Since you ask, there is just one very small secret you should know about. If you had received my letter, you would already know.'

'And? What is it, Lucy? What is it you have to tell me?'

'It—it concerns a baby. Our baby,' she said quietly. 'You—we—have a son, Charles.'

Whatever Charles had been expecting her to say, it wasn't this. Not a muscle of the handsome, authoritative face moved. He recovered himself quickly. 'And am I to believe this?' he finally said into the reverberant silence, which to Lucy seemed almost a lifetime later. 'The child is mine?' He stopped abruptly, aware that what he had said would be deeply hurtful and offensive and that now the words had been said they could not be retrieved.

Lucy bristled with indignation, suddenly angry that he might doubt his part in Edward's parentage. 'Yes, Charles. What I have just told you is the truth. I am not trying to deceive you. I did not get myself pregnant. I did not do it alone. You had some part in it—it was not all my doing. It takes two to make a child. We—you and I—made Edward.'

'Of course—and I'm sorry if you think I doubted you. I don't—not for one second. But—good Lord!' he said, getting to his feet and shoving back the heavy lock of hair that had fallen forward on to his brow with his long fingers. 'You are telling me that I have a son?'

'Yes, Charles. You have a son. Edward. Although, when I sent the letter informing you I was to bear your child, I truly thought you might have forgotten all about me.'

'I confess that when I returned to England it was with mingled fears of regret and concern that you might be pregnant. If you remember, I did mention that it was possible that it would be the result of our night together,' he said.

Then he smiled in disbelief of the very idea that he had a son, shaking his head as he tried to absorb the fact. 'Of course I couldn't forget you, Lucy. In fact, every day I have been here I hoped a letter would arrive from you telling me exactly this—that you were to bear my child. When no such letter arrived, I was resolved to return to India. Can I see him?'

'Yes, of course you can. Come with me. He has a nap at this time so he will be asleep, but he should soon be awake.'

As if in a trance, Charles followed Lucy into the nursery. She spoke quietly to the nurse, asking her to give them a moment. Charles's gaze went straight to the crib, where his son was deep in slumber. Slowly he moved towards it and stood looking down. Edward was lying on his back, his arms flung out on either side, breathing softly, his lips slightly parted. The child was so perfect it was as if a sudden pain twisted Charles's heart—as if it had been pierced by a sharp blade. Unable to tear his eyes away from him, he stood quite still in those first moments, his eyes seeking the truth, which in his heart he already knew. This was indeed his son.

There was a silence, a stillness. The moment seemed to go on for ever, though it lasted only seconds. The child was the most beautiful child Charles had ever seen. Charles could not yet speak, for his throat was clogged with words he wanted to say but couldn't.

He touched a tentative finger to the child's rosy cheek, then to his hair and finally, with a gesture that was lovely to see, to one of the tiny hands shaped like a starfish on the pillow. To his delight Edward's hand gripped his finger.

'Is he not beautiful, Charles?' Lucy whispered, returning his smile. 'The most beautiful little boy you have ever seen?'

'Most certainly,' he said, his voice hoarse with every kind of emotion as he stared down, feeling an immense closeness and love for the child. As if sensing he was the focus of someone's besotted admiration, Edward stirred, opening his eyes and blinking at his father for the first time. Without more ado Charles gathered him up and held him in the crook of his arm, his face soft, the softness melting away the harshness, the determination that ruled his everyday life. His expression was loving and proud.

'This is my son—such a handsome little chap. He is perfect—and he looks like you, Lucy—although he bears my likeness.'

'He is your image, Charles. One only has to look at him to know whose son he is.'

Edward's eyes opened and he blinked and blinked again, then blue eyes stared into blue eyes, the child's steady and curious, and then he smiled, a wonderful, toothless smile. With a great wave of tenderness washing over him, Charles placed a kiss on his forehead before carefully placing him back down in his cot. He reached down and touched the tiny hand.

For the first time in his life, he was experiencing new and confusing emotions. He saw the world in a different light, a world that no longer centred around himself, but around his tiny son. He looked at Lucy and smiled, this little boy holding them together with a thread, however fragile.

'Thank you, Lucy. I wish I had been present at his birth.'

'Now you are here you will have to make up for the time lost.'

'I can imagine you have not had an easy time of it.

But our son is a beautiful child, a credit to you, and I thank you for what you have done for him in my absence. I have missed seven months of his life. Believe me when I tell you that had I known of his existence I would have moved heaven and earth to come to you before now. From now on Edward's interests will be paramount. So you see, Lucy, already he is very precious to me. I am an utterly devoted and besotted father.'

When the nursemaid came back into the room, they left the nursery. Mrs Yates brought refreshments to them and when she had left a silence stretched between them, filled with the intensity of the emotion that suddenly linked them.

Placing his cup on the occasional table that separated them, Charles looked across at Lucy. 'It cannot have been an easy time for you when you realised you were pregnant,' he said calmly after a short pause in which neither of them seemed to want to break the silence.

'No, I confess it wasn't. I was living in Madras with Mrs Wilson's daughter at the time. They were very good to me. Indeed, I don't know how I would have coped without them. When I got over the initial shock of my condition, my duty was to the child. I remained in Madras until Edward was born. When he was two months old, I came to London. I decided to look to the future, to my new life—with or without a father for Edward— life is too short to squander on ifs and wherefores. My day-to-day life would change, I knew that, and that in all probability I would be shunned. But after much soul-searching I discarded any resentment and self-pity I felt about my situation. Now I spend as much time with my beautiful son as I possibly can.'

Charles gave her a look of admiration. 'It appears to me that you are a capable young woman. I can only apologise for not being there to support you. However, things have changed. I have much to think about before I have to leave for India.' There was a tension about his mouth. He hesitated, as if searching for the right words, then, getting to his feet, he said, 'I will leave you now and consider how best to proceed.'

Lucy watching him go, wondering in what way he wished to proceed. Perhaps he would offer some kind of financial settlement for Edward's future. The only other way she could think of that would put things right would be if he were to offer her marriage, but somehow, she doubted he would do that—or that she would accept.

The following day it was a worried Charles who arrived at his brother's town house in Mayfair. The instant he saw the tall man with dark hair coming towards him, his handsome countenance lightened. The two strode across the hall towards each other, where they clasped arms and hugged warmly, laughing.

'Good to see you before you have to leave for India. When? Do you know yet?'

'Not the precise date, but it won't be long—although I have some loose ends to tie up before I go.'

'Bet you can't wait to get back.'

'How are things with you, William? You look tired. Working too hard?'

'You might say that. It's backbreaking work running an estate the size of Cranford Park.'

Dismissing the subject with a casual wave of his hand, William drew him towards the sitting room. 'Anna will be sorry to see you go. I think she's got used to having you around.'

They entered the sumptuously furnished sitting room, where Anna was sat at a desk writing letters. Since the birth of her last child, she had bloomed like a beautiful English rose. On seeing Charles, with an exclamation of delight she went to embrace him.

'Charles! This is a wonderful surprise. I hope you're staying for dinner. Come and sit down. William will pour you a drink. I envy you going back to India. I would love to go back.'

They sat in a companionable threesome, conversing on familiar matters, the sun slanting through the tall windows. The brothers each held a glass of brandy from which they sipped appreciatively, while Anna preferred a cup of tea.

'And how are the little ones?' Charles asked, crossing his long legs in front of him.

'They are very well—though a handful. They're up in the nursery. You must go up and see them before you leave, otherwise Thomas will never forgive us if he knows Uncle Charles has called and not seen him. They're a delight, are they not, William?' Anna said, looking lovingly at her husband.

They talked of things that were of interest to them all, until Anna placed her cup down, a serious expression on her face. 'I almost forgot to tell you. I had a visitor the other day—Lucy Quinn, would you believe—Johnathan's betrothed. I was most surprised.'

Charles stared at her in shocked amazement, staying his glass halfway to his lips. It was as though all the air had been sucked out of the room.

'Lucy Quinn?' William said. 'Good Lord! I didn't expect to hear of her again—although I always did wonder what had become of her.'

'Yes—well, you'll be able to meet her again. She's a delightful young woman—such a tragedy what happened to her.' Her eyes filled with sadness on being reminded that they might have been sisters-in-law. 'I'm going to invite her round for dinner—you must come, too, Charles. I'm sure you'll find her interesting and have much to talk about.'

'Yes,' Charles said tightly, having recovered himself from the shock of realising who she was. 'I imagine I will—since Miss Lucy Quinn and I are already acquainted.'

Anna stared at him. 'You know Lucy?'

'Yes. We met in India.'

'You never said anything.'

'I had no reason to. I had no idea she was girl who had been betrothed to your brother, Anna. At the time, when you and William arrived in London, I had other matters to take care of. I was unaware of all the details concerning your brother's death.'

'But—you know what happened to her—which resulted in Johnathan's death?'

'I do now. She told me. I'm sorry, Anna. I really did not connect the Lucy I know with your brother. And she had no idea who I was. I didn't even know the name of the girl your brother was betrothed to.'

'Lucy came to see me, Charles. She was severely traumatised by events back then. But—I am curious. How well do you know her?'

Charles shifted uncomfortably in his chair. 'We—we met when I was wounded and ended up in the hospital she worked in. She was a nurse.'

'That wasn't what Anna asked you, Charles,' William said. His expression was one of calm speculation as he regarded his half-brother. He quirked a brow in amused enquiry, waiting for him to speak. 'I recall Lucy as being a very attractive young woman. You cannot have failed to notice what a dear, sweet girl she is.'

Charles got up sharply, agitated suddenly, as he put some distance between them. 'I would not describe Lucy Quinn as sweet,' he replied, turning to face them, his tone impervious, irritated because William seemed to be enjoying his predicament enormously. 'It has taken me a year and a half to appreciate that high-minded young woman is the most exasperating female I have known in my entire life.' He paused, becoming thoughtful. After a moment, he said, 'She is also the woman I want for my wife.'

Anna gasped. 'Your wife?'

William laughed. 'Pardon me, Charles, but I have to say that you do not look in the least like a man in the full flush of love.'

'I am not.'

'Then why do you want to marry her?' Anna asked. 'Have you come to care for her?'

'Of course I care for her—more than I have cared for any other woman, which is why I want her to be my wife,' he replied, annoyed when he saw William's victorious smile widen on hearing his confession. 'Lucy and I have a son—Edward. He was born in India and is seven months old. I did not find out about his existence until yesterday—but,' he said on a softer note when an image of his precious son entered his mind, 'he really is the most beautiful boy.'

Anna and William both stared at him in amazement, speechless. After a moment William let out a low whistle and said, 'Good Lord, Charles, I'm stunned—surprised— even shocked. You say you didn't find out about him until yesterday. Did Lucy intend keeping it from you?'

'Apparently not. She wrote to me from India via the Foreign Office. I never received the letter. I have looked into it. She did write, but they failed to pass it on.'

'I knew that Lucy has a child, but I'd no idea that he is also your son, Charles. She hinted that there was some bad feeling between her and the father. However, whatever has passed between you two, I look forward to meeting our new nephew,' Anna said, as shocked and surprised by Charles's news as her husband. 'Have you proposed to her, Charles?'

'No—not yet.'

'Is there a problem?' William asked. 'Are you afraid she will turn you down? Although with a child between you, it is the obvious solution.'

A wide smile lit Anna's face. 'But—that would be wonderful. I would love Lucy to be my sister-in-law— which she would have been had she married Johnathan.'

'Not so very wonderful,' Charles replied drily. 'She might very well turn me down.'

'I can't imagine why. Most women would be happy for the chance to marry a British diplomat.'

'Lucy is not most women.'

Suddenly Anna frowned as a thought occurred to her. 'Charles, when you ask her—do that, will you? Don't *tell* her. Knowing you and your autocratic manner, she might very well tell you to go to the devil.'

Charles found it irritating that Anna might be right. 'She can be very stubborn. She is a very independent young woman with strong opinions regarding marriage— and even after all this time, she is also still very much in love with Johnathan.'

'I don't believe that is so. She is still consumed with guilt about what happened, believing it was all her fault and that, having deprived Johnathan of his life, she does not deserve to be happy. But things have changed. She now has her son to think about. It is in the child's best interests that he grows up with both his parents. She hasn't been in London two minutes, Charles. Perhaps it would be a good idea to court her before you propose to her. You do want her, don't you?'

Of course he wanted her, his mind raged. Seeing her again was like a sunburst in his life. Suddenly he was catapulted backward through time while the image of Lucy abruptly blended into another image—that of an enchanting golden-haired young woman who had once looked up at him with unconcealed desire glowing in her eyes. All that passion was within her still. It sim- mered just under the surface. He had been driven to unleash it and that was coming back to taunt him now, for he wanted to unleash it again.

Within him, he felt a pang of nostalgia mingled with a sharp sense of loss because the woman he had known was gone now. His worry and confusion of the previous day when he had called on her had been replaced by a deeper, darker feeling of uncertainty. It was still a new emotion to him and one of which he was not particularly fond.

'Yes, I do,' he replied quietly, in answer to Anna's question.

'Then you must use all your powers of persuasion. Charm her—which shouldn't be too difficult, having seen how the ladies fawn over you. Show her that you care. Do not forget that you are to leave for India very soon so unless you want to say goodbye to her and your son, missing out on his childhood, then you must woo her in earnest.'

'Anna is right, Charles. And whatever happens, you will have our support,' William said on a more sombre note.

'Yes, we must,' Anna agreed softly. 'You are right when you say she still feels the guilt for what happened to Johnathan after all this time. She is reluctant to place her well-being in another's hands after what happened before—to rely on another person is difficult for her. But Johnathan would have wanted her to be happy.

'I realise that after what happened to her, she found it difficult forming any kind of relationship—and who can blame her—until she met you, Charles. She must care for you a great deal even if she does not show it.'

Going to him, she stood behind his chair and put her arms about his neck, fondly resting her cheek against his. 'I do believe it will come right in the end.'

'Thank you, Anna. I hope you are right.'

'It's very important that we make her feel welcome and unafraid of the kind of reception she will receive.' She looked at her husband, noting his pensive look. 'You knew her, didn't you, William?'

He nodded. 'I did—but not all that well. I wasn't always with Johnathan when they were together. What I do know is that Johnathan thought the world of her and they would have married had he lived. Of course we will do our best to make her feel welcome. She deserves our absolute support.

'There is the Rutherford ball coming up. They're close friends of ours so I doubt they'd object if she accompanied us. It would be an opportunity for you to begin courting her properly, Charles. Out in India she never had the opportunity to enjoy the luxuries in life and I imagine she could do with a few.' He grinned across at his brother, raising his glass. 'A few flowers wouldn't go amiss.'

Charles looked at his brother as if he'd taken leave of his senses. 'Flowers? You are joking? What the—' He broke off and his eyes narrowed as the suggestion took hold. 'Oh, I hadn't thought of that.'

Anna laughed. 'Clearly. Although Lucy deserves all the niceties life has to offer.'

'You're right, Anna,' Charles agreed, a positive light entering his eyes. 'You always are and, by God, I will shower her with all the luxuries I can afford.'

'There's no time like the present,' Anna said, pleased to see his enthusiasm. 'Flowers are as good a place as any to start.'

'Very well, Anna. I will take the task of courting Lucy seriously. I shall be politely considerate, attentive and indefatigable in my attempts to please her. I know exactly how to treat a woman and to adjust my attitude to what I believe will please her best. In fact, I shall be patience and consideration personified.'

'Goodness me, Charles! With so much consideration, I am almost tempted to divorce William and marry you myself,' Anna said, laughing and winking at her adoring husband.

Later that same day when a beautiful bouquet of red roses had arrived, Lucy couldn't believe her eyes. The note that came with them told her they were from Charles. Her surprise deepened the following day when two more bouquets arrived, each banded with a red ribbon. Reading the attached note, she saw they were also from Charles, telling her how he was looking forward to calling on her shortly. Touched by the extravagance of the gifts and wondering what he was up to, but unable to think of an answer, she gave them to Mrs Yates, telling her to accommodate them where there was room.

Going into the quiet, scented garden while Edward was taking his mid-morning nap, deep in thought she wandered along the paths, absently touching flowers, then sitting on a bench in a small arbour. The garden was well established and her grandmother, who'd had a love for all things that grew, had stocked it well with flowers and fragrant shrubs.

When Charles appeared on the terrace, instantly all her anxieties returned. She had not seen him since he had left two days ago—enough time for him to consider the best way for them to proceed into the future. Standing up, she waited quietly and calmly for him to reach her, her eyes enormous in her pale face. With his dark hair and tan coat and buff trousers, he looked incredibly attractive as he strode towards her. How handsome he was, how striking. Her heart wrenched as she allowed her eyes to dwell on his face.

It was never easy to remain composed when she was with him, for his face was so intense that she was affected by the force of passion that emanated from him, that seared her flesh and melted her bones. She wanted to tell him how deeply she had come to care for him, how much he had come to mean to her, but until she knew he would reciprocate her feelings she would keep them locked in her heart.

His eyes looked directly into Lucy's, his expression unreadable, neither warm nor cold. The torment in Lucy's mind showed on her face and, seeing it, he didn't have to guess at the reason.

'Anna told me of your meeting, Lucy. I was never more surprised to learn that Johnathan was her brother, that there was a connection between the two of you.'

'Why should you be surprised? I didn't know you were William Lancaster's half-brother either. I thought it only courteous that I should make Anna's acquaintance since I was betrothed to her brother. I always wondered what she was like. She's nice and very gracious—just as I imagined Johnathan's sister to be.'

'She is. Did you like the roses?' he asked, seating himself on a bench and pulling her down beside him.

'Yes, thank you, Charles. They were exquisite. They were the first flowers ever given to me. Somehow, I didn't associate you with presenting ladies with flowers.'

'I don't. You are the first.'

'What message did you hope to convey to me by sending them?'

'I wasn't conveying anything. I merely thought it would be nice to send you something. Red roses, I am told, have a significant meaning. Although I believe the flower reigns as the ultimate symbol of passionate love.'

Lucy stared at him, not having expected him to say that. 'I believe it also began its symbolic history in Greece, where it was associated with Aphrodite or Venus—the goddess of love.'

He grinned. 'There you are then. At least I've got that right. In some countries I believe it is the custom for a married woman to wear a flower on her dress to tell her husband of her desire.'

Lucy laughed. 'Since I don't have a husband that doesn't apply. Perhaps I should put one behind my ear.'

A wicked gleam appeared in his eyes. 'I believe that means an unmarried lady is available.'

'In which case I shall leave the roses where they are. In a vase.'

'I'm happy you like them.'

'Hmm,' she breathed, giving him a suspicious glance.

'Now why do I think Anna might have had a hand in your sudden decision to send me flowers?'

'She might have said something,' he answered nonchalantly. 'I am to return to India very soon, Lucy, so I would like to spend as much time with Edward as I can—and you, of course.'

'I see. So, what do you suggest?'

'I've come to take you for a drive. It's a fine day, so we might as well make the most of it.'

She raised her eyebrows in surprise. 'What? Now?'

'No time like the present.'

'Then I will go and get my bonnet.' Standing up, she looked down at him, her brow puckered in a frown. He was watching her with a strange and tender smile on his lips. 'Why, Charles, if I didn't know you better, I would think you are intending to court me,' she said in soft amusement. Her mouth curved into a tantalising smile. 'Of course, we both know such a thing is quite ridiculous.'

Getting to his feet, Charles caught her eyes. 'I thought you would think that—but would you mind if I did?'

'Goodness me, I have no idea. Apart from being betrothed to Johnathan—being very young at the time—I've never really been courted before—not properly.'

'Would you welcome my attention?'

'It would be…challenging, I think,' she said, giving him a thoughtful look. 'And the outcome might be…interesting.'

'Then we will see what happens—and Anna told me that if I am to court you, then I have to do it properly.'

'Hence the flowers,' she said drily. Was he set on a course in which he was to play the part of a considerate betrothed, because if so then he seemed completely assured of his success. 'It's all right, Charles, I understand perfectly. It's reassuring that you've decided to do things properly—but please don't imagine for one minute that there is anything to be gained by it. While you're waiting you might like to take a peek at Edward. He's having his nap. He likes his sleep and I swear a string of stampeding horses wouldn't wake him.'

It didn't take Lucy long to tidy herself and put on her bonnet, and in no time at all Charles handed her up into a shiny black carriage. When she was settled and her skirts arranged properly, he instructed the driver to head for St James's Park.

'You were right, Edward was asleep,' Charles said, seating himself across from her. 'I would like to spend more time with him—when he's not sleeping.'

'Perhaps when we get back to the house he'll be awake. You can go up and see him then if you like.'

Lucy sighed, relaxing into the upholstery and tingling with exuberance. A warm breeze floated across the park. People and rosy-cheeked children were milling about, some strolling while others gathered and sat in clusters to gossip. Flowers in beds and borders added a splash of colour to the park and the grass was like soft green velvet.

Charles suggested they leave the carriage to stroll along the paths, which they did, her arm in the crook of his elbow.

'While I remain in London, I would like to show you more of the city.'

'I have lived here before, Charles. I am no stranger to it.'

'I mean the real London. I want you to look on this time as a holiday.'

'And how much longer is it before you have to return to India?'

'Roughly about four weeks. I want to remain here until Tilly and her family come up from Devon. They're due any time soon.'

'Then I hope she arrives before you have to leave.' Lucy was aware that they were attracting some attention. 'I can't help feeling conspicuous,' she said. 'I'm sure everyone is staring at us.'

Completely impervious to the curious eyes flashing their way, Charles cast a glance around them, then shifted his gaze to Lucy's flushed face. 'Don't let it worry you. No one will know who you are.'

'Maybe not, but you are recognised in society and everyone will be curious who it is you have on your arm. It's a good thing I'm a nobody, otherwise my reputation would be destroyed.'

'When we have decided on the best way forward for us both—what is best for Edward—then you may do as you please. Which, as I remember from India,' he said with a conspiratorial smile, 'you did anyway, always prepared to cock a snook at anyone who dared to criticise.'

'I did, didn't I? Most unashamedly. The best way forward, you say. You have given it some thought, Charles? If so, then perhaps you would enlighten me.'

'I will—very soon,' he said with absolutely finality.

Lucy opened her mouth to argue, but he turned his

head to acknowledge an acquaintance in a passing carriage. Sternly, Lucy reminded herself of the arrogant and high-handed way he had negotiated this carriage drive, then she shrugged the thought aside. Charles was determined they were going to be together in whatever form. He had decided that and his indomitable will was going to prevail as surely as night followed day.

On returning to the house, Lucy removed her bonnet and asked Mrs Yates to have refreshment sent into the drawing room while Charles went to the nursery to see his son. It was a while before he came back down, looking quite pleased with himself after, he told her, frolicking on the rug with a wide-awake Edward.

To Lucy's chagrin, instead of seating himself in one of the many chairs in the room, he chose to sit beside her on the sofa and watched as she poured the tea. Beneath his watchful gaze he was making her nervous, so much so that she almost dropped the teapot.

He sat with his long legs stretched out, studying her imperturbably. His body, a perfect harmony of form and strength, was like a work of Grecian art and most unsettling to Lucy's heart. Unable to endure his scrutiny a moment longer, with the teapot poised in mid-air, she turned and looked at him, her eyes locking on his.

'Why do you look at me so closely when I am trying to pour the tea? You're making me nervous.'

Quite unexpectedly he smiled and his eyes danced with devilish humour. 'You don't have to look so uneasy to find yourself the object of my attention. As a matter of fact I was admiring you.'

Unaccustomed as she was to any kind of compliment from the opposite sex, the unfamiliar warmth in his tone brought heat creeping into her cheeks. To divert the conversation away from herself, she said, 'What do you do when you are in London—besides driving unattached ladies around in your carriage?'

'I have business meetings to attend as well as taking instructions from ministers at the Foreign Office and in Parliament as to what is expected of me when I travel to foreign parts.' A faint smile touched his lips when he observed Lucy's expression of bewilderment. 'I realise that spending most of your life in India, you will know very little about English politics.'

'You are a politician?'

'No—at least not in the professional sense.'

Lucy was impressed. 'It all sounds extremely grand to me.'

'I imagine it does and I take my duties very seriously, but I like what I do.'

Lucy leaned back on the sofa and they sipped their tea in companionable silence. When Lucy placed her cup and saucer back on the tray, Charles did the same.

Turning sideways to face her, seeing she had her eyes closed, he said, 'You look tired, Lucy. Have a nap if you wish. I promise not to disturb you. I can return and play with Edward and wake you when I leave.'

Lucy's eyes shot open. She was tired and would like a nap, but she wouldn't do so in front of Charles. 'I don't feel in the least like sleeping. Anyway, I could not sleep with you sitting next to me.'

'Why on earth not?'

'It's not often I'm alone with a gentleman—in fact, I'm never alone with a gentleman.'

'We have been alone together in the past.'

'That was different,' she said, her cheeks turning red when she recalled the passionate moments they had spent alone together in India. 'That was then—this is now. Things change.'

'They needn't. Why are they different, Lucy?'

Lucy also asked herself the question and to her consternation found the answer. It was because he encroached so closely upon her, because he seemed too near, because she was afraid of him coming closer still. Her body reached out to his, wanting to feel his lips on hers, but if that were to happen it would be her undoing. However difficult it would be, she must learn to resist these feelings and step back.

Quietly, in answer to his question, she said, 'Because now we have Edward.'

'I agree. Edward changes everything,' he agreed. The smile vanished from his lips, his expression became grave. 'But what there is between us, Lucy, is too special to deny.'

'Special? How special?'

'I think about you constantly. I don't want to lose you.' Meeting her steady gaze, he uttered a sound of exasperation. Her calmness provoked him. 'Damn it all, Lucy. What I feel for you is…different to anything I have felt before. Perhaps I am halfway to being in love with you—I don't know the answer,' he said, having great difficulty in putting his feelings into words. 'What I do know is that you make me forget that accursed affair with Amelia. I admire and respect you and I am never more content that I am when I am with you.'

His words took Lucy off guard. She had not expected this. Desire was there in his vivid blue gaze and something more, something so profound that it held her spellbound.

'I want to marry you, Lucy. I want you to be my wife.'

Lucy stared at him. He had it all worked out. She remembered his views on marriage and love when they had discussed it in India. She could not imagine they had changed. She knew she should be gratified that he had offered to marry her, but she did not feel particularly flattered or complimented by the manner of his proposal. What he offered was not enough.

He was watching her reaction from beneath lowered lids. 'Marry you? But—I can't marry you, Charles,' she said, getting to her feet and looking down at him. 'We agreed that night—no commitments. Nothing has changed.'

'Yes, it has,' he said, his voice adamant. 'We have a child. His birth changes what we said. It is right that we wed.'

'Why?' she said with a proud lift to her chin. 'Because you say so? Marriage is important and serious and not something to be undertaken lightly—especially not for me. I comprehend perfectly how you feel. But what makes you imagine I want to be your wife? You have certainly said nothing that can tempt me into accepting your proposal.

'I reciprocate your feelings. I am strongly attracted to you and desire you, but to marry without love is not for me. I have always made no secret of the fact when we've been together. You said you might already be half in love with me. That is not enough. When—*if*—I marry, the man I will choose for my husband will have to love me completely—or be more than *half* in love with me. I will settle for nothing less than that.'

Getting to his feet and shoving a heavy lock of hair back from his forehead, Charles sighed heavily. 'You are a stubborn woman, Lucy Quinn.'

'You have no idea how stubborn I can be. So far you have only scratched the surface.'

'Have you any idea how unreasonable you are being?'

'Why? Because I won't be coerced and cajoled by you? You are the one being unreasonable. To give myself in marriage now, without love, would not seem right for me.'

As if he was aware of the struggle she was battling with, as if to add oil to the flames, he said, 'You do not mention Edward in all of this, Lucy. For his sake, if nothing else, you will have to marry me. You do realise that, don't you?'

'I don't *have* to do anything I don't want to do. Are you asking me, Charles, or ordering me to marry you?'

'I am asking. Who else could possibly suit but the woman who inspires me with feelings and emotions I have never felt before—a woman who has given me the most precious gift of all. A child.'

Had he declared his love for her and told her he couldn't possibly live without her, Lucy would have been suffused with happiness. But he didn't. Raising her chin, she looked at him squarely, resolute in her determination not to weaken. 'Edward's birth doesn't change anything for me. I am not without wealth. I will see that he is properly raised. He will want for nothing.'

Charles's expression tensed. 'You insult my honour and your own. Damn it, Lucy! I am not asking you to become my mistress. I am asking you to be my wife.'

'Because you feel obligated. Well, you needn't,' she retorted coldly. She didn't want him to ask her to be his wife because he felt obligated, as if it were some kind of duty now they had a child between them. She wanted him to ask her because he loved her. But he didn't. Perhaps he felt affection for her, but no more than that. That realisation was what hurt the most. 'Please do not feel you have a duty towards me. Whatever I want, it is not that—to hold you through some obligation that would make a mockery of what we shared in India, however brief it was.'

Charles stared at her, his eyes like chips of ice. 'This is no longer about you and me, Lucy. It is about our son and doing the decent thing by him.'

'Do you think I don't want that, too?'

'Then what are you saying? That I set aside my own child?'

'No, that is not what I am saying, but you don't have to sacrifice yourself on the altar of matrimony for my sake or Edward's. Accepting your support for him is one thing. Marrying you is something else. When we were in India, I told you that I expected nothing—I wanted nothing from you. You are not required to marry me, Charles. It was never part of our agreement to go beyond that one night. What happened was entirely my fault when I invited you into my bed. I accept that and you are under no obligation to marry me.'

Charles's jaw tightened, his eyes burning furiously down into hers. 'In all conscience it would appear I have no alternative,' he said, his voice harsh in the quietness of the room. 'But it is certainly not to save your reputation that I do so. Marriage between us is in the best interests for Edward—who is paramount to all else.

'You imply that you have made your decision. I am asking you to reconsider and I will not ask you again. I strongly suspect that you are still living in the past, Lucy, that you still carry a candle for Johnathan—that you continue to blame yourself for his death and that you do not deserve happiness because he was denied the same. Don't you think it is time you laid him to rest and to look to the future?'

Lucy paled visibly. 'That was uncalled for,' she flared, even though there was a great deal of truth in what he said. 'You know nothing about it. Whatever I carried in my heart for Johnathan is my affair and nothing to do with anyone else.'

'I apologise if my words cause you pain, but they had to be said. I will not compete with a dead man, Lucy. What I am offering you is also a way of maintaining your honour and dignity.'

'Do not assume that marriage to you is a solution to all my troubles,' she flared, deeply hurt and angry at his comments about Johnathan, even if there was a ring of truth in what he said.

Charles's eyes blazed suddenly, with the incredible blueness of a sapphire, as her words goaded him to further anger. 'I don't, but it is the truth. You are right on one count. You brought this on yourself. You chose your own fate when you asked me to take you to bed. You wanted it so badly that you were prepared to run any risk. If you play with fire, you must be able to take the consequences. As I must do.

'I do not blame you. I never have. I was equally to blame. The time we were together was too precious to me to want to hurl recriminations at each other now. Can't you see that I am trying to make the best of a situation which involves our son and to me that means the obvious solution is for us to marry?'

'Do not press me further on this, Charles. You know my feelings. I am not ashamed of what we did, nor do I regret it—not for one moment. I will not marry you, because, despite this attraction, this desire you have for me now, you do not love me, nor care enough for me in any way that would make for a happy marriage. I hope you understand my reasons for refusing your—generous offer. Try to see it from my point of view. Should I accept your offer, I should lose all respect for myself—and for you, too, for putting me in a position of feeling obligated to you and for that I would not forgive you.'

'Yes, I can see that now. Believe me, the last thing I want is for you to feel obligated to me in any way.'

'Good. At last we understand each other. I will not live the rest of my life with any man in a loveless marriage made as a result of a temporary passion, to expunge his guilt.'

Charles's anger began to melt and he looked at her thoughtfully for a moment, moved, despite himself, by her argument. 'Lucy, you must be sensible,' he said on a gentler note, his expression grave. 'You cannot bring up a child on your own. You will never endure the disgrace and humiliation when it becomes public knowledge. People can be extremely cruel in such situations. The scandal will be intolerable. You will never withstand it alone.'

Anger rose up like flames licking inside Lucy. 'Why not? I have withstood much worse,' she flared. 'I could do so again.'

Her stubbornness provoked Charles's eyes to blaze with renewed fury. 'Edward belongs to me as well as you, don't forget. I *will* have a say in how he is reared and I refuse to have him brought up a bastard, being forced to endure the scourge of public scorn just because his mother—in her abominable stubbornness and pride—refuses my offer of marriage. It is not an offer I make lightly, Lucy, and believe me when I tell you that you are the only woman I have ever asked to be my wife—the only woman I have *wanted* to be my wife.'

Without another word he turned and strode to the door, where he turned and looked back at her. 'I won't accept your refusal. I know from your responses to me that you're far from immune to me. I will not ask you to be my wife again, but I swear this is not the end of it.'

'As to that we will have to see,' she retorted angrily. 'I think that now we understand each other.'

When he had gone Lucy stared at the closed door, her chest heaving as she tried to conquer her emotions. There was a silence occupied by her examining the words they had exchanged in anger. When he had asked her to be his wife the words had been forced from his unwilling mouth. As though he had not wanted to ask them, but had felt obligated. Tears clogged her throat. He should have fallen in love with her. He should want to marry her for herself—for love. He didn't want her because he worshipped her. That was all she had hoped for, all she had wanted.

Deep inside her she knew that Charles was right, that they had Edward to consider in all of this. The stigma of his illegitimacy would strike a bitter note. People would avoid them. Innocence was a technicality when loose morals were involved. Did she want her son to grow up without a father to guide him?

Was it time to sacrifice her pride and marry Charles? If so, what kind of future could she expect, living in a loveless marriage with a man who was a diplomatic envoy for the British government, riding hither and thither across the Indian plains, while she withered away for months at a time in some distant town awaiting his return? The thought was intolerable to her.

Chapter Ten

The following days were a kaleidoscope of shifting emotions for Lucy. Determined to take her under her wing, pointing out that it was what Johnathan would have wanted, Anna insisted that she accompanied her and William to social events. More often than not Charles was present.

On their first theatre attendance, Anna and her husband arrived on time to collect her. Coming out of the drawing room, Lucy saw William Lancaster for the first time in seven years and all the old unforgettable memories of Johnathan and that awful time came flooding back. Swallowing down a lump of nostalgia in her throat, she stepped forward to welcome them. William strode across the hall to greet her. Unexpectedly, tears gathered in her eyes. She dropped a small, polite curtsy.

'Lucy, my dear.' His voice was deep and he extended both hands and drew her close in the warmest of welcomes. 'How charming you look and how wonderful that you were able to join us this evening. I can't tell you how much I've looked forward to meeting you again. You haven't changed. You're just as lovely as I remember.'

Raising her eyes to his, Lucy saw he was sincere.

'Hello, William.' She held his gaze, sensing his pleasure at seeing her again. 'I haven't changed, although I feel as if a lifetime has passed since last we met.'

'I'm sure it must feel that way and I do understand, Lucy. I was sorry to hear of your father's death. You must miss him.'

Her smile did not falter, though the unexpected reminder of her loss stabbed at her heart. 'Yes, I do. When he died there was nothing to keep me in India any longer.'

'And you had your grandmother's legacy, which brought you back to England. Charles, who is to join us later, tells me he has asked you to be his wife. I sincerely hope you accept his proposal. How ever it came about, I cannot express my exultation that, by meeting you, it has prompted him to take a more serious interest in marriage.'

Try as she might, Lucy couldn't suppress her smile. 'I haven't accepted his proposal.'

William gave her a knowing smile. 'That is between you and Charles, Lucy, but I cannot deny that Anna and I are hoping for a happy outcome. Charles has told us about young Edward—proudly so. My brother is a lucky man.'

Dressed in a fashionable gown of saffron silk, Anna embraced Lucy warmly. 'What a pleasure it is to have you with us tonight, Lucy. I'm so pleased you agreed to come.'

'Thank you for inviting me. It was thoughtful of you.'

'Not at all—and how charming you look. Now come along. We mustn't be late.'

* * *

Lucy hadn't seen Charles since he had proposed marriage. He drew her aside when they were in the foyer. Theatregoers mingled around them and William and Anna had paused to speak to some friends.

'You look lovely tonight, Lucy,' Charles said, drawing her to a quiet place. 'I'm glad you don't intend what passed between us on our last meeting to stop you enjoying yourself.'

She looked at him squarely. 'I don't. It was very kind of William and Anna to extend the invitation for me to accompany them to the theatre. I knew you would be coming along and I have no intention of avoiding you. Despite what you think and regardless of our differences, I like being with you, Charles.'

He smiled wryly. 'That's something, I suppose. It doesn't change what I said, Lucy. I want you to consider my proposal of marriage seriously.'

'I've already given you my reply.'

'I'm hoping you're open to persuasion.'

'You said you weren't going to ask me again.'

'I'm not. All I ask is that you reconsider. I will always keep you safe.'

'No one can promise that,' she said, snapping her fan open and beginning to fan her face vigorously, already feeling the heat of so many bodies milling about. This really was a ridiculous situation. She had thought Charles had more pride than to come after her, especially when she had refused him so finally. Maybe that was the reason he was persisting—his pride. She had dented it badly by turning him down and now he meant to repair the damage by trying to get her to change her mind.

'I can be very determined,' he answered, his expression grave. 'I am not perfect, far from it, in fact. But if you become my wife, I will do all in my power to see that you come to no harm. You have many attributes, Lucy—confidence, as well as a sense of humour, although I have seen very little of it of late. And your compassion for others compels my admiration and respect.'

Lucy trembled, staring at him. 'Anything else?' she asked, hoping he would say something of a romantic nature.

'You are also brave. The fact that you have worked your way through adversity in your life inspires my admiration and bespeaks your courage and good sense. It makes me feel that I can trust you, trust in your integrity, which is a rarity for me. It is not often I come across a person I can trust.'

Lucy looked at him. It would seem he did understand her a little better than she had given him credit for, but he still did not speak of the romantic love she wanted to hear.

The tantalising channels in his cheeks deepened as he offered her a smile that seemed every bit as persuasive as it once had been. 'Will you relent, Lucy?'

'You have given me much to think about, Charles— but not now. This is neither the time nor the place.' The way he looked at her told her he was not done yet and that he would try another method of persuasion. His eyes delved into hers, seeking she knew not what.

'We have much to reminisce over.'

His voice was low, incredibly warm, melting her, Lucy feared, from the inside out. She couldn't believe what he was able to do with her emotions and with such little effort.

Sighing softly, he touched her cheek with the tip of his finger, uncaring that they were being observed. 'I remember our time together and our conversations and the first time I ever heard you laugh—the first time we kissed and the first time we made love,' he said, his voice low and fierce and wrenching to hear.

'I have an image imprinted on my mind of an enchanting golden-haired woman who once looked up at me with unconcealed desire glowing in her eyes. I remember the feel of her arms around my neck, the delicate aroma of her perfume, the heat of her body pressed close to mine. Most of all I remember her face after we made love, the genuine pleasure of her smile, pleasure that my kisses had given her, pleasure she gave me willingly.'

Flushing hotly, Lucy looked away, wafting her fan more vigorously. 'Please stop it, Charles. I refuse to listen to this.'

'But you will,' he murmured, leaning closer to her ear. 'All that passion is within you still, Lucy. It simmers just under the surface. I feel driven to unleash it again. You cannot blame me for feeling a pang of nostalgia mingled with a sharp sense of loss if I find that woman has gone now. You see, I remember how it felt to hold you, how your skin felt to my touch. I remember how you looked in the moonlight with your face upturned to mine—wanting to kiss you.'

'Stop it,' she repeated. Lucy felt her body burn beneath his eyes and she turned from him, trying to still the trembling in her limbs. The sheer wickedness of the slow lazy smile he gave her made her catch her breath against the tightness of her buttoned bodice.

All of a sudden, she longed to be rid of it, rid of all her clothing, when he looked at her that way. Her strong determination to hold herself from him, which she thought had worked when she had turned his proposal down, was completely overwhelmed by his palpable expertise and she thought again of what it was like to have him make love to her, to caress and kiss her boy into insensibility—she was tempted.

Charles moved closer to her, bending his head so that his mouth was close to her ear, his breath warming her neck. 'I remember how you liked me to touch you, how you would say my name over and over again, of how you filled my senses until I could not think straight.'

'Be quiet, Charles. You are cruel,' she told him in a fierce whisper. 'You should not say these things to me when we both know it is only to get me to do what you want that impels you to say them.'

'*You* accuse *me* of being cruel when you are trying to keep my son from me.'

'But I'm not. That is the last thing I want. But— please stop. I will not listen to this.'

'Then close your ears all you like, but I remember everything and I cannot believe you have forgotten. If you have, I will make you remember. I swear on my life I will.'

Staring into those vivid blue depths that ensnared her

own, Lucy felt as if she were being swept back in time. Drop by precious drop she felt her confidence along with her resistance draining away. How could she have deluded herself into believing she could sway him from his purpose? 'I dislike this situation, Charles, and I have decided that it would be for the best if we did not speak of it just now.'

Elevating a dark brow and folding his arms to restrain his hands from touching her, he continued to gaze down at her. His eyes narrowed because he could not link the figure standing before him with the woman who had given herself to him with such passion.

'Do you think that making love to you meant nothing to me, you foolish woman?' he said abruptly, his lips curling in slight mockery. 'Do I look like a man playing games? The hell I am. How dare you dismiss me without any sort of explanation? Exactly who, Miss Quinn, do you think you're dealing with?'

Lucy fought the urge to shrink from his show of bluster and forced herself to sound as calm as possible. 'I know precisely who I am dealing with. That's the trouble. We do not suit.'

'Why?'

'Because we are too different. We have been through this when you first proposed. I don't want to go through it again.'

'And neither do I. But it has to be discussed at some point.'

'Do we have to do this now, Charles?'

'No, we don't,' he said, brightening suddenly and

stepping back. 'You will be relieved when I tell you that I have decided not to speak of marriage again.'

She stared at him with surprise at this sudden change in him. 'You have?'

'You are right. We have come to enjoy the play, so smile. Here come William and Anna. I think it is time we went to our box and settled down.'

'And you really are not going to pressure me about marrying you.'

He held up his hands in a pose of surrender. 'You have my word. I will not speak of it.'

Lucy sighed and pinned a smile on her lips, glad that the uncomfortable moment had passed.

When Charles's time was not taken up at the Foreign Office, as a foursome they visited the theatre once more and went to the gardens at Marylebone where they drank tea. Anna accompanied him to the house on a couple of occasions when he came to see Edward. True to his word, he did not mention his proposal of marriage, but he was always watchful.

Lucy was as happy and carefree as she had ever been and revelling in Anna's company in particular. She was aware of Charles's moods, but always at the height of her pleasure she was aware of a warning voice telling her to have a care. She knew she was falling completely under Charles's spell, but she need have no fear, she told herself firmly. She was not an innocent girl. She would always remember the man she was dealing with—worldly and determined—and she would always pride herself on her common sense.

There were days when she learned a great deal about him. He was extremely knowledgeable. He was something of a connoisseur of music and the arts. But, she reminded herself every time they were together, it was ephemeral. It would end when he returned to India, so she clung to each moment, savouring it to the full, although she had an uneasy feeling that she was becoming his victim as he had all the time intended that she should.

Lucy was nervous about going to the ball, her nervousness superseded by a blissful sense of unreality. Taking particular care to choose what to wear, she selected an off-the-shoulder emerald and eau de Nil silk gown. It suited her, its colour catching the glow of light in its folds, shading the richness of the silk from light green to a dark shade. It fit her perfectly, with a fitted bodice and a tight waist that dipped into a vee.

Martha, one of the maids she had set on to take care of her clothes and assist her to dress when she attended social events, had been right about this particular colour. It set off her hair and the dark green of her eyes. Her hair was demurely swept back into a coil at the nape. A touch of rosewater perfume and she was ready to face whatever the evening had in store for her.

William and Anna had come to collect her. The scene that confronted them at the Rutherfords' fashionable house in Mayfair was a kaleidoscope of colour. The house was ablaze with light, with large urns of sweet-scented flowers overflowing. They climbed the curving staircase to the ballroom, where she was met by a wave of light and heat and music. The buzz of conversation was punctuated by the fluttering of fans and the swishing of silk gowns. Footmen dressed in formal dark green velvet livery stood at attention. The ballroom with its tall windows and marble pillars was very grand.

Set against this background of unashamed opulence, the rooms of the house were swarming with titled, wealthy and influential guests, their beautiful gowns and jackets competing with each other. The whole house resounded with careless gaiety and glowed with the brilliance of the immense chandeliers dripping with sparkling crystals reflecting the dazzling kaleidoscope of gowns and jewels. Lucy felt strangely inadequate, knowing she could never compete with the worldly experience of these people. She felt vulnerable and gauche. Dancing was in progress, ladies and gentlemen dipping and swaying in time to the music.

Expecting Charles to appear at any moment, a warm, aching sensation of anticipation spread through her.

Taking two glasses of sparkling wine from a footman, William handed them to Anna and Lucy.

'If Charles does not show himself soon, you will have no shortage of partners, Lucy.'

'I fully expect to spend my time observing the dancing rather than taking part.' Taking a sip of her wine, she glanced around, her gaze arrested by a gentleman across the room. 'I think Charles has already arrived.' She felt his gaze light upon her.

Charles stood with his back to the open doorway through which bright lights from beyond were shining, his face partly in shadow, the light gleaming on his dark hair. He had been there for several minutes, observing William and Anna as they introduced Lucy to people they were acquainted with, but he only had eyes for Lucy.

The loveliness of her smiling face was flushed and, when she moved her slender, though softly rounded form, she moved with a fluidity and grace in the simple elegance of her dress over the highly polished floor. Charles's breath caught in his throat as he watched the irresistible curve of her generous lips as she laughed with Anna. He had never thought to see her looking so at ease, so provocatively lovely, glamorous and bewitching. He yearned to hold her in his arms, to feel her warmth, smell her hair, her skin.

He recollected himself, his dark eyebrows dipping alarmingly and his lips thinning. Every time he thought of her, of kissing her, he felt a sharp needle of exasperation drive through him, directed at her, as though, like a witch, she had cast a spell on him, which was totally absurd.

It was not her fault that he couldn't seem to put her out of his mind. No woman had clouded his judgement and stolen his peace of mind so completely. Never in his life had he felt a bond so great and a feeling so all consuming. He had told her he was half in love with her. After much soul searching and deliberation, he now realised it was more than that. He loved her with his whole heart and soul, more than he had loved anyone in his life, but until she could banish her past love from her heart, then it would remain his secret.

Jolted from his reverie when the centre of his attention looked his way, he forced a smile to his lips.

Charles would be surprised if he knew how Lucy was feeling as she looked at him, how her heart skipped a beat when her eyes met his. His mouth was a firm, grim line and there were shadows under his tumultuous eyes. He was splendidly dressed in a well-cut coat of dark blue superfine cloth edged with silver trim, his dove-grey waistcoat was embroidered with silver thread and he wore a pristine white neckcloth. He was more magnificent, more intimidating, more brooding, more remote than Lucy had seen him. Never had any man looked so attractive or so distant and never had her heart called out so strongly to anyone.

She wanted to do something to make him look at her, to see she had the ability, the mind, perhaps, to capture his masculine attention. She so wanted to see that look in his eyes that would tell her she was the most important person in the world to him at that moment. Somehow, she forced herself forward, her head held high, wishing she could cool the waves of heat that mounted her cheeks.

'I can't tell you how delighted I was when Anna told me you had agreed to come tonight, Lucy. Where are they, by the way?'

'Dancing, which is the whole point of being here.'

His expression softened as his gaze swept over her. 'You look lovely. Are you enjoying the ball?'

'We've only just arrived—but I would like to.'

'And yet I notice how you seem to prefer to stand on the fringe.'

'The truth is, that as a woman of limited importance, I am apprehensive of being among so many important people. I'm the proverbial wallflower, I'm afraid. I confess to feeling a little overwhelmed by it all. I'm unused to such a grand gathering. When I entered the house, it reminded me of a tableau set up to tell a story. I find it rather awe-inspiring to stand on the edge of a gathering such as this and simply watch everyone.'

'You really are the most unconventional woman,' he said, his lips twisting.

'I have to agree with you. A conventional woman would not have done the things I did in India. I have never been to a ball before and I am finding it all rather overwhelming.'

'Then we must do something about it right away. Come, we will have our first dance together—the first of many, I hope.'

Lucy gave him a wry look. He was watching her, his teeth showing in a lazy smile. 'I don't think that would be wise—at least, not if you value your feet.'

'I'll risk it if you will.'

Unable to refuse, not that she wanted to, Lucy placed her hand on his arm and allowed him to lead her on to the dance floor. 'I hope your leg doesn't still cause you any discomfort, Charles.'

'It is quite recovered—thanks to the ministrations of a wonderful nurse,' he said, taking her in his arms and spinning her round, as if to prove the point.

Gazing openly at him, Lucy decided she liked the

crinkles at the corners of his eyes caused by smiling. He had lovely eyes and she wondered if he knew it. Then, pulling herself together, as he drew her into his embrace, she wickedly chose that moment to lift her head and turn the full impact of her brilliant smile upon him. It was a waltz, a swirling, exciting dance that brought couples into close contact as no other. Charles swung her into the rhythm with a sureness of step and she followed with a natural grace.

'Everyone loves to dance the waltz. Do you remember how it was between us—that magical night we spent together at the palace in Guntal?'

'Yes, I remember it all too well. How could I forget?' Her body was heating up because she could not forget what they had done that night. She wanted to think about it, linger on it, close her eyes and squirm with pleasure at the thought of those hot, blissful moments.

'You were not telling me the truth when you implied you were a poor dancer, Lucy,' Charles said at length. 'You dance as beautifully as you make love.'

Lucy felt a sudden warmth infuse her body and she knew her cheeks had pinked. 'I must say, Charles, that you do pick your moments.'

'I meant what I said. I will not accept your refusal to marry me, Lucy.'

Leaning back in his arms the better to see his face, she met his gaze. 'I know.'

'And I never say anything I don't mean. At some point very soon, I will have persuaded you to overlook your refusal.' The heat of his desire lent the weight of truth to his words.

'You are so sure of yourself, Charles. Have I given you reason to believe my feelings have changed since you made your proposal?'

'The days I've spent calling on you to see Edward combined with the evenings I've been squiring you around to this and that with William and Anna, we have come to know each other better, so it is something that I sense.'

'So you persist.'

'Because I cannot get you out of my thoughts—and I now have a son to think of and must do what is best for him—which is two parents, not one.' He halted by the French doors leading out to the terrace and the garden beyond.

'Perhaps you will honour me by taking a turn about the gardens. You will find it cooler outside.'

Lucy did not have a chance to refuse. She found herself drawn through one of the long open doors and out on to the terrace.

'Charles—I don't think…'

He grinned wolfishly. 'I want to talk to you, Lucy. I cannot do that when we are surrounded by so many people and constantly on the move.'

In the diffused moonlight he took her hand and led her down a flight of shallow stone steps. He pulled her along a path into an ornamental shrubbery, hiding them from view. It was a place for lovers hiding from the lights and music.

Lucy came to a halt. 'I think we have come far enough, Charles. Why have you brought me out here?'

'It is my hope that I can persuade you to be my wife

without being watched by the whole of London's elite while I am doing so.'

Lucy sighed with exasperation. 'Please do not speak of it tonight, Charles. We are here to enjoy the ball after all.'

'We can do both. Have you any idea what you are doing to me—holding yourself from me? I can't stop thinking about you. I remember the times we were together—the time we made love,' he said, his voice low and fierce and wrenching to hear. 'I remember everything about you—the softness of your flesh, the way you responded to my touch, to my kiss, the way you filled my senses until I was unable to think. Yes, Lucy, I remember everything.'

'Stop it, Charles.' Her face was flushed under his watchful gaze. Memories of him and their night together were etched into her brain like carvings on a stone. 'You are trying to provoke me.'

'We made love, Lucy. Afterwards, when I discovered the consequence of that night, my whole concern was for you—that I do the honourable thing. I see now that I should have chosen my words more carefully.'

'You were being honest. I would ask for nothing less. You have meant well for speaking so plain, but somehow it seemed to me like the worst insult of all. I do not want to marry any man if it is all for duty and consideration—without love.'

'If my words have hurt you, then I'm sorry. It was certainly never my intention. I care for you deeply and I will not give up on you, Lucy, or our son. I am determined. And what of you? You hide your feelings well.'

His words, carelessly thrown on her already roiling emotions, ignited like oil thrown on to a fire. 'How ever I may seem to you, I am neither cold nor indifferent,' she said in a shaky, indignant voice. 'And with the birth of our son things have changed since—since we parted in India. What do you think I am? I am not made of stone. I am not without feeling. I have desires and needs just like any other woman. How could you think I do not?'

'Perhaps that's because you turned me down. When I first met you, you were so lovely I was attracted to you like a moth to a flame. For a time, I held it against you, which was stupid of me. But I was on my guard. Suddenly you posed a threat, a danger to my peace of mind—which somehow made you different, gave you added appeal. I had no wish to become shackled in that way to another woman ever again.'

'Regardless of that you still asked me to marry you.'

Lifting his hand, he traced the outline of her jaw. 'When Amelia left me, I persuaded myself that I would never fall in love again, that I would have the strength of character to withstand such a debilitating emotion.'

'And now?'

'Everything has changed.'

'It has? How?' she asked, awaiting his answer with bated breath.

'When I sent you the roses it was the truest way of expressing my feelings that I could give you. I know you, Lucy. I believe that marriage between us is the most sensible course to take. Get used to the idea, to the knowledge that you are very special to me, that I will make a decent life for us as a family, that I will take care of you and Edward and that you have nothing to fear. What we feel for each other is quite unique, that is evident, and all it needs is time—and we have plenty of that. I'm hoping you come to understand, too, before it's too late.'

'You're speaking in riddles, Charles.'

'No, I'm not,' he replied. 'It merely seems that way because you refuse to see what is before you—what is in your heart.'

'I know what is in my heart. I know who I am.'

'If only that were true.' He spoke softly, tenderly. His eyes were sad and reflective. He claimed to know her, but he didn't, not really, and she realised she didn't know him either. He was complex, a man of many moods. Beneath that handsome façade were depths she had never fully appreciated. Looking towards the house, she saw others coming out into the garden. She shivered when a cold breeze touched her bare shoulders.

'It's coming in cold, Charles. I'll go back inside if you don't mind.' She smiled up at him. 'Just think, you'll soon be back in India so you won't have to suffer the cold English winter.'

Charles looked into the distance. His face, sculpted in moonlight, was without expression now. He seemed remote, untouchable. 'You're right. I will,' he said. His voice was hard. 'And you will be here in London, still dreaming and grieving about your past love.'

'Charles, I…' She hesitated, feeling suddenly deflated. 'It isn't like that…'

He looked at her, his eyes hard. 'No? Then what is it like, Lucy? I had hoped there might be a chance for us. I hoped that you might come to your senses. I was wrong. I was a fool to hope.'

'I'm sorry. I hadn't meant to cause you pain...'

'It's not your fault. You cannot help how you feel,' he said tersely. 'Each of us creates our own kind of hell. We've no one to blame but ourselves. We just have to get on with it.' He scowled and looked towards the house. 'You're right. It's blowing cold. Come, we'll go back inside.'

After that the night passed in a haze for Lucy. She danced with people she did not know, people whose names she could remember, and she danced with William, but Charles did not ask her again and left before the end of the ball. Soon the night was over and she was thankful.

Charles, travelling with William and Anna in their carriage on their way home from the ball, was to spend the night at William's house. Staring fixedly out of the window, he was despondent and more disturbed than he realised over his angry dispute with Lucy, to such an extent that he could think of little else.

Concentrating on what Anna was saying proved difficult, because he couldn't stop thinking about how he was going to get that stubborn, headstrong, beloved woman to agree to be his wife. Whenever she was in a room with him, he had trouble keeping his eyes off her. When she was absent, he couldn't seem to keep his mind off her. He'd wanted her from the moment he'd first laid eyes on her.

The revelation of just how much she had come to

mean to him, how much he loved her, pounded in his brain, but in the face of her defiance to keep on rejecting him, he felt helpless. Meeting her again in London, he had tried desperately to reach out to her, but his own stupidity over Amelia, and his pride—along with Lucy's determination to cling on to Johnathan— had been between then.

But there was Edward to consider, so something must be put in place between them before he left for India. Lucy was not immune to him, he knew that, but time was running out. With the revelations of how deep his love was for her, it was as though his mind had become free of its burden of pain, the kind of freedom he hoped and prayed Lucy would feel when she finally let Johnathan go.

'I couldn't help noticing that you and Lucy seemed to be avoiding each other, Charles,' Anna remarked, dragging Charles out of his despondency. 'You hardly spoke to her all evening. You—do have feelings for her, don't you?'

'Of course I do. I have the kind of feelings for her that a man can only feel for one special woman, though what the hell I'm to do about it I don't know. She continues to turn me down, Anna. What more can I do?'

Chapter Eleven

When an opportunity arose, in the true spirit of a matchmaker, two days after the ball Anna went to see Lucy. As always Lucy was delighted to see her and after Mrs Yates had placed light refreshment before them and left the room, Anna came straight to the point. 'Charles has told us that he has proposed marriage to you, Lucy.'

'Yes, he has,' she replied, her expression guarded, wondering just how much Charles had divulged to William and his sister-in-law. She was uneasy about people gossiping about her behind her back and would like to hear Anna's account of what Charles had told her. 'Has he told you that I refused his offer?'

'Yes, he did.'

'What else did he tell you, Anna?'

Anna gave a wry smile. 'Charles is always so guarded about his private life, but having found out that he had a son, he felt marriage was the only solution to a difficult situation. Are you quite certain that you don't want to marry him?'

'No, Anna, I am not—in fact, I am quite confused about the whole idea of marrying Charles. So please do not counsel me on the wisdom of my refusal and tell me how foolish I am being.'

'I wouldn't dream of doing any such thing. You are a grown woman with a mind of your own. You do have a great deal to consider, I accept that,' she said, watching Lucy closely. 'You have only recently arrived in London and wish to make your life here. But then, you do have Edward to consider—both of you,' she said pointedly. 'This is no longer just about the two of you, but how your estrangement will affect him in the future.'

'Exactly. Edward's well-being is paramount.'

'Of course it is. So you must consider this carefully. A woman alone with an illegitimate child is prey to all the pitilessness of society that believes the sin is all the woman's fault, that she is to blame for conditions she has brought on herself.'

'I know that, Anna. I have thought about nothing else.'

'You know, Lucy, I find it strange how the two of you met. It was as if it was meant to be. When he was wounded, it was fortunate that you were there to nurse him back to health.'

'There were others, Anna, not just me.'

Anna sighed, placing her hand over Lucy's folded in her lap. 'Johnathan wouldn't want this, Lucy. He would want you to be happy. Most women would be delighted to accept a proposal from Charles.'

'Then the world is full of silly women,' Lucy replied flippantly.

'And yet you abandon him, the father of your child,

so you can continue mourning a man who has been dead for seven years.'

'I am not abandoning him—and—and I no longer grieve for Johnathan. He is in the past, I accept that now.'

Anna studied the dark eyes regarding her solemnly from beneath a heavy fringe of dark lashes and asked the question that had been plaguing her ever since she had known of Lucy's connection to Charles, for she was not convinced by anything Lucy had told her. 'You have feelings for him, don't you, Lucy?' she said softly.

Lucy looked down at her hands resting in her lap, her throat aching with the tears she had refused to shed. She nodded, unable to deny it any longer. 'Is it so very obvious, Anna?'

She smiled. 'It's written all over your face.'

Lucy gave a wobbly smile. 'Oh, dear. I thought it might be. I cannot ignore what I feel.'

'Why would you want to, if you love him?'

'Sadly, I cannot choose who to love, but love Charles I surely do with all my heart and soul.'

'Then what is the problem?'

'Charles does not feel the same way. It's his inability to return my love that makes me hold back, because I will settle for nothing less. I love him and I want him to love me. Is it so very wrong of me to want what my mother and father had—that perfect love?'

Anna heard the anguish in her voice, saw it in her eyes. 'Of course not. It's quite natural to feel that way. I am not convinced that Charles doesn't love you. I believe he does—although perhaps he doesn't realise just how much just now. I believe his pride might have something to do with that. He believes the reason you turned him down is because you are still grieving for Johnathan—that you continue to blame yourself for what happened to him—which is what you told me when first we met.'

'Yes—that did have something to do with my decision. But not any longer.'

'That's good.' Anna got up, picking up her gloves and pulling them on. 'I must go. I promised William I would accompany him to visit friends just out of town.' Lucy followed her to the door. 'I hope you enjoyed the ball, by the way?'

'Yes, I did—very much.'

'Then I will make a point of seeing you are invited to the next. Pity Charles won't be there,' she said as she was about to depart the house.

Lucy looked at her retreating back sharply. 'Oh? Why…?'

'At present he is on a ship in the London docks.'

Anna had Lucy's full attention. 'Ship? What ship?'

'A ship that is about to sail for India.'

'When?'

'Today.'

'Today?' Lucy gasped, unable to comprehend her words. 'But—he said he wasn't leaving for another month—until after his sister arrives from Devon.'

Anna turned and looked at her. 'There must have been a change of plan. The vessel sails later today.'

A stone seemed to hit Lucy a heavy blow over the heart. 'But—he—he can't possibly… How can he do that—without telling me? Without saying goodbye.'

'I believe he called on you yesterday, but you weren't at home.'

'No—I had taken Edward to the park with Alice. Oh, Anna,' she cried, gripped by panic when Anna was about to climb into her carriage, 'what shall I do? He can't leave like this.'

Anna smiled at her. 'He can and he will, Lucy. I believe the ship won't depart until later this evening—depending on the tide, of course. So, it is up to you. Now I must be off,' she said, kissing her cheek lightly. 'But remember what I said, Lucy. Charles cares about you a great deal. I am sure of that.'

Alone, Lucy paced the room in anguish as she tried to fight off the burden of doom which was descending on her. She was unable to comprehend why Charles was doing this to her at a time when she could no longer deny her love for him and at the very moment when happiness seemed finally within her grasp. Memories of Charles stirred as she stalked the house, unable to settle her thoughts.

The past came back to haunt her now that he was about to leave for India. She saw again Johnathan's beloved face, blurred now and fading. On a cry, she banished his image from her mind. What a fool she had been not to grasp what was before her eyes.

Impatience and anguish had plagued her since Anna had told her Charles was leaving. Lucy suspected that this was the reason for her earlier visit, so she had time to do something about it if she wanted. *'I believe Charles does love you,'* she had said. Anna's words had brought her closer to this moment and a flood of joy swept over her.

It was time she faced the fact that she did want Charles, that she did love him quite desperately. What she wanted now was to hear Charles say that to her. Had she been seduced, not by Charles, but by her desire for him? She knew in the depths of her heart that it was a most pertinent distinction. This desire was of the kind that had trapped women since time began into loveless unions. She had every reason to distrust the emotion, to avoid it, to reject it.

But she could not—perhaps before today, but now this rogue emotion was too strong, too compulsively within her, for her ever to be free of it. But this in itself brought no sadness, no pain, and indeed if the act itself could elicit such power and joy, such boundless excitement, such pleasure that she was addicted to it, then given the choice she would have the experiences rather than live the rest of her life without it.

Having made her decision, she was aware of a kind of peace stealing over her. But like a dark cloud coming over the sun, she knew this small sense of peace and happiness she had felt so briefly in Charles's arms would be short lived if she did not speak to him before he sailed for India.

The noise and bustle of the East India dock was jarring and chaotic. It was a scene of great variety. The smell of tar and coffee beans, timber and hemp, permeated the air, along with other aromas which titillated the nostrils. Stevedores carrying crates and trunks swarmed up and down the gangplank. Charles stood on the deck of the giant vessel that was soon to depart for India. He surveyed the crowded dockyard below him, his eyes sliding over the people milling about, then his glance instantly came to a halt and froze when it reached a breathtaking vision. It was Lucy.

She was attired in a dark green dress, the colour complementing the pale blonde of her hair which was swept back off her forehead and held in place by a clip, then left to fall artlessly about her shoulders in a wealth of luxurious glossy curls. Charles saw only perfection. She was too exquisite to be flesh and blood, too regal and aloof to ever have let him touch her. But, he thought, drawing a strangled breath, what in God's name was she doing here?

'Good Lord!' exclaimed Sir Humphrey Lloyd beside him. 'See that young woman, Charles? Who is that gorgeous creature? Is she real?'

'My thoughts exactly,' said Sir Humphrey's companion, helping himself to a pinch of snuff. 'She shines like a light in the midst of all that chaos below. I hope she's sailing with us. Her company will certainly make the voyage more enjoyable.'

At that moment the lady in question looked up at the ship, her eyes searching, finding and fastening on Charles.

Charles smiled, turning to the two gentlemen who were about to embark on this, their first passage to India. One of them, Sir Humphrey, was a diplomatic envoy like himself, the other gentleman a businessman going out to India where he hoped to make his fortune.

'I can confirm that the lady is perfectly real, gentlemen, and I'm sorry to disappoint you, but she is looking for me. She is my future wife,' he said with a confidence he was far from feeling, but he continued to live in hope. 'If we meet up in India, it will be my pleasure to introduce you, but for the time being I wish you *bon voyage*.'

With that he left the ship, unable to believe that Lucy had done something so foolhardy as to come to the docks alone. On reaching her, he took hold of her elbow and led her to her carriage and only when everyone's attention was taken up with what was happening on the dock did he lean towards her.

'What the hell are you doing here?' he demanded, his voice low. 'It's not the place for an unaccompanied young woman to be.'

Beneath his icy calm Lucy flinched, but in the face of his anger her own fury rose. 'I'm sorry if you're not pleased to see me, Charles, but what do you think you are playing at, leaving London without a by your leave to me? How could you do that?'

Taken off guard by both her anger and her words, he cocked an eyebrow in puzzlement. 'What are you talking about?'

'You—deciding to go back to India at a moment's notice, leaving me here with Edward and failing to put anything in place for his future.'

Suddenly Charles understood what had happened, that she must have been speaking to Anna and had got hold of the wrong end of the stick—which was what Anna would have intended to snap Lucy out of her stubborn refusal to marry him. 'I told you I am here for another four weeks, Lucy. I have no intention of leaving before we have settled our issues.'

She stared at him in surprise. 'You're not leaving?'

'No. I am here merely to bid a friend of mine farewell. Hopefully we will meet up in India some time.'

'But—but Anna said…'

'I think you will find that Anna's intention is to bring us together by whatever means at her disposal, Lucy.'

'Oh—yes,' she said, bemused by the whole thing. 'I think I see it now.'

'Don't be downhearted,' he said, opening the carriage door. 'You can give me a lift to my house in Chelsea. Not knowing how long I was going to be with my companions, I sent my driver away.'

After giving Lucy's driver directions, they left the docks behind. They were silent as the carriage rattled its way along the rough roads to Chelsea village. They both had things to say, but not in the carriage with the driver listening in on their conversation. Arriving at the house, Charles sent the driver back to Kensington, telling Lucy his own driver would take her home later.

Charles's home was a charming house that stood in its own grounds back from the road. It was quiet when Charles let them in. He explained that it was the housekeeper's day off.

'We don't have to stand on ceremony with each other,' Charles said harshly. 'We are, after all, almost family.'

There was a tense silence in the room for several seconds before Lucy looked at him. 'Why?' she asked bluntly. 'Do you really think that I am going to marry you?'

'I do not,' he said easily, 'see how you can get out of it. Not if you want to live in society, which cannot happen if you are seen as a fallen woman.'

'I can always return to India—or go somewhere else. It's unlikely the story will follow me. I can afford it now.'

'But you will never be sure. What will you tell Edward when he asks about his father? That he is dead? You won't be able to lie, Lucy. You are too honest and honourable to do that.'

As he removed his coat and flung it over a chair, Lucy looked at his handsome face and thought of him waiting at the altar for his bride, a man brought to his knees by shattered pride because she had rejected his proposal of marriage. He was waiting for her to go to him. That he was hurting deep inside she could see in his eyes. A lump of poignant tenderness swelled in her throat and she unthinkingly walked towards him. She felt the heat of his eyes upon her and they warmed her more than any verbal reassurance. The message in those compelling eyes was as clear as if he were whispering it.

You will marry me.

'I'm so sorry,' she whispered achingly when she stood before him, wanting so much to reach out and touch him, but it was as if her arms had lead weights attached to them that kept them planted firmly by her sides. She gazed at the sensual mouth only inches from hers. It was an inviting mouth.

The eyebrows snapped together over cool blue eyes. 'Sorry? Sorry for what? Sorry for refusing to marry me and leaving me to kick my heels?'

Her lips curved in a wobbly smile and she had to

clear the tears from the back of her throat before she could go on. 'Which tells me you are as determined to marry me as you were when you first proposed. I deserve to be thrashed to within an inch of my life for daring to provoke you, but all that would achieve would be a delay in the wedding, for it would be unthinkable for a bride to walk down the aisle covered in bruises.'

'I would never harm a hair on your head and you know it.' His heated gaze seared her. 'Does that mean you will marry me, Lucy?'

'I shall be proud to be your wife, Charles.' Stepping closer, she slipped a hand behind his head and pulled his face close to hers and kissed his lips until his sanity began to slip away.

The desire Lucy had ignited in him and which been eating away at him for so long... He lifted his head and looked at her. 'I think an arrangement to our problem can best be solved upstairs?' he said, a half-smile curving his lips.

Lucy's excitement was almost unendurable as she let him lead her up the stairs to his bedroom. Once there he closed the door and leaned against it. The air inside the room was sultry and warm and the gentlest of breezes stirred the curtains. Lucy was the first to break the silence, looking at Charles wide-eyed and uncertain, relieved to see his mood had lightened.

'Well, Charles, here we are,' she said softly.

He sauntered towards her, scrutinising her intently, his eyes drawn to her mouth. 'This is what you want, isn't it? This is what all this is about—the reason why you hastened to the ship in case you were too late and I had sailed for India?' His eyes were beginning to glint with wicked amusement. 'I should hate to disappoint you,' he murmured, his voice low and husky.

'You won't—but if you have changed your mind and prefer it if I left...'

'And if I don't wish you to leave?' he breathed, reaching out and very slowly tucking a thick strand of her hair behind her ear, the warmth smouldering in his eyes as he looked at her, emphasising his desire to remain. 'If I want to find out if what we experienced together once before can be as good between us again? If it is, then I think that should settle the argument about whether or not you will be my wife. Do you wish to leave?'

'No, I want to stay,' she whispered, her heart beginning to pound with helpless anticipation.

Charles placed a finger under her chin, turning her face up towards his. He searched the depths of her glowing eyes for a moment, seeing the pupils large and as black as jet in their centres, then he sighed, shaking his head. 'You wanted this all along, didn't you, Lucy— along with a little collusion from Anna, I don't doubt.'

'Not really. I didn't know what she was playing at until you told me you weren't about to sail for India. She's a very shrewd lady is Anna. But after we parted at the ball, I realise it was foolish of me to try to distance myself from you. I couldn't. I'm glad Anna came and gave me the impression you were about to leave. It was what I needed. I couldn't bear the thought of you not being here and it does not suit me to live the life of an unmarried mother.'

He arched a sleek black brow. 'I see. Well, what are you going to do about it? Show me.'

Lucy stared at him, unsure how to proceed now the moment had arrived when it was within her power to win him over. He was so incredibly masculine and stood so close that she was overwhelmed by him. A faint mocking smile curved his mouth as he waited patiently for her to make a move, his heightened senses darkening his eyes and tensing his features, but she would not be afraid of him.

Following her instinct, she rose to the challenge in an impulsive attempt to communicate with him the only way she knew how. With an enticing smile, she raised herself on tiptoe and left her hands slide slowly over his silk shirt, feeling his muscles tauten as she placed them lightly on his shoulders and began to spark the passion that had lain dormant between them for too long.

'I would do this,' she whispered, reaching up and placing a kiss on his mouth with gentle shyness, her lips as light as a butterfly's wings, her heart hammering like a wild, captured bird's. 'And this—and even this.'

And she continued to place tantalising little kisses on different features of his face, her warm breath caressing his skin, before stepping back.

Charles responded with another questioning lift to his brows, giving no indication of the feelings her soft lips had aroused in him. 'No woman I have ever known has been capable of igniting such an uncontrollable rush of lust with just a few featherlight kisses. But I'm sure you can do more?'

Lucy's delicate brows drew together in confusion. 'Are you criticising me? What else would you have me do?'

'Oh, I'm sure you can think of something. I'm in no hurry. You can take your time—as long as you want.'

Tentatively she put a hand over his and smiled, drawing a deep breath. With no notion of whether what she was doing was right or wrong, she moved closer, love her only instinct to guide her. All along his arm his muscles were tense as he watched her, a savage, wolf-like look in his eyes. Slowly she uncurled his fingers that were clenched in a fist, raising his hand and stroking the palm with the tip of her finger, lifting it a little more and placing her lips to its warm centre, feeling the sinews tense and then relax. She slid her fingers through his, lacing them together, feeling his eyes watching her, burning into her bowed head.

Still holding his hand, she drew him towards the bed, sitting and pulling him down beside her. They lay back and, smiling softly, she leaned over him, her breath warm as she kissed his mouth, and then held back a little, looking to see if she had reached him. His breathing had quickened and his eyes held hers like a magnet, but when she lowered her head and would have kissed him again, he took hold of her and pushed her back on to the bed, suspending himself above her, the sudden ferocious depth of his desire for her roaring in his ears.

'No, Lucy. No more,' he said huskily, unable to resist temptation, to withstand the glorious beauty of her. 'This is where I take over.'

Lucy gazed up into his smouldering eyes, while his

hands plunged into her hair on either side of her face, holding her captive as he looked down at her. 'I may have given you reason to think otherwise, but I am still a novice at all this,' she breathed after his mouth had claimed hers in a kiss of violent tenderness.

'You seem to be doing very well to me, but I am sure you can do better. I remember I taught you well and it is not too long ago for you to remember.'

'And if I don't?'

'Then I shall have to teach you all over again.'

'And you will continue to do so when I am your wife,' she whispered.

'When you are my wife,' he repeated softly, trying to control his hungry passion, looking down into her velvety eyes, now huge with desire. 'Enough conversation for now. That is not what I want from you.'

'Then what do you want from me, Charles?' she asked, a provocative smile curving her lips.

'Only that you let me love you, my adorable lady of pleasure,' he murmured, proceeding to make love to her, pausing only long enough to discard his clothes and remove hers, flinging them to the far corners of the room in his impatience to be with her.

Lucy became lost in the beauty of his body, his touch, with a sensual joy she had not felt since that night when Edward had been conceived. His lips were warm, first on her mouth and then sliding down the long, graceful column of her neck, gentle, harmless, with the merest whisper of a caress. Then slowly, easily, where his lips had led, his hand followed and stroked, cradling her breast, soft to his touch, and then to the smooth flesh of her stomach.

Completely absorbed, she was aflame, her body responding to Charles's caresses like an explosion of raging thirst. He held her in a state of bemused suspension, the sensations she had experienced once before melting her inside and out. He raised his head and looked down at her, his eyes travelling in wonder and rediscovery over her body, ripe and more mature after the birth of their child.

He pressed her back against the pillows, his breath warm on her throat as his arms dragged her fully against his hardening body, which moved over hers. Their skin touched with a burning warmth and Lucy moaned under the power of his body as her own unfolded and opened to him, like a flower opening in the warmth of the sun, and they made love as passionately as they had done before.

Afterwards Charles rolled on to his back, pulling Lucy close so that her cheek rested on his chest. She sighed, sleepy and languid, her expression one of perfect tranquillity, her slender, silky limbs entwined with his. Lifting a hand, she brushed her fingers lightly over his chest, smiling serenely as she raced the outline of his muscular shoulders, wanting this moment to go on for ever. With the sheet draped carelessly over them and his arms around her, Charles gently kissed the top of her head, glorying in the sheer heaven of holding her.

'Well,' he murmured, 'was it as good between us as the last time?'

'Yes. Better, I think.'

'And it will get even better—when we are married.'

'Yes,' she agreed, 'for marry we must, otherwise we might find another little Edward on the way and I doubt I could withstand the stigma of being an unmarried mother of two illegitimate children.'

'There is that, I suppose,' he said, chuckling softly. 'I cannot believe you actually thought I would leave you here alone and go to India without you. I couldn't do that. I would have resigned my position with the Foreign Office and sought another occupation to remain close to you.'

'You would have done that—for me?'

'Yes. You see, my darling, when I saw you refused to marry me, I was the most wretched of men. The plain and simple truth is that I wanted you so much I was miserable when I was away from you and I realised how much you had come to mean to me—how much I care for you. I love you, Lucy. Deeply. And I know you love me. I can feel it when I hold you in my arms.'

'Yes, I admit it. I do love you, Charles. I love you as much as it is possible for a woman to love a man— although I was so wrapped up in the past and reluctant to let go of it that I didn't realise how much. The past has not been easy and the years have been filled with tragedy, but when I met you, I knew a happiness as well as joy that sang in my blood without my being aware of it. I know with a certainty that I have survived the past and, in doing so, I have experienced a shattering love that reaches my very soul.'

Charles sighed with contentment. When he clasped Lucy in his arms the bewildering melancholy that had had him in its grip for so long vanished for ever. 'You belong to me, Lucy. Your place is by my side along with our son. You will come with me when I go to India?'

'Gladly. I have been a part of India for so long. England could never stir the feelings I have for that country inside me.' A swift vision of that lovely, mysterious country with all its smells, its vibrancy and blistering heat sprang into her mind with a mixture of pleasure and pain. England was a plain comparison.

'In India, you will forget everything that has gone before and share with me a future that will be filled with joy few women are fortunate to know. All the anguish and conflict of the past will be behind us at last. You are a beautiful and truly wonderful woman,' he said, with a raw ache in his voice, bending his head and kissing her lips tenderly, all the love that had been accumulating over the years since Amelia's betrayal delivered in that that kiss.

'And am I to believe you love me for my beauty alone?' she teased gently, her lips against his.

His features became solemn. 'No. I am not so stupid that I would have let your beauty alone make me love you. You have a multitude of other assets that I admire and love. You are a rare being, Lucy Quinn. You are everything I dreamed a woman, a wife and a mother could be—and more.'

Lucy tilted her head up to his and could see he was perfectly serious. 'That is a compliment indeed, Charles. Thank you.'

The following afternoon Charles arrived to collect Lucy. They were to dine with William and Anna. Having been let into the house by Mrs Yates, he stood in the hall and watched as Lucy descended the stairs, aware of the sudden pounding of his heart and the way his breath caught in his throat. Silver threads gleamed in her hair and her eyes sparkled bewitchingly.

The low cut, scooped neckline of her gown framed her shoulders and gave a provocative hint of her breasts. She looked quite exquisite and the exultation he felt at the sight of her nearly overwhelmed him. He realised with a start that all that really mattered was that she was to be his wife.

He nearly groaned aloud at the surge of desire that swept through him. Stepping forward, he took her hand as she reached the bottom of the stairs and drew her close. After kissing her lips, he held her from him.

'Is Edward awake? I would like to see him before we leave.'

'Yes, you're in luck. He's woken from his afternoon nap.'

They entered the nursery to find Edward sitting on the floor with his favourite bricks around him. Charles knelt down on the carpet by him. He saw the dark curly hair clinging in tendrils around a rosy face which was squared at the jaw, a little like his own. Standing up, he took hold of the child and held him in his arms. Grasping a brick to his chest, Edward smiled. Charles gazed at him. He had the same startling blue eyes framed with long black lashes. Feeling all the instinctive poignancy, the yearning love he had felt when he had first laid eyes on him in his crib just days before, he could not tear his eyes away from him.

'He's a fine boy, Lucy.'

'He resembles his father,' she remarked with a smile. 'Even at so young an age he has the same arrogant way of holding his head, the same jut of his chin as his father.' With mock severity she sighed. 'I suppose I'll just have to get used to having two such men in my life.'

Charles gave him a kiss on the forehead, then put him back on the carpet, placing his arm about Lucy's waist without taking his eyes from Edward. 'Count yourself fortunate. With two such men around you'll never be bored.'

She laughed, punching him playfully on the shoulder. 'That's just the kind of reply I can expect from you. Now come along else we'll be late for dinner with William and Anna.'

Reluctantly Charles dragged himself away from his son, determined not to miss a day of seeing him. He had been deprived of him for far too long as it was.

The four of them went into the sitting room where a sherry was put in Lucy's hand and the conversation was about the ball and then became general mostly. William and Anna were highly delighted that the two of them were to marry—and Anna blushingly apologised for deceiving Lucy when she had implied that Charles had been about to leave for India. Lucy laughingly told her that it was forgotten. Without her interference they would not be where they were now.

It was mentioned that Tilly and Lucas with their little family were travelling up from Devon within the next week, give or take a day or two. Charles was impatient to see her again. Tilly, the Countess of Clifton, was his sister and he loved her dearly, although he had yet to meet her children, two boys, Gideon and Andrew. Tobias at six years old was Lucas's nephew, who lived with them. His parents had died in Spain while Edmund Price, his father, had been a soldier in Wellington's army.

When dinner was announced they went into the dining room to take their places at the large formally laid table. The food was sublime, the wine superb, the conversation relaxed and about anything and all things that came to mind. Anna was the first to mention the wedding when the last course had been served and eaten and they had retired to the sitting room.

'Now,' she asked, as they settled on two sofas facing each other, a low table between them, 'when would you like the event to take place?' She glanced from Lucy to Charles, who looked a little bemused by her question. 'I take it you have discussed it with Lucy, Charles?'

'Not yet, but we will. As far as I am concerned the sooner the better.'

'How soon?' Lucy asked, turning to look at her betrothed who sat beside her.

'Three or four weeks at the most—if Lucy is in agreement.'

'Three or four weeks! But that's far too soon,' Anna exclaimed. 'You can't possibly mean that. It's virtually impossible. Clearly you have never had to arrange a wedding before, Charles.'

Charles laughed. 'No, Anna, I haven't, and I sincerely hope I never have to arrange another. You must take into account that we have to leave for India shortly so the sooner the wedding takes place the better.'

'Have you any idea what has to be done? A guest list has to be drawn up, the flowers and bridesmaids—Lucy's dress to be made—the church.'

'The church. Do you have a preference, Charles?' William asked.

'Not at the moment. I haven't given it a thought.'

'St George's Church in Hanover Square, where Anna and I tied the knot, is Mayfair's most fashionable church. How does that strike you?'

Charles looked at Lucy, who was quietly listening. 'Do you have a preference, Lucy?'

'No, not at all—only—I don't want a fuss. The mere thought of anything ostentatious terrifies me. I would prefer a small affair with few guests. My father has not long been laid to rest—albeit over a year now, but I feel I must respect that.'

'Of course you must, Lucy,' Anna said, 'and I apologise for not taking that into account. I can understand you not wanting a fuss. That was exactly how I felt when I married William. Might I make a suggestion that I hope you will consider? It might be the solution.'

'Please do,' Lucy answered.

'Cranford Park has its own chapel. It's not often used these days—the local village has a fine church that we attend most Sundays when we are in residence. If you want a quiet wedding, then I'm certain it would be suitable.'

Charles looked at Lucy. 'I can't say that I've seen this chapel, but I'm sure it would suit. What do you say, Lucy?'

'It sounds perfect. I would like that. Thank you.'

'Then that's settled,' William said, draining his glass and nodding to the hovering footman, who went to an alcove where a huge trough of Sicilian jasper was filled with iced water and bottles of champagne. Taking out a bottle, he filled glasses and handed them out before leaving the room.

Lucy and Charles made scant conversation on the journey back to Kensington. They were both preoccupied with their own thoughts. For Lucy, the evening had been eventful. It had been an evening of stirred memories, each one bittersweet—some welcome and nostalgic, others not so welcome and better to be set aside.

Over the following days Lucy saw little of Charles. His work at the Foreign Office kept him occupied. They were to travel to Berkshire shortly. In the meantime, Anna was a constant visitor. And then it was time for them to leave for Cranford Park.

The Lancaster crested coach carrying Charles, William and their ladies passed through huge, wrought-iron gates bearing the distinctive Lancaster insignia. From there the road wound its way through meadow and pasture to the great house itself.

Cranford Park was set in the county of Berkshire, with a commanding view of the surrounding countryside where honey-toned cottages were tucked away into folds of the land. It was a brilliant late summer's day, with fields gilded with ripening corn. Surrounded by breathtaking parkland and glorious gardens, there was power and pride in every line of this gracious house that stood like a silent, brooding sentinel, the home of the Marquess of Elvington. Lucy was enchanted by it all.

'Oh, my,' she whispered, her eyes wide as they took in every detail. 'I've never seen anything quite so beautiful—and there's a lake. See how it glints between the trees like a rush of quicksilver?'

Anna, seated beside her, laughed at her enthusiasm. 'I felt exactly the same when I saw it for the very first time. It really is a beautiful house, Lucy. I will enjoy showing it to you.'

At the main entrance the four bay mounts pulling the coach at last danced to a halt and William got out, gallantly extending his hand to help Anna and Lucy. The coach carrying nursemaids and children pulled up behind them. Uniform-clad footmen appeared out of the house and descended on the coaches to strip them of the mountain of baggage.

'Welcome to Cranford Park, Lucy,' William said, taking her arm and escorting her inside.

'I'm sure you must want to freshen up and see Edward settled, Lucy,' Anna said, looking back at the door as the children were ushered inside, fractious after being confined for so long, Martha carrying a sleeping Edward. 'I'll ask the housekeeper to show you to your rooms.'

Charles disappeared into William's study to partake of liquid refreshment while Lucy was shown to their rooms. At a glance, she became aware of the rich trappings of the interior. The opulence and elegance of what she saw took her breath away. It was like nothing she had experienced before.

* * *

During the first few days she familiarised herself with the house, but what she liked most of all was exploring the extensive grounds. She became a familiar sight at the stables where Charles joined her and, together, they rode further afield to enjoy the delights of the countryside. There was great excitement when Tilly and Lucas and their boys arrived, expressing their surprise and absolute delight on seeing Charles.

After Tilly had thrown herself into her brother's arms and declared passionately how much she had missed him, as the nursemaids ushered the children up the stairs she was introduced to Lucy. When Charles gave her the news of their impending marriage, she expressed her delight and was more than happy to welcome Lucy into the family. Tilly was gay and spirited and it was clear she loved her brother deeply and had worried about him being so far away in India.

Later, when the family were gathered together on the terrace, the eldest of Lucas and Tilly's three boys came to Lucy and smiled up at her. At six years old he had a mop of dark brown curls and deep blue eyes.

'Hello,' Lucy said, smiling down at him. 'And what is your name?'

'I'm Tobias and I'm going to build boats when I grow up.'

Lucas laughed, playfully ruffling his curls. 'Like his father before him. His parents would have been proud of him.'

'Tobias has been with us since his birth,' Tilly explained, placing her arm protectively round the child's shoulders. He fell into her embrace before running off to join Thomas scampering about after a small dog beneath the trees. 'He's the son of Lucas's sister—who died in Spain along with her husband—he was with Wellington's army. Tobias is a delightful child and we love him dearly. He already has a sense of what his life will be.'

'You have lovely children,' Lucy remarked. 'Although I imagine they're a handful.'

'They are—but I wouldn't have them any other way. Lucas disciplines them as best he can, but he's a softy where they are concerned. I'm just going to check on Andrew—he was rather tearful when I left him and I want to make sure Florence has settled him down and he's not about to go down with something awful, then I'll be back.

'I want you to tell me all about India and how you and that brother of mine got to know each other. We have a lot of catching up to do. Perhaps now he's home you'll come and see us in Devon. Honestly, Lucy, it's so lovely down there that you'll never want to leave.'

Lucy watched her disappear into the house, wondering what she had done to deserve to be welcomed into this warm and loving family. Charles had told her so much about Tilly, the sister he adored. With her shining black hair and warm violet eyes, she was just as she imagined.

Three days before the wedding, the few guests accompanied by their personal servants arrived and were easily accommodated in the great house. It was Charles and

Lucy's decision to limit the wedding guests to immediate family and close friends only, which avoided offending the sensibilities of friends and made it a quiet, intimate affair. Lucy had insisted on inviting Mrs Wilson and Alice and her husband Henry, along with their daughter, who was more than welcomed in the nursery. Anna was ready to greet them and insisted Charles and Lucy were by her side.

'Let them get a look at the bride and groom right away,' she said.

The following day, with the house ringing with the children's voices and laughter, everything had taken on a sense of urgency as wedding preparations got under way. Some members of the house party who wished to ride jaunted off to the nearby village, then settled down to cards and the like in the evenings.

Lucy had found herself spending a great deal of her time with Anna and Tilly. She had become very fond of them both and would be sorry when they had to part. Anna spoke of Johnathan when they were alone, but she accepted that Lucy had Charles now and was sensitive of his feelings and careful not to dwell on Lucy's past.

Sitting under the trees where tea tables had been laid, Lucy sat drinking tea out of china cups and eating dainty cakes with Mrs Wilson and Alice before they left her to stroll along the garden paths. When Mrs Wilson left for London after the wedding, secure in the knowledge that Alice was well and having seen her grandchild, she was to make arrangements to return to India to join her husband. She was to travel with Charles and Lucy, much to Lucy's delight. Lucy sighed, watching mother and daughter, arm in arm, saunter across the lawn. She tilted her face to the sun, her thoughts melancholy as memories of her time in that wonderful land crowded in to her mind. She was so happy to be going back.

Seeing her sitting alone, Tilly's husband Lucas came to sit with her, stretching his long athletic legs out before him and fixing her with his light blue gaze.

'How are you settling in, Lucy? I imagine you find the splendour of Cranford and its extended tribe daunting after being in India.'

'It is certainly very grand, but I am very happy to be here. I don't think I've ever been made to feel so welcome.'

'The Lancasters are famous for their hospitality. I cannot get away from the feeling of family that I always find when I come to Cranford—more so when the children are present. At home in Devon, I find myself a frequent visitor to the nursery for tea.'

Lucy smiled. Tilly had told Lucy a little about Lucas's family, how his parents had drowned when the vessel they were on went down in the Channel when they were sailing to Jersey to visit friends, and how his sister had died in Spain shortly afterwards after giving birth to Toby.

'You have no other immediate family in Devon?'

'No. I have cousins and aunts scattered about the country, but no one close. I thank God for Tilly.' He grinned. 'I confess there were some ups and downs when we first met, my dear wife being as wilful and spirited as an unbroken horse, but I wouldn't have her any other way.'

His feelings for his wife were clear for Lucy to see. Tilly was a passionate, lively individual. They were well matched.

'And you and Charles are to return to India. Does that excite you?'

Lucy sighed. 'Yes, I have to confess it does. Like my father before me, I love India. Charles's work will take him far and wide. I'm looking forward to seeing places I haven't seen before.'

She looked past Lucas to where Charles was in conversation with William, having discarded his jacket over a nearby chair. With his hair falling over his brow, the recklessly dark, austere beauty of his face, the power and virility stamped in every line of his long body, she felt a familiar twist to her heart. They would be man and wife two days hence.

She was glad they were to leave for India soon. She could never be happy living her life in the metropolis. She did tell herself that she would be happy living anywhere providing Charles was with her. But—*India*? She was almost able to smell and taste the dust of the vast and beautiful Indian plains and feel the heat and smell the scents of that precious land.

Epilogue

It was a beautiful sunny morning for the wedding. The ceremony was to be conducted in the thirteenth-century church which stood in its own grounds close to the house. It contained monuments and effigies which reflected the ancient lineage of the Lancaster family. Anna, Tilly and Lucy had filled it with flowers from Cranford's glass-houses and the scent was intoxicating. The ceremony was to take place in the early afternoon and the guests would sit down to a splendid wedding breakfast on the wide terrace overlooking the gardens.

Shortly after midday, having been to see her son in the nursery, Lucy was ready, dressed in a gown of ivory silk overlaid with fine gauze and tiny seed pearls. Her lustrous fair locks were drawn back from her face into a chignon. Looking into the mirror at her reflection, it was not sentiment alone that brought tears to her eyes.

There was an ache in her heart for her father, who had not lived to see the day his daughter realised her own dream of becoming a wife to the man she loved, a situation she had thought could never be. For her it was both an end and a beginning. Never again would she fear that all she loved might be snatched from her by forces beyond her control, that fear would stalk her footsteps and make a mockery of her dreams. She would never look back.

Anna's image appeared in the mirror when she came to stand beside her.

'You look absolutely wonderful, Lucy. Charles has left for the church. Are you ready?'

Lucy turned and looked at her. 'As ready as I will ever be. Thank you, Anna, for all you have done for me. I feel coming to Cranford, being with the family gathered together and how you have embraced me as one of you, your presence and your company gives me peace. Peace and a sense of belonging I thought I would never know again when Johnathan died—and then my father.'

'I'm glad of that. It cannot have been easy for you leaving India alone to embark on that long sea journey back to England, but here you are—and about to be married.'

Now, standing beneath the chevron-moulded arch at the entrance to the church, Lucy focused her eyes on the groom dressed in dove grey standing at the altar with William beside him. Her heart surged with love. Charles's presence was like a tangible force, powerful and magnetic. They stood facing Reverend Bucklow, waiting patiently for the bride to appear.

Lucy was caught up in the moment as she moved slowly down the knave, her hand tucked into Lucas's arm. All the radiance in the world was shining from her large dark green eyes, which were drawn irresistibly to the man who was waiting for her at the front of the church, overwhelming in stature, his dark hair immaculately brushed and gleaming. His plum-coloured coat, dove-grey trousers hugging his long legs, matching silk waistcoat and crisp white neckcloth were simple but impeccably cut.

Every head turned to look at the bride.

'Oh, isn't she simply beautiful?' one of the maids seated at the back of the church sighed.

'Exquisite. And did you ever see such a gown?' whispered another as the bride passed through the south transept which housed an alabaster tomb chest and life-size figure of a knight and his lady.

Unable to contain his desire to look upon Lucy, Charles turned. The vision of almost ethereal loveliness he beheld, her face as serene as the Madonna's, her body slender, breakable, snatched his breath away. And he loved her. It was as simple as that. He loved her intelligence and her unaffected warmth. He loved the way she felt in his arms and the way her mouth tasted. He loved her spirit and her fire and her sweetness, and her honesty. My God, that he should feel this way about her. After a succession of meaningless affairs, he had finally found a woman he wanted, a woman, despite all her denials when she initially turned him down, who wanted him.

To have lost her would have been an appalling devastation too dreadful to contemplate. Lucy stirred his heart, his body and his blood to passion, to a love he could not have envisaged. He could not face a world without her in it, without her humour and fearless courage and angry defiance, that passion he had experienced in her arms, her lips smiling at him, her beautiful dark eyes challenging him.

Something like terror moved through his heart. Dear Lord, he prayed, make me cherish and protect her all the days of my life and give her the joy and happiness she deserves. With William by his side, he stepped out and took his place in front of the minister, waiting for her in watchful silence.

Lucy's eyes were irresistibly drawn to him, clinging to him, and she met his gaze over the distance without a tremor, surprised to find she felt perfectly calm, her mind wiped clean of everything for the moment. There was a faint smile on Charles's firm lips and her heart warmed as if it felt his touch.

When Lucy reached him, she looked up into his eyes, and the gentle yielding he saw in those liquid depths almost sent him to his knees. Still smiling, he took her hand, his long fingers closing firmly over hers. She responded to his smile—in that moment in complete accord, her marriage, too, seemed right. As he looked down at her, she saw his deep blue eyes were misted with emotion as he surveyed her. His smile said it all—that he adored her.

'You look adorable, Lucy,' he said quietly. 'And I love you.'

'And I you, Charles.'

Together, side by side, they faced the minister to speak the marriage vows that bound them together, the words reverberating through Lucy's heart—unaware as they did so of Anna and Tilly dabbing away their tears of happiness. Lucy could feel her eyes misting as she repeated her own vows and she lowered her gaze to the strong, lean hands that held hers in a gentle grip.

Suddenly it was over and she was his wife as long as they both would live. Charles bent his head and gently kissed his bride on the lips, unable to believe this wonderful creature belonged to him at last. They walked back to the house with a happy coterie of guests following in their wake.

The wedding breakfast, with everyone gathered around the enormous table that had been erected on the terrace and covered with the finest linen and shining crockery and bowls of pink roses to match those in the bride's bouquet, was a truly impressive affair, with course after course of elaborate dishes.

Charles leaned close to his wife, the sweet, elusive fragrance of her setting his senses alive. 'What are you thinking?' he asked quietly.

She turned and looked at him, her face lively and bright. 'About all this—our wedding. I never believed it possible that this could happen.' A cloud crossed her eyes and a note of regret entered her voce. 'My only regret is that my parents are not with us.'

Charles squeezed her hand comfortingly under the table. 'They will not be far away. I am certain that they are watching you from that mysterious place where we all go to one day.'

'Do you really think so?'

'Yes. Perhaps our children will produce their likeness,' he said softly, his eyes gleaming into hers, lazy and seductive, feeling a driving surge of desire at the sultriness of her soft mouth and the liquid depths of her eyes.

Lucy stared at him. 'Children?'

'At least half a dozen,' Charles replied, laughter rumbling in his chest. 'But you have to promise me one thing.'

'And that is?'

He stretched his arm possessively across the back of her chair without taking his eyes off her, slowly running his fingers along the back of her neck. 'At least one of them must look like you.'

She smiled, enjoying his caress. 'I'll do my best.'

After the meal which continued to early evening, when the sun was dipping in the sky and toast after toast had been drunk to the happy couple, Lucy rose to go upstairs. Seeing Charles about to follow her, she placed her hand on his shoulder.

'Give me half an hour, Charles, and then come up. I have a surprise—don't spoil it.'

Raising an eyebrow, he settled back in his chair and looked at her suspiciously, his lips curving in a half-smile. 'Then I will wait. What can it be, I wonder?'

'You will soon find out.'

And Charles did. Lucy could see he was not disappointed. When he entered their room, with bare feet she walked towards him dressed in a sky-blue silk sari finely threaded with gold, so fine yet so delicate that she imagined it would filter through his fingers like liquid when he removed it. It clung to her body like a sheath.

Memories of how she had looked in India when she had worn Indian attire came flooding back and Charles's heart turned over. She was exquisite. She was smiling up at him, a smiled that brightened the room, and the closeness and sweet scent of her heated his blood.

'The sari takes me back, Lucy. There is a radiance about you, a radiance I saw in India.'

'I dressed just for you—so that your eyes alone could see me like this. Although it's not the same, is it? Not the same as being in India.'

'It will be, when I take you back. It's a beautiful sari.'

'The material was given to me by Ananya before I left the palace—which I had made into a sari in London. I sincerely hope to see her again one day.'

'You will. I will make a point of taking you back to Guntal. Are you happy?'

'Ecstatic.' She ached with the happiness she felt. Slowly, deliberately, she leaned into him, the peaks of her thinly clad breasts pressed to his chest, rousing his blood to boiling as the heat of her touched him. 'The wedding was perfect. It's been a perfect day.'

'It's not yet over,' he said, his voice low and husky as his long-starved passions flared high as he folded her in his arms, crushing her to him. 'We don't have to return to the others right away.' His eyes shifted to the bed. 'There is time to seal our union—in bed.'

Laughing softly, she took his hand, drawing him in that direction. 'Then what are we waiting for? We aren't likely to be disturbed. I told Martha not to come back for at least—two hours.'

Grateful of the opportunity to be alone, they officially became man and wife in the best way possible, leaving them sated and warm and pulsating with pleasure.

Lucy lay exhausted and drowsy in her husband's arms,

her breath softly stirring the furriness of his chest. How she loved him and gloried in being able to respond to him in their bed. A warm and gentle breeze stole in through the open windows and cooled their heated bodies. Some moments later she lay on her stomach and, leaning on his chest, looked up at him, her gilded tresses spread in thick waves of silk over him, her eyes dark and sultry.

His expression held no laughter when he searched the hidden depths with his own. When he spoke, his voice was low and emotional.

'Thank God the past is behind us, Lucy, and you still have the capacity to love. I am so proud of you and all you have achieved.'

'I have you, Charles. A future with you and our son. That is all I want.' Raising her hand, she cupped his cheek and looked at him lovingly. 'Be assured that I love you. I love you in a way I never loved Johnathan. Yes, I loved him with all the innocence and the heart of my youth, but this, what we have, is something more, something deeper and more intense. Sometimes, when I think back to that night we were together, what we did, how you made me feel, the depth and fierceness of my feelings and emotions are disturbing—frightening, even.'

A great tenderness welled up in Charles and caught his throat. His hand moved out and gently touched her cheek. 'Then it is my responsibility to see that there is nothing to fear in the future. My attraction to you is both powerful and undeniable. I have wanted you from the moment I first saw you, one minute formal and strait-laced, and the next a woman filled with newly found passion. You are still full of strange, shifting shadows and I ask myself if I shall ever truly know who you are.'

'Know only that I am the woman who loves you, the woman you made love to. Your wife. That is the truth.'

He looked into her eyes, as if the only peace he could know would come from locking gazes with her. 'I'd like to gamble all I've got on the fact that I'll be the envy of every man who meets you.'

Charles's strong, lean hands left her face and folded round her, drawing her close to his hard chest and rolling her on to her side. Again, his lips were on her eyes, her cheeks, seeking her mouth. Trembling with a joy that was almost impossible to contain, Lucy abandoned herself to his embrace, pressing herself close to him and closing her eyes. No one could truly know what she'd gone through, how terrifying it had been for her and how it had influenced the path she had chosen.

'I can't wait for us to return to India,' she murmured, her lips kissing the hollow in his throat where a pulse beat rapidly. 'I hope it will be soon.'

'A week at the most, my love—so you'd better start packing. How will you feel, living the life of a nomad, travelling from one state to another—for I refuse to leave you and Edward behind in some far-away city to await my return.'

'It is what I want—more than anything.'

'Then in that we are in agreement.'

Lucy felt a rush of joy so intense she was sure she would faint. 'It will be like going home. What shall we do about the houses we own? It will have to be thought about now the wedding is over.'

'We will think of that later. I have a feeling Lucas would buy the house in Devon. The house in Chelsea I will keep on. It will be convenient for Lucas and Tilly to reside there when in London. Which leaves your house in Kensington.'

'I will sell it. I see no reason to hold on to it.'

'Whatever happens—if we do return, I shall see that we are together always.'

Fresh from their lovemaking, after looking in on their son, unaware of the importance of this day as he slumbered away, they returned to their guests. Ecstatic bliss glowed inside Lucy like golden ashes, long after the explosion was over.

Lucy was happy. The past was history and the future lay ahead, full of promise and hope.

* * * * *

*If you enjoyed this story,
see how it all began with the first two books in the
Cranford Estate Siblings miniseries*

Lord Lancaster Courts a Scandal
Too Scandalous for the Earl

*And when you're all caught up,
you're sure to love more of
Helen Dickson's thrilling historical romances!*

To Catch a Runaway Bride
Conveniently Wed to a Spy
The Earl's Wager for a Lady